Wild Weather Soup

for
Emily

written and illustrated
by Caroline Formby

W9-ATA-325

Published by Child's Play (International) Limited

Swindon   Chicago   Toronto   Sydney   Bologna
1995 Mission   ISBN 0–85953–950–4   Printed in Singapore

Winifred Weathervane
lived up in the clouds,
where the air was always cold.

But Winifred was much too busy
making weather to worry
about frost on the windows
or icicles hanging from the ceiling.

The gas fire in the kitchen
kept her nice and warm,
while she prepared weather soup
in her big black cauldron.

Every day, Winifred squeezed rain
for the rainforests in South America …

... and baked hot dry weather
for the African savannah.

She made mists
for the mountains
in Japan …

… and winds to blow
across the cold
Atlantic Ocean.

Sometimes, Winifred whisked wispy little cirrus clouds for Paris ...

... and big fluffy cumulus clouds for London.

And sometimes, she made them the other way round.

Whatever weather was needed,
Winifred worked hard in her kitchen to make it.

She froze snow for Alaska in the morning …

... curried a hot spell
of sunshine for India
in the afternoon.

... and fried a sunset
for the Pacific Ocean
before bedtime.

But every so often, like the rest of us,
Winifred would say to herself,
"I need a break."

So, one spring morning,
she prepared a settled spell,
blew bubbles of weather round the globe,
and left her home in the clouds
for Australia ...

It was warm and sunny on the beach,
as Winifred settled down for a nap
in the shade of a big, blue beach umbrella.

But as she snoozed, it grew hotter and hotter,
much hotter than it should have done,
and much hotter than Winifred had planned.

Something was wrong with the weather!

"Oh, dear!" sighed Winifred.
"No rest for the wicked!
I must go home and see what's the matter."

But before she could move,
a tremendous thunderclap flung her out of her chair.

An icy blizzard swept across the beach.

Clutching the big, blue beach umbrella, Winifred was carried on a jet of warm air straight up through the wind and snow.

High above the clouds,
where the air was calm and still again,
Winifred set off to find her home.
But where was it? North, south, east or west?

Wherever she looked, Winifred could see
nothing but topsy-turvy weather.

In the rainforests,
it had stopped raining …

The African savannah was a huge muddy swamp.

In the mountains in Japan,
hurricanes were blowing.

The Atlantic Ocean had almost disappeared
under a blanket of fog.

Tropical storms
raged over London.

Monsoon rains cascaded on Paris.

It was baking hot in Alaska.
The ocean boiled
and the glaciers were melting.

Snow was falling
on the Taj Mahal in India ...

Then Winifred saw
a big round hole
in the ozone layer,
that protects the Earth
from the sun's harmful
ultra-violet rays.

She flew through the hole to find out
what had caused it.

To Winifred's surprise,
she landed with a bump
in her very own kitchen.

"Oh, dear," she sighed,
"I must have left the gas on again."

The lid had blown off her pressure cooker.

Quickly, to stop the weather
getting any worse,
Winifred turned off the gas.

But her problems were not over yet ...
She still had to mend the hole
in the ozone layer.

Then Winifred remembered
the big blue beach umbrella.

It was just the right size and shape.
"The very thing!" she exclaimed.

As soon as Winifred had fixed
the hole in the atmosphere,
the weather began to settle down.

New clouds formed
and drifted north and south.
The west wind blew from the west
and the morning sun shone
in the east.

Everything was in balance again.

Well done, Winifred!

One good thing came out of it all.

Winifred hitched her kitchen
to a weather satellite,
high up above the clouds,
where she can look after the ozone layer.

She still takes a holiday
now and again,
but she tries to remember
to switch off the gas.

The world can do without
any more wild weather soup.

Bernie,

I hear you love politics. I hope you enjoy my book.

All my best, Mike

The Progressive Revolution

The Progressive Revolution

Revolution

How the Best in America Came to Be

Michael Lux

WILEY

John Wiley & Sons, Inc.

Published by John Wiley & Sons, Inc., Hoboken, New Jersey
Published simultaneously in Canada

For general information about our other products and services, please contact our Customer Care Department within the United States at (800) 762-2974, outside the United States at (317) 572-3993 or fax (317) 572-4002.

Wiley also publishes its books in a variety of electronic formats. Some content that appears in print may not be available in electronic books. For more information about Wiley products, visit our web site at www.wiley.com.

Library of Congress Cataloging-in-Publication Data

Lux, Michael, date.
    The progressive revolution: how the best in America came to be / Michael Lux.
        p. cm.
    Includes bibliographical references and index.
    ISBN 978-0-470-39511-0 (cloth)
  1. Democratic Party (U.S.)   2. Progressivism (United States politics)
3. United States—Politics and government.   I. Title.

    JK2316.L89   2009
    320.510973—dc22

                                                    2008047045

Printed in the United States of America

10 9 8 7 6 5 4 3 2 1

Since this book is about history, I want to dedicate it to
two who have gone before:

To my father, John Lux, who gave me my love for history and
politics, and my passion to do something about injustice.

And to my Republican grandmother, Hazel Carne, who thought of
herself as a conservative and would probably have been a little
concerned about having a book such as this dedicated to her, but
who fed the poor from her own table when she was poor herself,
which I've always thought of as pretty darn progressive.

CONTENTS

PREFACE

My conservative friends will be delighted, I'm sure, for me to acknowledge upfront that I come by my progressive nature, in part,
because of being brain damaged. I'm not kidding.

When I was a few months old, I got a toy wedged in my throat
that cut off my air supply for a couple of minutes until my mom
noticed me turning a deep shade of blue. She figured out what was
going on and got the air flowing again. But the oxygen supply was
cut off long enough for me to suffer a degree of brain damage that
resulted in a mild form of cerebral palsy. I had a lot of trouble walking for a while and remained exceptionally slow and uncoordinated
throughout my childhood—one of those slowest-in-school, last-
one-picked-for-the-team kids. I was not, in Newt Gingrich's classic
term of art, "a normal American." Fortunately, my family did not
care that I wasn't normal. In fact, they gave me special care and
attention and support, a sort of abnormal kid's affirmative action.

Through our church, my family also hosted two families
from apartheid-era Rhodesia (now Zimbabwe). When I was in elementary school, I walked one of these families's two younger kids
to school. Although I was too gimpy to protect them very well

physically, I knew it was my job to stand by them and be there for them when the bullies in our school screamed "nigger" at them.

Having the kind of family who took such good care of the weak and looked out for their neighbors made me want to live in a country that did the same.

These experiences—of being the other, and of standing with the other—gave me my progressive faith. I call it faith because it was also fed by the Bible verses I learned growing up. I was taught to be my brother's keeper. I learned to treat others the way I would want to be treated. I was told that Jesus had been sent to bring good news to the poor, to proclaim liberty to the captives, and to set the downtrodden free. Most of all, I was taught that living a good life meant feeding the hungry, giving clothes to the naked, and visiting the sick and those in prison—that these were the things I would be judged on.

So I grew up determined to do all those things. But I don't have the patience to be a good social worker, and I wanted to attempt something that would bring longer-lasting change. So I became a community organizer and from there was drawn into politics. I find politics to be endlessly fun and exciting. It has been my great good fortune to have knocked on thousands of doors and played a role in registering millions of people and turning them out to vote. I have produced television and radio ads, been a part in one way or another of presidential politics in seven elections, served as a senior staffer in the Clinton White House, been involved with scores of organizations, and written on a couple of different blogs.

Because my career has been in the political world, I am in no way a professional historian. I am, however, a thoroughly devoted history buff. I have devoured every American history book that I had time to read, beginning at a young age when I pored over my father's history books. I have noticed a pattern over the years: the debates of the past are remarkably similar to the debate I am engaged in now. The eras were vastly different. The names of political parties sometimes changed. The specific issues were different some of the time. But I noticed that the fundamental arguments and themes and even the basic political alignments remained remarkably the same over the years. People were arguing over voting rights back when our country began, and they still are today. Today people disagree about whether government should pursue policies that favor business and the wealthy, and they also disputed this at the nation's founding. In 1776, people clashed over whether Jefferson's words about all of us being created equal should be taken seriously, just as they debate this issue today.

That ongoing argument, between the forces of progressive thought and those of conservative thought, is what inspired this book. In the introduction, I lay out my basic theory about how the debate between progressives and conservatives has been a permanent conflict throughout our country's history. Furthermore, when progressives have been on the winning side of that debate politically, the country has made dramatic progress, whereas when conservatives have won the day, the country has suffered as a result. In chapters 2 and 3, I focus on the debate in the days of the Founding Fathers and how the ideas they advanced and the progress and the mistakes they made carry over into today's political battles. In chapters 4, 5, and 6, I turn to three of the biggest and broadest areas of conflict—civil rights, economics, and issues around what kind of democracy we want to have—and trace the evolution of those battles to modern times. In chapter 7, I detail the history of the modern progressive and conservative movements, starting with Joe McCarthy on the right and Martin Luther King Jr. on the left, and show how those movements have developed and reacted to each other. In chapters 8 and 9, I bring the discussion fully up to the present and make my argument on where the country should go from here.

I want to thank several people who have helped me enormously in the creation of this book.

First are some of the authors who most inspired and influenced my writing. Arthur Schlesinger Jr.'s superb book *The Cycles of American History* was one that I drew on and referred to heavily throughout my book. I never would have been able to track down all of the information on voting and the debate over democracy without Alexander Keyssar's comprehensive *The Right to Vote: The Contested History of Democracy in the United States*. Lerone

Bennett Jr.'s classic *Before the Mayflower: A History of Black America* has inspired me for thirty years (even though Bennett is far more critical of Jefferson and Lincoln than I am). Harvey Kaye's *Thomas Paine and the Promise of America* and Garrett Epps's *Democracy Reborn: The 14th Amendment and the Fight for Equal Rights in Post–Civil War America* both enormously influenced my overall thinking in writing this book. And no author affected me more in terms of my book's subject than Garry Wills in his *Lincoln at Gettysburg*. Learning how conservatives then and now have opposed the ideas in the Gettysburg Address and how Lincoln crafted his arguments in that speech to win the debate was a revelation.

Second, I want to thank a couple of people on the business end of getting this done: my agent, Cathy Hemming, and Hana Lane of John Wiley & Sons. Since I am a first-time author and a novice in the book business, their help, guidance, and general forbearance in putting up with my foibles have been absolutely essential. I also want to thank John Javna for helping to inspire the idea of this book initially.

I am thankful as well for my wonderful staffers, Carla Ohringer Engle and Peter Slutsky. Their patience and help throughout this process have been truly wonderful. My research interns, Josh Phillips, Leigh Ann Smith, and Cara Wittekind, have been essential in tracking down multitudes of random quotes and facts.

I want to especially thank Adam Bink, the staff person who has organized the book's editing, sourcing, researching, fact checking, and so on, ad infinitum. His help has been monumental, above and beyond the call of duty. It is no exaggeration to say that this book never would have been written without him.

My wife, Barbara Laur, also deserves enormous credit for helping me get this book written, and not only for being generally wonderful and supportive and thought-provoking, though she has been all that and more. She also edited the entire book. Her help and support have been an inspiration and a joy, and however good or bad you think the book is, I guarantee that it's a lot better because of her editing.

Finally, I want to thank my family. My sisters, Linda and Barbara, and my brothers, David and Kevin, somehow managed to put up with me when I was an obnoxious kid, although sometimes it was probably a close call. They all continue to inspire me and teach me as an adult. All of them have amazing families, and among them, their spouses, and my wife's family, I am lucky enough to be graced with twelve nieces and nephews, seven great-nieces, and a great-nephew. That youngest generation inspires and entertains me but isn't yet old enough to discuss much history of politics. The dozen older ones teach me new things and give me fresh ideas pretty much every time I talk to them. I want to especially thank my conservative Republican nephew Eric, who challenges my thinking and forces me to be at the top of my game when we spar verbally. He probably won't agree with a single sentence in this book, but knowing I would have to defend each argument from his challenges has made the writing that much better.

It was my mother, more than any other person in my life, who modeled for me what compassion is and who taught me to look out for others. She is the living embodiment of the progressive spirit that I argue for in this book.

The History of American Progress

The two parties which divide the state, the party of conservatism and that of innovation are very old, and have disputed the
world ever since it was made. Now one, now the other gets the
day, and still the fight renews itself as if for the first time, under
new names and hot personalities.

—*Ralph Waldo Emerson*

I t is the contention of this book that American history consists
of one long battle between the forces of reaction and the defense of wealth and power, on the one hand, and the forces
of progressivism and community, on the other.

If you look at our country's long history, from the days of the first
stirrings of our revolutionary impulses against Britain to today, progressive leaders and progressive movements have moved this
country forward in the face of bitter—and frequently violent—
opposition from reactionaries and defenders of the status quo.
Consider the major advances in American history:

- The American Revolution
- The Bill of Rights and the forging of a democracy
- Universal white male suffrage
- Public education

- The emancipation of the slaves
- The national park system
- Food safety
- The breakup of monopolies
- The Homestead Act
- Land grant universities
- Rural electrification
- Women's suffrage
- The abolition of child labor
- The eight-hour workday
- The minimum wage
- Social Security
- Civil rights for minorities and women
- Voting rights for minorities and the poor
- Cleaning up our air, our water, and toxic dump sites
- Consumer product safety
- Medicare and Medicaid

Every single one of these reforms, which are literally the reforms that made this country what it is today, was accomplished by the progressive movement standing up to the fierce opposition of conservative reactionaries who were trying to preserve their own power. American history is one long argument between progressivism and conservatism.

The striking thing about this long debate is how much the arguments that have occurred are repetitive over time, in terms of their rhetoric, constituencies, philosophy, and the values they represent. From generation to generation, the conservatives who oppose reform and progress have used the same kinds of arguments over and over again. Arthur Schlesinger Jr. described the division as one between "public purpose and private interest." If you sketch out the broad lines of the conservative case against the progressive case, it flows something like this:

The Conservative Argument

Successful businessmen and their allies make America great, and we should not undermine their authority or cost them money because that will mean bad things for the economy and all of us. Their freedom to run things as they like benefits everyone in the long run. And they should be the ones who control our government as well, because they know how the world works, and we can trust them to protect our national interests because of their knowledge and wisdom. An excess of democracy is a dangerous thing.

We must adhere to tradition because once we tamper with tradition, society goes to hell. It's a scary world out there, and the people who have always run things can protect us, but only if we stay with our traditions and keep things the way they have always been. People who are different from us create problems, and we don't want our traditions or the carefully built structure of our society undermined.

If people are poor, it's probably their own fault because they are too lazy to work, didn't study in school, and are generally bad people. Society shouldn't spend any money on helping people who can't help themselves, and we can't afford it anyway. Ultimately, each of us is responsible for ourselves in the world, and we shouldn't be relying on government or anybody else to make it.

We should fear change and be wary of hope because when things change, we just don't know what the unintended consequences will be.

The Progressive Argument

We are all created equal and deserve both equal rights under the law and equal opportunities to make good lives for ourselves and our families. That means that the laws should not be formulated to favor one race of people or to help the wealthy over the poor. And it means that we all should have a good education, enough food to eat, adequate health care if we get sick, and a decent place to live.

Our society works well only when it has a sense of community, an understanding that we are all interdependent on one another, that we are all diminished if any one of us is suffering, and that we look out for those who can't take care of themselves.

America is a democracy that should be a government of, by, and for the people. We don't trust elites to look out for the rest of us, and we want everyone to have a say in how the government and the economy are run.

Fear and Hope

The arguments by conservatives all too frequently invoke fear—of change, of one another, of foreigners and foreign enemies, or of certain people. They proclaim a loud and fervent patriotism and a love of traditional values, quite often quoting the Bible to justify their point of view, while ignoring those patriots and Bible quotes that don't fit in with their agenda.

Progressives, on the other hand, have called for hope, rather than fear, and for changing things for the better, rather than just leaving things the way they have always been. We have been for more power for regular folks and less power for elites. And we have been for a stronger sense of community, rather than the sense that each of us is on his or her own.

The central theme of this book is to show how these political arguments have been repeated time and time again since the American Revolution, how the same alternative visions of America keep being argued over and over, and how when progressives have won the day politically, the country has moved forward.

The good news is that a more progressive vision of what America can aspire to has prevailed enough times over the years to make us a far better country. While it is certainly true that the United States is more conservative by many measures than the industrialized countries in Europe, and that progress has been uneven and painfully slow, we are also the country that invented the modern notions of democracy and equality, and that legacy has echoed down through the generations and inspired new movements to make their claims on the American dream.

American history has always been a mixed bag, with vision and courage and progress mixed together with slavery, the brutal killing of many millions of American Indians, wars we shouldn't have fought, and altogether too much greed. There have been plenty of times when the progressive movement was too weak and small to stop bad things from happening, or when it settled for compromises on fundamental issues, such as slavery and women's suffrage.

Even leaders who pushed for progressive policy in some areas failed us in others. As I discuss more in chapter 4, this is especially true in terms of the way otherwise progressive leaders, such as Jefferson, Jackson, Wilson, and FDR, have failed us on racial justice issues. But it applies to other leaders as well. For example, Teddy Roosevelt created the national park system, partially broke apart the big trusts, and brought us some measure of food safety, but he had no use for unions or women's suffrage, allowed some of the worst lynchings in the nation's history to occur in the South, and was a military adventurer. Woodrow Wilson brought us the single most important economic reform in the country's history—a progressive income tax—and his ideas set the stage for many New Deal–era reforms and the United Nations, but he got us into a stupid, wasteful world war that we had no business being in. Kennedy and Johnson helped push through civil rights laws, Medicare, and Medicaid, but got us into the Vietnam War.

Yet even with all of the disappointments that are part of America's history, we also know that progressive arguments and movements have prevailed again and again and have created a democracy where progress is always possible. Movement leaders such as Tom Paine, Frederick Douglass, Sojourner Truth, Elizabeth Cady Stanton, Susan B. Anthony, John L. Lewis, Walter Reuther, Martin Luther King Jr., Cesar Chavez, and Rachel Carson have always been ahead of the politicians and have pushed our country to become better. Our history is full of progressive leaders fighting the good fight, and winning much of the time, to create a better nation. The battle between conservatism and progress will continue to be fought as long as there is a United States of America.

1

The Big Change Moments

Major change happens in history for three major reasons. The first are what I call earthshaking events: wars, revolutionary new technological advances, and other types of cataclysmic incidents (natural disasters, large-scale acts of terrorism, and economic meltdowns). Many people subscribe to the myth that only when these milestones take place does big change happen. Clearly, however, when you look back at history, you can see that this myth is false. For example, the Jeffersonian expansion that was epitomized by the Louisiana Purchase, the mass democratization of politics in the Jacksonian era, the economic changes of the Gilded Age, the Progressive Era reforms, the ending of Jim Crow, and the passage of Medicare-Medicaid all happened during periods of peace and relative economic stability.

A second kind of change results when groundbreaking new policies are enacted that literally change the way people live and think and affect how political power is distributed. The final category of change moments encompasses what I call intellectual change moments: debates over fundamental issues and ideas, such as may be expressed in speeches and books. Obviously, all of these various kinds of change interact with one another. Debates over issues and dramatic speeches and books cause new policies to be enacted and can even provoke wars. Life-changing events such as wars or technological developments certainly create extreme intellectual ferment and frequently result in new laws being passed. But for the purposes of this book, I want to focus on the latter two: the speeches and the books that reframed our political and legislative debates and the policy changes that moved the country in a new direction.

I would argue that a very small number of moments in our political and intellectual history were truly harbingers for major change. Here are the ones that I think have been most crucial.

On the policy side of things, I believe that eleven key new laws— or, in the case of Supreme Court rulings, interpretations of laws— signified big, dramatic moments in the history of the United States that created long-lasting change:

1. The enactment of the U.S. Constitution (1789)
2. The enactment of the Bill of Rights (1791)
3. The set of reforms Lincoln and the Republicans passed in the 1860s that derived from the Civil War and the ending of slavery
4. The 13th, 14th, and 15th Amendments to the U.S. Constitution, passed by the Republicans after Lincoln's death, which abolished slavery and forever changed the relationship between the federal government and the states
5. The terrible deal that ended Reconstruction and sold out African Americans in 1877
6. The series of conservative Supreme Court decisions, culminating with *Plessy v. Ferguson* in the late 1800s, that created a structure of corporate dominance over individual rights and white dominance over African Americans
7. The Progressive Era reforms of the early 1900s, which included breaking up corporate trusts, creating the national park system, passing food safety legislation, establishing a progressive income tax, and women's suffrage
8. The New Deal reforms of the 1930s
9. The civil rights and voting rights legislation of the 1960s

10. Medicare and Medicaid

11. The environmental legislation of the 1970s

These are the laws and the policies that reshaped history, that are affecting us even as we sit here today. Some are conservative, like those awful Supreme Court decisions in the late 1800s, and some are a blend of conservative and progressive, such as the U.S. Constitution. But they were all policies that had a deep and fundamental impact on how the country is structured.

Less dramatic and less sudden have been the long and gradual battles, many of which continue to this day, over issues such as who gets to vote or who gets a quality education.

These policy battles will be discussed throughout this book, but even more central to my narrative will be the debates and the ideas behind them, which in many ways have had a bigger impact on America's history than the policy changes have. By my count, there have been ten books, speeches, documents, and debates that have fundamentally changed the history of the nation.

1. Tom Paine's *Common Sense* (1776)

2. The Declaration of Independence (1776)

3. The debate over the Constitution and the Bill of Rights (1787–1791)

4. The debate over the Alien and Sedition Acts (1798–1801)

5. John C. Calhoun's states' rights movement (which began in the 1830s)

6. Abraham Lincoln's Gettysburg Address (1863)

7. William Jennings Bryan's "Cross of Gold" speech (1896)

8. Rachel Carson's *Silent Spring* (1962)

9. Martin Luther King Jr.'s "I Have a Dream" speech (1963)

10. Betty Friedan's *The Feminine Mystique* (1963)

All of these books, debates, and speeches literally shifted the way people thought about politics and issues and the role of government, and many of them inspired movements that changed the country.

Later, I will discuss these policies and political ideas and the way they moved history, but I want to make some observations at the outset about some broader patterns in the debate.

If you look at the two lists in terms of the timing of all these events, what first jumps out at you is the way that big changes seem to be all bunched together: six of the items mentioned on the two lists occurred in the 1776–1800 period; four in the 1860s and the 1870s; three in the period around the turn of the century, in the late 1800s and early 1900s; and six in the 1960s and early 1970s. That's nineteen out of twenty-one of the biggest change moments in American history concentrated together in four decades or, at most, four generations. Add in all of the huge changes resulting from the New Deal and World War II, and that's little more than five decades in which almost all of the biggest changes in American political history happened.

There are lots of theories about this concentration of change. Several scholars, including the brilliant historians Arthur Schlesinger Sr. and Jr., explain it via a "cycles of history" hypothesis: that periods of big change happen when demand for it gets pent up due to periods of slow change, and the slow change periods occur because people get exhausted during the big change period. Some historians have suggested a cyclical generational impulse, where one generation's lethargy or ambition causes a reaction from the next generation to do essentially the opposite.

I think these cyclical theories have some merit, but I also believe that they tend to discount how the ideas of major leaders or the activities and the fervor of an important movement cause ripples that make or allow other things to happen. There is absolutely no question, for example, that the energy, creativity, passion, and ideas of the civil rights movement inspired the women's, environmental, antiwar, and other progressive movements of the 1960s and 1970s. There is little doubt that the way Lincoln reframed the idea of America through the Gettysburg Address helped set the stage for the debate that culminated in the remarkable 14th and 15th

Amendments to the Constitution, which have become the legal basis for most of the great advances in civil rights and civil liberties in the modern era. Without Tom Paine's clarion call in *Common Sense*, the delegates to the Continental Congress who met later in that fateful year of 1776 probably would not have voted to declare independence, and Jefferson would not have written the Declaration of Independence. Nor would the Bill of Rights have been so politically urgent for the Federalists to pass fourteen years after that, without Paine and Jefferson's partnership in creating the idea of American freedom as fundamental to its nature. And absent the populist revolt against the conservative corporate domination of the American government in the post–Civil War era, neither the reforms of the progressive movement early in the twentieth century nor the revolution of the New Deal two generations later would have happened.

Ideas and movements beget more ideas and other movements. And that's an essential part of what causes change in this country.

Complications

When you make the kind of sweeping arguments that I am making about how the big debates continue throughout our entire history, you have to be wary of oversimplifying things, so let me get some caveats out of the way.

First, I want to make clear that there are excesses to American progressivism, and there are honorable things about American conservatism. For example, I personally have a great regard for tradition. I am a traditional fellow myself when it comes to family traditions and some church and political customs. And I think there are good things to be said about fiscal conservatism and being careful with tax dollars. I feel that we need to be careful about making change too fast and to be wary of unintended consequences. I also believe, as Ralph Waldo Emerson put it, that "reform in its antagonism inclines to asinine resistance, to kick with hooves; it runs to egotism and bloated self-conceit; it runs to a bottomless pretension, to unnatural refining and elevation, which ends in hypocrisy and sensual reaction." American progressivism has sometimes led to excesses. Government bureaucracies can get bloated and can take shape in ways that don't work well. People who think that they can remake the world anew in their idealism sometimes do make mistakes.

Both sides have their good points, and both sides have their flaws. My own view, though, is that I would rather take the problems of progressivism than the problems of conservatism because conservative principles are all too easily used to defend traditions that are actually rotten to the core and to shore up corruption, greed, and oppression. When conservatives defended slavery and Jim Crow, that was evil. When conservatives object to civil liberties because they might hurt the defense of the country, that is wrong. When conservatives stand up for greedy corporations that are hurting their workers and the environment and are denying health care to the sick, that is corrupt. The kinds of excesses bred by conservatism are far more dangerous and lead far more easily to corruption than do the kind of excesses that may arise from progressivism.

I will take progressivism's potential weaknesses—bureaucracies that sometimes get bloated, the unintended consequences of changing things too fast, the pretension and egotism that sometimes accompany trying to remake the world anew, the fact that "undeserving people" sometimes get government benefits—over conservatism's problems any day of the week.

Another caveat that it is important to acknowledge is the problem, mentioned earlier, that many of our political leaders were quite progressive in some arenas and awful or neglectful in other, very important, ones. This has been especially true with issues of race. Some of the great progressive statesmen who helped create our nation—most notably Thomas Jefferson—were slave owners. As I wrote in the introduction, Andrew Jackson and Woodrow Wilson had much to speak for them, especially in the realm of economic progressivism that truly helped the working class in this country, but they were both simply shameful on race issues. Teddy Roosevelt's era of domestic progressive reforms was outstanding on many different levels, but he continued and expanded on McKinley's imperialist policies, which had terrible long-term consequences in terms of the precedents he set. Far too many progressive leaders over the course of our country's history did nothing to stop the terrible treatment of American Indians.

Even great political parties and movements themselves frequently became a stew of good and bad ideas. The pro–working class Jacksonian Democrats became mired in the slavery issue and continued on this destructive course for more than 130 years, until the civil rights movement finally sundered forever the alliance between white Southern racists and Northern progressives. The Republican reform movement of Lincoln, Charles Sumner, and Frederick Douglass got entangled with the corrupting influence of Northern industrialists and lost its way. The abolitionist and early feminist movements, which were united in complete solidarity throughout the 1840s, 1850s, and early 1860s, were broken apart by the political deal-making of the post–Civil War period and, once broken apart, have never truly been reunified (note the bitterness in some of the discourse between Hillary Rodham Clinton and Barack Obama during the 2008 Democratic primary elections).

These contradictions have frequently made progress uneven or created an opportunity for conservatives to divide and conquer people who should have been standing in solidarity.

My third caveat is that although times and political and economic systems have changed, both conservatives and progressives may quote the same historic leaders to fuel their debates. Conservatives, for example, enjoy quoting Jefferson and Paine to support their belief in a small government. But, as I explain in the next chapter, Paine and Jefferson lived in very different economic and political times. They had watched in horror as King George and then Alexander Hamilton used a powerful central government to benefit the big bankers and manufacturers, rather than the small farmers and workers whom Paine and Jefferson cared about. Given whom they fought for their entire careers, they would have clearly been outraged at modern big business and would have wanted to use the federal government to restrain it.

So, how do we draw the lines in comparing thinkers such as Paine, Jefferson, and Hamilton to modern-day progressives and conservatives? It goes back to those fundamental definitions that I discussed in this book's introduction: conservatives believe in adhering to tradition, empowering elites, and championing individualism; progressives believe in political and economic equality for all and in a strong community and mutuality. By those definitions, Paine and Jefferson were clearly progressive, and Adams and Hamilton, for all of their important contributions to the nation's founding, were classic conservatives. The fact that different economic and political moments in history sometimes lend themselves to confusing rhetoric should not obscure those basic alignments. I will discuss all of this further in chapter 2.

These complications and disappointments sometime make messy attempts to suggest that the battle lines between progressives and conservatives have always been consistent, clean, or clearly defined. I still believe, however, that despite this complexity, the broad outline of progressive versus conservative thinking remains strong and clear from the vantage point of history. And the progressive movement, the movement that has pushed for political equality and economic justice, for a sense of community and mutuality, as opposed to the individual's selfish rights to exploit his fellow citizens, has continued to press for positive change that has made the United States a far better country.

The Implications of History and Our Current Political Debate

Those who don't study history, as the classic George Santayana quote goes, are condemned to repeat it. It is important to understand the echoes of all those past battles to engage effectively in the debates of our times.

When you hear a politician talk about states' rights and how the federal government should not involve itself in local issues, you hear the echoes of John C. Calhoun in the 1830s denouncing the federal government and defending states' rights; you hear the

Southerners, a generation after Calhoun, who seceded from the union and then violently opposed a federal role in civil rights; and you hear the arguments of the segregationists who opposed civil rights all the way through the 1960s.

When politicians or media figures such as Lou Dobbs condemn immigration reform, you can recognize them as modern versions of politicians from the 1800s who wanted to deny citizenship and voting rights to working-class Catholic immigrants from Europe. Dobbs evokes the Know-Nothing Party's hatred of new immigrants in the 1850s. He echoes the Southerners who fought against civil rights and voting rights in the 1860s by arguing that the law might also make the Chinese "Coolies" in California eligible to vote. He is following in the footsteps of the 1920s politicians who carefully imposed quotas to keep certain immigrants from coming to this country.

When Rush Limbaugh mocks "feminazis" or calls Barack Obama "Barack the Magic Negro," you can hear the derisive echoes of two hundred years of conservatism making fun of the idea of equal rights for women and minorities.

When you see politicians worshipping at the altar of free enterprise or spinning out their supply-side theories of how giving tax cuts to millionaires will help the whole economy, you can imagine the Social Darwinists of the 1880s and the economic royalists who hated FDR's New Deal.

When telecommunications lobbyists explain to you why they should be able to determine which content on the Internet gets the easiest and fastest access, you can consider them incarnations of the railroad lobbyists in the late 1800s and early 1900s who rationalized why railroads should be able to discriminate against carrying the freight of certain consumers whom they didn't like.

And when you hear the voices of progressives calling out for equal rights and more power for working people and an economic system where the wealth is not all concentrated at the top, you can hear the roar of a long line of leaders from Tom Paine and Thomas Jefferson, through the abolitionists, the early feminists, and the early labor leaders; through Abe Lincoln and the Radical

Republicans; through the populist and progressive movements of the late 1800s and early 1900s; and through FDR, Truman, John L. Lewis, Walter Reuther, and Martin Luther King Jr.

These are historical debates: Do we make progress, or do we keep things the way they are? Do we support more equality and more civil rights and more voting rights for more people, or not? Do we help our neighbors survive hard times, or do we look out only for ourselves? Do we provide a strong public education for all of our children, or not? What's most important: preserving our environment for future generations, or letting big business extract the maximum possible profit? Giving workers a decent wage or letting business pay those workers whatever it wants to pay them?

These are the questions that come up again and again, generation after generation, in American history. They are the questions our generation must answer as well, and our children and grandchildren will need to address the same issues. It is my contention that when we answer these questions one way, America moves forward and becomes a better country. When we answer them the other way, we make mistakes that send us backward as a nation. That's the way it once was and the way it will always be.

2

A Progressive Revolution
How Tom Paine and Thomas Jefferson Literally Invented the Idea of America

I n the span of six months, an unknown writer who had just
arrived from England and a quiet, unproven thirty-three-
year-old literally invented the idea of the United States as
we have come to know it and, in so doing, the concept of modern
democracy. Ever since then, their words have inspired the progressive movement, in the United States and all over the world.

Many heroes deserve a great deal of credit for America surviv-
ing and winning its incredibly uphill victory in the Revolutionary
War. The revolution would never have succeeded without George
Washington and his brave soldiers; without the Adams cousins, Sam
and John, and all of their steady work over many years; without
the willingness of John Hancock and the other gutsy members of the
Continental Congress who voted for and signed their names to the
bold document that Jefferson wrote; and without Ben Franklin
lending his stature, leadership, and progressive ideas to the cause.

But it was the writings of Thomas Paine and Thomas Jefferson
that gathered all of the anger and courage and work and intellect
of the times into two transformational documents that gave Americans, and soon thereafter the world, the idea of a new kind of
nation ruled not by a king or aristocratic elites but by the people
themselves.

Before Tom Paine's *Common Sense* was published, there was a general sense of outrage in the American colonies about British abuses of power and a steadily growing opinion that standing up to Britain was important. But no one had forcefully and dramatically articulated the call for revolution in a way that appealed to the broad majority of the colonists, including the working-class artisans who would make up most of Washington's soldiers. And when Paine did, his words struck the American consciousness like a thunderbolt. *Common Sense* fundamentally changed the shape of the debate, from one of "How do we best claim our rights as Englishmen?" to whether America should declare its independence. And because Paine framed the question and made such a compelling argument for it, the weight of public opinion moved strongly and irrevocably toward independence with amazing speed.

Common Sense was no more than a long pamphlet, an essay only eighty-four pages in length. It was published in January 1776 and was disseminated in a mostly rural colonial world without any of the communication technology or travel that we have today—no Internet, TV, radio, wire services, telegraph, cars, railroads, or major highways. Yet the pamphlet "went viral" with stunning speed. Within a month of its publication, opinion leaders such as George Washington were already telling their friends what a great argument for independence *Common Sense* had made, and within three months it had sold more than 120,000 copies (the equivalent in today's population of selling more than ten million copies). Given that only about 50 percent of the population was literate, the number of sales becomes even more stunning.

By the early spring of 1776, *Common Sense* was being talked about in every bar, restaurant, church, and club in America. Paine combined a razor-sharp wit with acerbic sarcasm about the British that delighted his readers. He thumbed his nose at conventional views and made fun of elitist British pretensions with statements such as "Male and female are distinctions of nature, good and bad distinctions of heaven, but how a race of men came into the world so exalted above the rest and distinguished like some new species, is worth inquiring into." Paine's clear, compelling case for the colonies to declare their independence and form a new government ruled by the people, rather than by a king, was a transformative event in American history. Without his urgent call and dramatic formulation of the case against Britain and for a new country, the Tories, who wanted to make more attempts at reconciliation, might well have prevailed, or Britain's combination of repression and minor concessions might have dramatically slowed or even stopped the move toward revolution. Even more important, without Paine's stirring vision of an independent nation governed by its own people, a new country might well have been born without the kind of democracy that the Founding Fathers eventually created. Paine's writing fostered a strong public opinion among everyday people, not only among intellectuals, that an entirely new form of government—a democratic republic—ought to be created. For all the inclinations toward democracy espoused by some (though hardly all) of the framers at the 1787 Constitutional Convention, it was *Common Sense* that firmly and irrevocably planted those ideas and ideals into the young nation's psyche.

Paine was not one of the groups of founders—such as Washington, Jefferson, Adams, and Franklin—who played a major role in the forming of the new government thirteen years later, but he was a soldier in the war and helped Washington immensely before the critical battle at Trenton. Paine inspired the troops by penning one of the most frequently quoted lines in American history: "These are the times that try men's souls. The summer soldier and the sunshine patriot will, in this crisis, shrink from the service of his country; but he that stands it now, deserves the love and thanks of man and woman."

Paine's contribution to the American Revolution was profound. It very likely would not have happened without him. But as we shall see, conservatives so hated Paine's progressive ideas that they strove mightily to denigrate his contributions, disparage his legacy, and limit his influence. Their negative efforts didn't work, but to the extent that they did succeed, the cause of American progress was hurt deeply.

Jefferson Takes the Handoff

Because of British arrogance, American courage, and Thomas Paine, what had been utterly unthinkable just a couple of years earlier was, by the summer of 1776, being hotly debated in Philadelphia. But it was still far from certain that the members of the Continental Congress would put their "lives, fortunes, and sacred honor" on the line and actually vote to declare independence. Many colonists—most historians estimate a third—still strongly opposed such a move. Their arguments were the classic arguments of conservatives in every generation. As one letter from a colonist to a British newspaper put it: "The balance for the present crisis lies both with the Colonists and the Government. The former have shown this by an extravagant zeal for liberty, without considering how it should be nourished and maintained, without considering that nothing is as essential as a due obedience to the government they live under." Samuel Seabury, the first bishop of the American Episcopal Church, argued, "If I must be enslaved let it be by a King at least, and not by a parcel of upstart lawless Committeemen. If I must be devoured, let me be devoured by the jaws of a lion, and not gnawed to death by rats and vermin." Many delegates to the colonial conventions in 1775 and early 1776 emphasized the need for caution, for trying to win over the British government, rather than making enemies of it.

As the delegates who gathered in Philadelphia rejected these conservative opinions and began to coalesce around the notion of declaring independence, they turned to a relatively quiet and remarkably young—only thirty-three years old—delegate from Virginia to write the first draft. The world would never be the same.

Jefferson rejected all of the old conservative debates about the "extravagance of liberty" and the importance of obedience to the existing order. He took Paine's bold arguments for liberty and set them into a dramatic and groundbreaking universal framework. His opening paragraph, tweaked and improved by Franklin, was so eloquent and so powerful that it became a clarion call for progressive democracy that has echoed time and again throughout the ages:

> We hold these truths to be self-evident, that all men are created equal, that they are endowed by their Creator with certain unalienable rights, that among these are Life, Liberty, and the pursuit of Happiness. That to secure these rights, Governments are instituted among Men, deriving their just power from the consent of the governed. That whenever any Form of Government becomes destructive of these ends, it is the Right of the People to alter or abolish it, and to institute new Government, laying its foundation on such principles and organizing its powers in such form, as to them shall seem most likely to affect their Safety and Happiness.

So in this incredible opening paragraph, you have Jefferson laying out these huge ideas that have dominated American political debate ever since.

- All men are created equal.
- Consent of the governed.
- The right of the people to alter or abolish their government.

We are so familiar with these words today that we can hardly fathom how bold and radical these arguments were at the time.

- Divine right of kings? Not anymore.
- Citizens owing due obedience to the government they live under? No, not if that government was unjust.
- Adherence to tradition? No one ever rejected tradition more profoundly.
- Rule by aristocracy? No—rule by the people instead.

All of those familiar conservative debates about upholding tradition and leaving things as they had been for hundreds of years were blown away by the bold strokes of Jefferson's pen. His words have literally put conservative thinkers on the defensive ever since, as they are forced to explain why equality shouldn't happen and why the elites should run things. In the opening paragraph of the Declaration of Independence (the rest of it being a fairly dry recitation of grievances against Britain), Jefferson reframed the debate for all time.

The ideas in the Declaration of Independence were not Jefferson's alone or original to him. He and the other delegates in Philadelphia that summer were greatly influenced by the Greeks' and the Romans' experiments in democracy, by the Magna Carta, and by philosophers like John Locke. Just as Tom Paine was not the first to advocate American independence, Thomas Jefferson was not the first to champion the equality of men or the consent of the governed. But as with Paine, the power of Jefferson's words in the crucible of that moment created an explosion that echoed throughout the colonies—and soon thereafter throughout the world. History pivoted at that moment and has been changing ever since. Progressive leaders and revolutionaries have quoted Jefferson's words more frequently than those of any other writer since 1776.

Jefferson's language about equality and the consent of the governed laid down a marker that has been difficult to walk away from, as generation after generation has demanded its place at the table of American democracy. When conservatives in the 1780s called for a monarchy and more power for elites, Jefferson's words were used to knock down their arguments. When those same conservatives opposed a bill of rights, Jefferson and his allies prevailed by espousing the same moral ideals as are stated in the Declaration. Following the passage in 1798 of the Alien and Sedition Acts, which contradicted the 1st Amendment, Jefferson and his supporters fought back using the Declaration's principles and won a big political victory in 1800. When Lincoln took up the cause of American democracy and spoke out against slavery in the 1850s and 1860s, he returned to Jefferson's words for guidance. When Martin Luther King Jr. spoke of the promissory note owed to African Americans, he again recalled the words in Thomas

Jefferson's Declaration. Abolitionists and feminists and the populists and union organizers and FDR all used Jefferson's words to make their case.

America is a country ruled by the people, who must give their consent and who have the right to alter their government whenever they are unhappy with it. The people are created equal under the law, and they have unalienable rights. The ideas underpinning our nation were truly radical at the time. The progressive argument won the day, and a progressive revolution in thinking and in governance became real.

The Conservative-Progressive Debate about Paine and Jefferson's Legacy

As I will discuss further on, Jefferson was viciously attacked during his political career and throughout American history ever since. His words and legacy have been alternately discounted, ignored, or co-opted by conservative thinkers. But because Jefferson was the writer of the Declaration of Independence, the nation's third president, and the founder of the world's longest-lasting political party, conservatives have found him difficult to dismiss or denigrate too severely.

Tom Paine was a different story entirely. Paine was vilified by conservatives throughout his life and was even left to die by one conservative leader, after being imprisoned in France by the French politician Maximilien de Robespierre. After his death, his philosophy was reviled, and his contribution to the revolutionary movement has been ignored or derided by conservatives for the two hundred years since.

Paine grew up in Thetford, England, the son of an interesting couple: his father was a working-class artisan and a Quaker; his mother was the daughter of a prominent Anglican lawyer. Paine had some schooling but was apprenticed to his father at age thirteen to learn corset, or stay, making. Paine left for London in 1756 to work as a journeyman, next as a sailor, and then as a stay maker. He got married in 1759, but his wife and baby died in childbirth, and his business failed. During the 1760s and early 1770s, as he worked at a variety of jobs in Thetford and London, he became more and more interested in politics and was a leader in a movement by excise officers to get a salary increase from Parliament. The effort failed, leaving Paine increasingly frustrated. Through that campaign, however, he ended up meeting Benjamin Franklin—a pretty strong progressive himself—who was representing the colonies in their increasingly troubled talks with Parliament. Franklin encouraged Paine to go to America and helped him make contacts in Philadelphia. In late 1774, only a year and a month before Paine wrote *Common Sense*, he made the move to the City of Brotherly Love.

Paine was instantly galvanized by the political situation in the colonies and became a fervent advocate for the American cause. Through Franklin's help, he became a journalist, the editor of the *Pennsylvanian Magazine*. His passionate writing drew attention from the beginning.

One of the things Paine was most excited about was furthering the cause of people like his father and himself—working-class artisans—and a politically vibrant artisan movement thrived in Philadelphia during those years. In Harvey Kaye's *Thomas Paine and the Promise of America*, the author described it this way:

> In Philadelphia itself, where the merchant elite had long controlled commercial and public affairs, Paine actually witnessed something of a "mechanics revolution." Artisans—Paine's own people—had not only militantly supported the boycott but also, in alliance with the city's radicals, run their own slate of political candidates and successfully challenged merchants for control of the Committee of Observation and Inspection. At the same time, poorer mechanics and laborers also became politically active. Having enlisted in Philadelphia's militia, they created their own Committee of Privates, through which they demanded the right both to elect their own officers and[,] regardless of their incomes, to vote in city elections.

Paine never forgot his working-class roots, and his writing reflected a passionate, pro-worker, anti-elite point of view during his entire life. *Common Sense* was written to appeal to working-class audiences; its simplicity and directness were what made it compelling and powerful to so many Americans. Paine's writing created a revolutionary spirit in the colonies that lit a fire under reluctant elites. The revolutionary idea became a movement backed by the broad majority, including the working class, and that movement gave courage to the leaders who were trying to decide what to do next.

Paine made enormous contributions to the revolution. He was a writer who in great part sparked the revolution in the first place, Washington's best propagandist and rallier of the troops, and a soldier himself in Washington's army. Yet his love of the working class, his strong opposition to slavery, and his denunciation of corruption by war profiteers during the Revolution made many of the elites in the new United States of America his enemies. Despite his fame, or perhaps because of it, he had trouble finding work after the Revolution and ended up going to Europe in the spring of 1787 to seek financing for a bridge engineering project that he was excited about. Although he probably wouldn't have had the political support from the elites who dominated Pennsylvania politics at the time to go as a delegate to the Constitutional Convention, his trip to Europe took him out of any role in that process, much to our country's detriment. But Paine quickly got involved in the storm of political debate, sparked by the American Revolution, that culminated in the French revolution of 1789. He moved to France, both to be at the heart of the action and to escape a wave of political repression in England (whose government naturally hated Paine passionately).

Paine participated in the early debates of the French revolution, arguing for a more democratic government and against the death penalty for the deposed king and queen. These viewpoints naturally put him on the other side of Robespierre, who had taken over the French government as a bloodthirsty dictator. Robespierre sent Paine to prison and scheduled him for execution, at which point one of the most shameful events in American history occurred.

The American diplomat to France at that time was a man named Gouverneur Morris. One of the delegates to the 1787 Constitutional Convention, Morris was a staunch conservative. He once said, for example, "There never was, and never will be, a civilized society without an aristocracy." He and Paine were old political enemies, and Morris had once described Paine as "a mere adventurer from England, without fortune, without family or connections, ignorant of even grammar." Morris refused to help Paine gain his freedom or escape the death sentence, even though he almost certainly could have, given that France was still trying to get American support for its new government. A stroke of pure luck kept Paine alive when a guard marked the wrong cell door for the upcoming execution. A new minister to France, a close ally of Jefferson's and the future president James Monroe, eventually gained Paine's release and, with his wife, nursed him back to health.

During his years in Europe, Paine added to his already remarkable legacy by writing three important books that, along with *Common Sense*, mark him as one of the greatest political philosophers of all time.

1. *Rights of Man* was Paine's powerful and compelling response to Edmund Burke's book *Reflections on the Revolution in France*, which essentially founded the modern conservative movement. In his book, Burke strongly rejected the ideas of republican government being proposed in America and France. Jefferson's idea that all men were created equal was anathema to Burke, as was the idea of the people governing themselves. He argued that the people of the day were bound to follow tradition and the precedents of the past, and that kings and aristocracy were a better form of government than democracy.

    Rights of Man was a stirring response. Paine stated that common people had genius and talents and that government should involve them rather than try to dominate them. His answer to Burke's concern about "mobs" was that the brutality of kings and the aristocracy created the conditions for mobs in the first place. Paine also challenged Burke's argument for tradition, insisting that no generation of people can bind future generations.

2. *The Age of Reason* was Paine's most controversial work. More theology than political theory, it laid out Paine's beliefs about religion and the church. Because it discredited the hierarchical beliefs of the organized religion of that era, it made Paine the target of hatred from conservative clergy from that time on. Paine explained that he believed in God, only not the God that was portrayed in classical Catholic or Protestant dogma, and he rejected the idea of linking the power of churches with government.

3. *Agrarian Justice* was Paine's major treatise on the economy. In it, he made the case for modern progressive economics and argued that government and society had the obligation to deal with poverty and inequality. He wrote, "Civilization has operated two ways to make one part of society more affluent, and the other more wretched, than would have been the lot of either in a natural state. . . . The accumulation of personal property is, in many instances, the effect of paying too little for the labor that produced it; the consequence of which is that the working hand perishes in old age, and the employer abounds in affluence."

These three books were so far-reaching and went so far beyond the bounds of the normal political and philosophical dialogue that were considered acceptable at the time that they turned Paine into an incredibly controversial figure. Although the books would inspire progressives in America, Europe, and all over the world for the next two hundred years, the short-term impact on Paine's political standing was devastating. Conservative political elites and clerics turned on him with a vengeance and made it their mission to destroy his reputation and political standing.

In fact, the only politician who was willing to take a chance on Paine was his old ally Thomas Jefferson. On becoming president, Jefferson took the very big political risk of writing to Paine and encouraging him to come back to America. Jefferson even offered him passage on a U.S. naval vessel. Paine accepted and returned to America in 1802, where he spent his last years writing and agitating for change (proposing, among other things, a United Nations–type international organization and a Social Security system). He died in 1809, the year that Jefferson retired as president.

Jefferson was vilified for welcoming Paine back into the country, but that certainly wasn't the only thing he was disparaged for. Jefferson was called an atheist, a freethinker (God forbid!), an infidel, a libertine, and a Jacobin (which was the equivalent of being branded a communist). Pro-business elites like Hamilton were convinced that Jefferson would bring economic ruin to the nation, with his love of the common man and his hostility to the financial movers and shakers of New York City, Philadelphia, and Boston. The coalition of business elites and conservative clerics that emerged against Jefferson and for John Adams in the 1800 election looks very similar to the Republican Party coalition of today.

In terms of the religious side of their opposition, the pamphlet most used by Adams's Federalists was one written by the Reverend William Linn, titled "Serious Considerations on the Election of a President Addressed to the Citizens of the United States." In a rather odd passage, which exposes Linn's close philosophical ties to wealthy elites, he takes great offense at a story circulated about Jefferson that, upon seeing a small dilapidated church, Jefferson said, "It is good enough for Him that was born in a manger." Linn was outraged, saying that such a comment could only "issue from the lips of no other than a deadly foe to His name and His cause." I guess poor people's churches weren't worthy enough for highbrows like Linn.

In his pamphlet, Linn asked, Does Jefferson ever go to church? How does he spend the Lord's day? Is he known to worship with any denomination of Christians? These questions sound a lot like current conservative attacks on godless liberals.

On the economic and political side of their argument, the Federalists were remarkably blunt. To them, *democracy* was a word of derision and insult, and the fact that Jefferson was for the rabble was the worst thing one could say about him. As Saul Padover wrote in his biography of Jefferson, the Federalists were clear in their opinions: "A democrat had no caste and no character. He was not respectable, did not belong to the best clubs, and wore no silk on Sunday. A democrat, a follower of Jefferson, was a common man, an ordinary American who worked with his hands and hoped for a better life. The Federalists regarded such men as the lowest dregs of humanity."

While these types of arguments seem strange today, it is important to remember that they were much more politically popular in 1800, when only the owners of property were allowed to vote, and when elites were highly suspicious of the newly forming democratic republic.

Jefferson, however, made the politically risky decision to align himself with the common man. While his campaign vigorously defended itself from the attacks on his religious beliefs and marshaled clerical supporters to write pamphlets arguing against the Linn attacks, Jefferson was happy to claim the mantle of advocate for greater political rights and economic benefits for the people. In fact, Jefferson's campaign even distributed Paine's book *The Rights of Man* as an argument on his behalf.

This open embrace of democracy flipped out Federalists such as Alexander Hamilton, who, at a dinner in New York City, shouted at a man who expressed pro-democracy ideas: "Your people, sir— your people is a great beast." One Federalist polemist wrote, "A democracy is scarcely tolerable at any period of national history. Its omens are always sinister. . . . It is on its trial here, and the issue will be civil war, desolation, and anarchy. No wise man but discerns its imperfections, no good man but shudders at its miseries. No honest man but proclaims its fraud, and no brave man but draws his sword against its farce."

This strident-sounding article represented the views of Adams and the Federalists perfectly. In fact, it was reprinted in every major Federalist newspaper in the country.

When Jefferson won the presidential election in 1800, democracy spread. The voting rights of white men of all classes began to be expanded, and the Federalists faded as a political party. But the battle to shape the way history was written and interpreted had just begun.

Over the years, conservatives have used three basic strategies for dealing with Paine, Jefferson, and their powerful philosophies of equality and of democratic and economic empowerment for the "common man": direct attack, ignoring or discounting their role in the nation's founding, and co-opting their legacy by trying to claim it as a conservative one. The first two of those strategies were a lot easier to employ with Paine, because Jefferson's stature in history made it tough to attack or ignore him. But, as we shall see, a combination of all three strategies has been used in regard to the ideas of both men.

Direct Attack

All throughout America's history, Tom Paine's ideas have been the subject of intense attack. For decades after Paine's death, traditionalist ministers assailed him by name in sermons, and conservative writers denigrated him repeatedly as a drunk and as a dangerous infidel. And even in recent times, conservatives seem happy to keep maligning Paine. Irving Kristol, one of the founders of neoconservatism, commented, "To perceive the true purposes of the American Revolution, it is wise to ignore some of the more grandiloquent declamations of the moment—Tom Paine, an English radical who never really understood America, is especially worth ignoring." Harvard professor Bernard Bailyn, who reacted angrily to the campus turmoil of the 1960s, called Paine "an ignoramus, both in ideas and the practice of politics," and said that his ideas were "rejected by the Revolutionary generation." In the era of McCarthyism, federal loyalty officers asked questions about whether employees or applicants were reading subversive authors, with Tom Paine's writings being on their list of frowned-on books. The State Department at that time took Paine's selected works from its libraries, and J. Edgar Hoover sent agents to the nation's main library systems, bearing instructions to remove and destroy, among other books, a biography of Tom Paine. Conservative intellectuals such as Daniel

Boorstin wrote in *The Genius of American Politics* that "the greatest defender of the Revolution—in fact the greatest political theorist of the American Revolution" was not Tom Paine at all but rather "the great theorist of British conservatism—Edmund Burke" (the man who rejected Jefferson's ideas in the Declaration of Independence).

The attacks on Jefferson were, of course, more subtle. It's hard to get much traction directly attacking a revered founding father. Most typically, conservatives would contrast the "great genius" Alexander Hamilton or the steady and reliable conservative John Adams, Jefferson's most bitter political rivals, with Jefferson and his romantic attraction for agrarian ways and common people. The influential twentieth-century conservative philosopher Russell Kirk, while praising Adams and Hamilton, suggested that Jefferson "came to sympathize with French egalitarian theories." Kirk at least gave Jefferson back-handed praise: his "doctrines always were more radical than his practice and [were] far less extreme than French notions of liberty." Kirk went on to say, as quoted in *The Conservative Mind*:

> In the United States, this struggle between true and false liberalism, qualitative and quantitative democracy, has been substantially the contest between Washington's liberty and Jefferson's liberty. Jefferson wished to emancipate men from external control; but he never understood, as Burke knew, how power without and power within always must remain in ratio; so that every diminution of power on the part of the state, unless it is to result in injury to society, should be accompanied by an increase of self-control in individuals. The Epicurean and speculative Jefferson disliked the whole idea of rigid self-discipline, to which the house of Adams was devoted; and Jefferson's example encouraged the expansive and coarsely individualistic tendencies of Americans.

In the mid-1800s, after Jefferson's political career was over and he had been elevated to iconic status, conservative senator John Randolph from Virginia expressed perhaps the most open hatred of

Jeffersonian principles. Randolph completely rejected the philosophy of the Declaration of Independence. He considered the Declaration to be the foundation of the "leveling" ideas of American
democracy, and he described Jefferson as the pied piper of equality
and democracy. Here is one example of his sarcastic attacks on
Jefferson: "As the Turks follow their sacred standard, which is a
pair of Mahomet's green breeches, we are governed by the old red
breeches of that Prince of Projectors, St. Thomas of Cantingbury;
and surely Becket himself never had more pilgrims at this shrine
than the saint of Monticello."

Randolph made clear that he didn't believe that men were born
free and equal: he said that their physical, moral, and intellectual
differences were obvious, and that differences of birth and wealth
were more important as well. He suggested that Jeffersonian doctrines, if taken literally, would result in anarchy. The following
truly remarkable quote, which Kirk quoted approvingly, is one of
the bluntest conservative replies to Jefferson:

> Sir, my only objection is, that these principles, pushed to
> their extreme consequences—that all men are born free
> and equal—I can never assent to, for the best of all reasons,
> because it is not true; and as I cannot agree to the intrinsic
> meaning of the word Congress, though sanctioned by the
> Constitution of the United States, so neither can I agree to a
> falsehood, and a most pernicious falsehood, even though I find
> it in the Declaration of Independence, which has been set up,
> on the Missouri and other questions, as paramount to the
> Constitution. I say pernicious falsehood, it must be, if true,
> self-evident; for it is incapable of demonstration; and there
> are thousands and thousands of them that mislead the great
> vulgar as well as the small.

Ignoring and Discounting Paine and Jefferson

It was a challenge for conservatives to disregard and belittle Jefferson's role in America's founding, but you would be surprised at
how hard they tried.

One of their strategies over the years was to emphasize the more conservative Washington as the founder *über alles*, the father of his country. Although Washington's contributions to our country's founding were obviously extremely important, conservatives throughout the 1800s practically created a cult around Washington. They even built a phallic monument of him that towered far above any other building in Washington, D.C. In nineteenth- and early-twentieth-century history books, Washington's role was given far more prominence than Jefferson's, and Washington's alliance with the conservative heroes Hamilton and Adams against Jefferson was frequently emphasized. Americans today assume that Jefferson had a similar billing to Washington's throughout history, in part because of their monuments on the National Mall in Washington, D.C., but, in reality, it wasn't until FDR came along and brought a new emphasis to Jefferson's role that his monument was even built.

Another tactic conservatives have used is to emphasize the Constitution as our country's primary founding document over the far more progressive Declaration of Independence. Wilmore Kendall, a highly influential conservative writer of the mid-1900s, scoffed at the primacy of the Declaration as opposed to the Constitution. He attacked both Jefferson's and Lincoln's emphasis on equality and their interpretation of the progressive philosophy embedded in the Declaration as being more central to the idea of America than were the more conservative governing principles laid out in the Constitution.

But the memory and importance of Jefferson have been hard to erase, especially with FDR's renewed focus on his philosophy and writing as the inspiration for modern progressive politics. The attempt to eradicate Paine's even more radical message was, for much of our history, far more successful. Paine was not even mentioned at the 1876 centennial celebration of the Declaration of Independence. And until Gerald Ford repeated Paine's words about the times that try men's souls in an attempt to buck up Americans who were troubled by the economic problems of the 1970s, no Republican president since Abe Lincoln had quoted Paine by name or even mentioned his influence on the country.

While some conservative historians over the years completely ignored Paine's role, almost all of them consistently downplayed it. References to the Founding Fathers frequently left Paine off the list. William F. Buckley Jr.'s *National Review* magazine, the most influential conservative magazine over the last sixty years, as a general rule, had an informal policy of banning any mention of Paine at all.

Co-Opting Paine and Jefferson: The Role of Government

Since trashing and ignoring Paine and Jefferson didn't really work and was perilous, given their iconic status among so many people, a third major strategy of conservatives was to co-opt Jefferson's and Paine's words for their movement. The idea was simple: ignore all that inconvenient stuff about equality, democracy, and the economic rights of the common man, and take Paine's and Jefferson's most antigovernment quotes to lay claim to these great leaders as part of the small-government libertarian movement. At least in this strategy, conservatives have a plausible, if ultimately flawed, argument.

Paine and Jefferson grew up in an era where the greatest threat to their freedom and happiness was a tyrannical government. Even if King George did not have absolute power, he still had an enormous amount, and in most governments around the world, the king's rule was still absolute. And neither the American colonists nor the working-class artisans Tom Paine grew up with had much in the way of political power or a stake in the system.

The world back then also had nothing similar to today's big businesses, with their multinational economic and political power. As Arthur M. Schlesinger Jr. explained in *The Cycles of American History*: "Early American corporations were quasi-public agencies, chartered individually by statute. They were granted franchises, bounties, bond guarantees, rights of way, immunities and other exclusive privileges to enable them to serve specified public needs. In many cases state government bought shares in corporations and installed their representatives on boards of directors."

It is important to note that in the earliest days of the brand-new experiment in republican government that the United States was attempting, Alexander Hamilton was pushing the idea that a powerful, centralized government should be used in service to wealthy bankers and businesspeople. Hamilton was not arguing for the free market, as conservatives today do, because the times were so fundamentally different. He was contending instead that the federal government should use all of its powers to promote economic development, and his way of doing that was to cut deals with wealthy financiers and businesspeople to get them excited about the new nation. As the first secretary of the treasury, he laid out his case for the U.S. economic plan in his landmark *Report on Manufactures*, arguing that "a certain activity of speculation and enterprise, which if properly directed, may be made subservient to useful purposes."

In Jefferson's and Paine's experience, despotic kings and men allied with big-money capitalists such as Hamilton were the ones arguing for more government power. This is why, with Jefferson's and Paine's orientation toward democracy and common folk, they both at various times in their careers argued, as Paine did in *Common Sense*, that "society in every state is a blessing, but government even in its best state, is but a necessary evil." Jefferson, decrying business and bankers, once remarked, "Were we directed from Washington when to sow, and when to reap, we should soon want bread." Jefferson also used the idea of states' rights to argue for progressive principles, such as in the debate over the Alien and Sedition Acts.

Modern-day conservatives love to use those kinds of quotes to claim kinship with Jefferson and Paine. Ultimately, though, their argument falls on its face. As Schlesinger said, "Hamilton thought private property in danger of subversion from below by debtors, Jefferson from above by bankers." Jefferson, upon becoming president, used the powers of government very aggressively, but on behalf of regular people, instead of favoring Hamilton's bankers and big-business leaders. Jefferson's first State of the Union address said that government should help agriculture, industry, and trade by offering them protection and aid whenever needed. He repeatedly asked that surplus government revenues be applied to "the improvements of prosperity and union." He was the founder of the University of Virginia and a big supporter of public education in general. And, of course, his single most significant accomplishment as president was the Louisiana Purchase, which in one stroke of a powerful government leader's pen doubled the size of the nation.

It's even harder to make the case for Tom Paine as a modern-day conservative libertarian. Among the things Paine proposed in his long career as a political writer were:

- A progressive estate tax to keep families from an excess accumulation of property
- No taxation of the poor
- Welfare programs for the poor, including special relief for families
- A publicly financed system of social security for the elderly
- Public funding for education
- Employment centers for the jobless
- Redistribution of wealth through a progressive income tax

Paine completely discredited the idea that people in poverty were there because of their own fault and also rejected the then widely held view that property should afford privileges that the poor didn't have.

In the world that Paine and Jefferson lived in, so different from ours today, it is natural that they viewed government with some suspicion. But conservatives who pretend that Paine and Jefferson would be small-government libertarians today are either fooling themselves or trying to fool us. The progressive ideas of Paine and Jefferson always stood for more democracy, more equality, and more economic opportunity for the poor and the working class. They were freethinkers who were strong civil libertarians and who argued for a wall (the term originally came from Jefferson) between church and state. They were opposed by wealthy elites and conservative clergy in their own times, just as modern-day wealthy elites and conservative clergy oppose progressive ideas. Conservatives have denigrated Paine's and Jefferson's ideas since the founding of our country.

The Ideas of Paine and Jefferson in the Modern Debate

Paine and Jefferson created the idea of American democracy and equality. Progressives ever since have used their words and their ideas in the battle for progress. When the great liberal composer Earl Robinson was called in front of the House Un-American Committee in the McCarthy era and was asked to cite one poem or song he had written, encouraging schoolchildren to support the Constitution, Robinson recited his words from "The House I Live In": "What is America to me? A name, a man, a flag I see. A certain world called democracy. . . . The words of old Abe Lincoln, of Jefferson and Paine."

The first organizers of labor unions in America in the 1830s used Paine as their inspiration. The early abolitionists and feminists quoted Paine and Jefferson frequently. Abe Lincoln, as we shall see in chapter 3, was deeply influenced by Paine and Jefferson. FDR was inspired by Paine and especially by Jefferson, so inspired that he finally built the memorial that Jefferson long deserved. The organizers of the labor movement of the 1930s were motivated by Paine, and civil rights movement leaders such as Martin Luther King Jr. used Jefferson's words in the Declaration as a cudgel to beat down Jim Crow's door.

But inspiration aside, the ideas of Paine and Jefferson are still part of a hotly disputed debate, along with those of their historical opponents—Burke, Randolph, Hamilton, Adams, and Calhoun. Russell Kirk, one of the most important conservative writers of the last hundred years, makes clear his disdain for Jefferson and Paine's "levelling" ideas. Another critic of Jefferson and Paine's brand of democracy is Samuel Huntington, the modern conservative scholar who is most famous for his nasty diatribe against the Muslim world in *The Clash of Civilizations*. In his influential report "The Crisis of Democracy," he wrote, "Some of the problems of governance in the United States today stem from an excess of democracy."

In the report, Huntington mentioned that "the 1960s witnessed a dramatic renewal of the democratic spirit in America," but he sure wasn't happy about it. He suggested that public interest groups, minorities, women, students, unions, and "values-oriented intellectuals" (nothing worse than intellectuals with values) had created a democratic distemper. He further observed, "A democratic political system usually requires some measure of apathy and non-involvement on the part of some individuals and groups." Yes, that apathy thing is essential.

Huntington, while perhaps blunter than some, is no outlier in terms of conservative discomfort with too much democracy. Columnist David Brooks, incensed that his pal Joe Lieberman had lost to Ned Lamont in the 2006 Connecticut Democratic primary, remarked, "Primary voters shouldn't be allowed to define the choices in American politics." And new organizations and media forums, such as MoveOn.org and blogs, that have gotten more people involved in the democratic process have truly driven conservatives crazy.

The battle goes on. The ideas of Paine and Jefferson have been making conservatives crazy for 230-plus years. In the 1770s, conservatives opposed the American Revolution because they hated the idea of rebelling against their king, and today conservatives fear new civil rights, "excessive" democracy, and equality of economic opportunity. As progressives carry our fight forward, we bring the words and ideas of Paine and Jefferson along with us. Their ideas became the central guiding principles behind the idea of America.

Just as a religion founded on the ideas of a man who believed in the Golden Rule and Matthew 25:31–46 can be corrupted or twisted by conservatives hundreds or thousands of years later, so, too, can the original idea of America created by Paine and Jefferson be corrupted and twisted. But their actual words, just like those of

Jesus and other ancient religious prophets who preached love and compassion, keep coming back unfiltered to new generations and inspire them to continue fighting for progress.

Historian Joseph Ellis noted in his book *American Creation*, "It is no exaggeration to observe that between the summer of 1775 and the spring of 1776 the entire liberal agenda . . . of American history made its appearance for the first time." Between Tom Paine's direct frontal assault on monarchy and his compellingly straightforward arguments on behalf of equality and justice and Jefferson's opening words of the Declaration of Independence, not only a new nation but a new progressive vision was born. In the words of Paine, "We have it in our power to begin the world over again." And they did.

3

The Constitution, the Bill of Rights, and the Right to Think and Speak Freely

Neither Tom Paine nor Thomas Jefferson was present at the Constitutional Convention in 1787, and their absence not only made for a worse document, but it almost caused the whole process to come crashing down. What the mostly conservative and elitist framers at the Constitutional Convention did not realize was how difficult that Constitution would be to ratify without a clear delineation of the freedoms that Americans had already come to see as their birthright. Only eleven short years had passed since *Common Sense* and the Declaration of Independence had been written, yet citizens had grown used to having new freedoms and a voice in the new nation's government. Had Paine and Jefferson been there, the Bill of Rights almost certainly would have been a part of the original document.

Unlike the Declaration of Independence and *Common Sense*, the Constitution was a more conservative document, written by far more conservative men. The anti-Federalists, who did not want a new Constitution—at least, not like the one that emerged—did not participate in the Constitution-writing process. The delegates who ended up going to the Constitutional Convention were essentially self-selected and tended to be the wealthy elites who were most worried about the flaws in the Articles of Confederation. Although there were some progressive thinkers present, including Ben Franklin and George Mason, the delegates who gathered in Philadelphia that summer were overall fairly traditional.

While tending toward conservatism in their own right, the framers were aware of public opinion and understood the opposition they faced. Some of them were also genuinely mixed in terms of their own political opinions and had more progressive points of view on certain issues, so the Constitution ended up being a combination of more conservative-elitist ideas and some progressive ones.

Frankly, many of the things debated in Philadelphia that summer were neither conservative nor liberal; they were merely structural and balance-of-power issues that needed to be resolved if the country was to stay together and be unified. Debates over the balance of power between big and small states, for example, didn't break along conservative versus progressive lines. Neither did an issue such as whether to have a unitary executive or an executive council. But structural issues like these took up most of the delegates' time and energy.

The crowning idea of the Constitution—the system of checks and balances and dispersed power embodied in a government with a chief executive, an independent judiciary, and two legislative bodies—was also neither progressive nor conservative, although both sides have alternatively claimed and rejected it over the years. Some progressives have argued that the separation-of-powers structure dramatically slows down the ability to change government policies quickly and is not as responsive as it should be to the popular will; others are thankful that when conservatives are in power, they don't have the ability to run roughshod over the rights of the minority (consider the Senate confirmation battles in recent years when Bush and the Republican majority in the Senate were trying to push right-wing judges through). Some conservatives, such as Bush and Cheney, have argued that the chief executive does not have enough power to do what he or she needs to do. Most political leaders over the years, however—progressive and conservative alike—are inclined to be satisfied on balance with the doctrines on the separation of powers that are embodied in the U.S. Constitution. And when you think about the themes of debates that progressives and conservatives have had throughout our country's history—more versus less democracy, more versus less economic justice for working families, more versus less equality of rights, more versus less freethinking, rather than tradition—I find it hard to argue that the structural decisions made in the 1787 Constitution about the separation of powers are essentially one philosophy or the other.

The conservatism of the Constitution's framers definitely showed up in other ways, however, and the mistakes they made have haunted us over the years. Much to our benefit, the mistakes have been corrected in many cases, especially in terms of slavery and the lack of a Bill of Rights and also on smaller issues such as the election of the Senate by state legislators rather than by the voters. Yet we have been stuck with certain mistakes, such as the dreadful Electoral College idea, which have caused repeated crises for our country.

The Fear of Democracy and the Electoral College

The Electoral College, the biggest legacy of the wealthy conservative framers' fear of democracy, remains in our Constitution. And it continues to cause disasters, near-disasters, and other problems for us to this very day.

The idea of even having a chief executive independent of the Congress, let alone the method of picking that executive, was perhaps the single most contentious issue at the Philadelphia convention. The leading idea that was discussed for much of the convention was whether to have Congress select the executive, perhaps by appointing an individual to a lifetime position or by electing an executive council of three, five, or fifteen people.

Some delegates feared that having the president elected by Congress would not create sufficiently divided power centers. And certain framers did make the argument that with Congress representing districts and states, someone should represent the entire country. In the end, that combination of arguments carried the

day, so the idea of having a national election for a single chief executive, the president, was adopted.

That left the conservative, antidemocratic framers with a problem, though: they didn't want the people, the rabble, choosing the
president directly. That would be giving way too much power to
even the landowning white men who voted in elections in that era.
Instead, the framers latched onto the idea of the Electoral College,
where voters would pick wise, thoughtful men who could then
make the presidential decision. And in a stunning lack of insight
that would soon cause the greatest crisis the country faced in the
years before the Civil War, they failed to recognize that political
parties would arise, and thus structured the college in such a way
that the top vote-getter would become president, and the second-
highest vote-getter would become vice president (each elector
could vote for two people). Just thirteen years later, this system
resulted in the 1800 election meltdown, which almost destroyed
the country right then and there.

The failure to trust in regular voters, as opposed to elites,
produced a system that was bound to create major political crises
from time to time, and it did—four full-blown meltdowns, and no
fewer than nine other near-misses in terms of big problems. But
beyond the crises, the Electoral College has become a system
where the vast majority of Americans know their votes don't matter
very much because they live in solidly Democratic or solidly
Republican states. Even in closely contested elections, only about a
quarter of the states or less is truly competitive. With the presidential nominating fights so frequently settled early, this means that up
until the 2008 primary battle, which on both sides continued longer
than it had in recent years, a majority of Americans under the age
of forty had never cast a vote for a presidential candidate that they
felt actually meant something. When the Obama-Clinton primary
went on so long, I had scores of friends and family members in
late-primary states excitedly calling me to say that they were so
thrilled that their votes would finally count. If the popular vote
elected the president in the general election, this problem would
be solved because everyone's vote would matter in the final result.

It's the Electoral College crises and near-crises, though, that have too often genuinely threatened our government. There have been four times where the Electoral College system caused a major crisis of legitimacy in the government.

- **1800.** Jefferson's Democratic-Republican Party won a narrow majority of electoral votes in the election, 73 to 65. The design of the original Electoral College, however, with each elector being able to vote for two people, threw a rather massive wrench into the election. The plan was for Jefferson to be president and Aaron Burr to be vice president, but members of Jefferson's party failed to organize themselves so that one less elector would vote for Burr. That threw the election into the lame-duck, Federalist-controlled House of Representatives. The resulting crisis almost destroyed the young country, as state militias supporting Jefferson were getting ready to march on Washington. In the end, Jefferson successfully maneuvered his way into the White House, resolving the crisis. The Electoral College was then restructured to the way it is today, with the president and the vice president running together on a slate.

- **1824.** The easy victories of the Democratic-Republicans from 1804 to 1820, culminating with James Monroe winning his second term unopposed, gave way in 1824 to an intense four-person contest between Andrew Jackson, John Quincy Adams, William Crawford, and Henry Clay. Jackson was the big winner in the popular vote but fell short of a majority in the Electoral College because all four candidates picked up a sizable chunk of electoral votes. Clay finished third in the popular vote but fourth in electoral votes, making him ineligible because only the top three candidates could be considered. Had he been third in electoral votes, he probably would have won the battle in the House of Representatives, where he was the speaker. Since he wasn't eligible, Clay cut a backroom deal with Adams: Clay gave Adams the support he needed to become president and Adams made Clay the secretary of state. The supporters of Andrew Jackson were not amused. They cried corruption and even talked of open rebellion. Adams became a failed president, losing to the Jacksonians in the 1826 congressional elections and to Jackson in his 1828 reelection bid.

- **1876.** Speaking of corrupt bargains, the 1876 election was the most rotten political deal in all of American history. The election that year was between Republican Rutherford B. Hayes and Democrat Samuel Tilden. Tilden won the popular vote easily and appeared to have won the Electoral College as well, 203 to 166. Republicans, however, disputed the 19 electoral votes of South Carolina, Louisiana, and Florida, saying that there had been fraud. By outmaneuvering the Democrats, the Republicans were able to essentially steal the election, but with Democrats threatening another Civil War, Republicans gave them a consolation prize: federal troops would be withdrawn from the South, and protection of the freed slaves would be ended. It was a hell of a deal for the racist conservatives in the South, one that resulted in almost ninety years of Jim Crow, and was arguably the worst miscarriage of justice in history.

- **2000.** Modern readers know all too well the absurdity that was the 2000 election. Al Gore won the popular vote by more than 500,000 votes nationwide, was just two votes short of the 270 electoral-vote majority needed to claim the presidency, and would have won Florida if tens of thousands of black voters hadn't been illegally stricken from the voting rolls by Florida secretary of state Katherine Harris, and/or if poorly designed ballots hadn't confused voters in two counties, and/or if a proper recount had been done. But Harris, Florida governor Jeb Bush, and the conservative Republican members of the Supreme Court used their raw political power to seize the White House.

In addition to these truly major crises, we have had nine other near-miss presidential elections where only a slightly different scenario might have provoked a crisis, or at least a huge dissatisfaction with the result. The last one was in 2004, where a switch of nearly 119,000 votes in Ohio would have made John Kerry the president, even though Bush had won the popular vote by more than 3,000,000 votes.

The framers' basic lack of faith in democracy and the people resulted in a tragically flawed presidential election system, which is still in place today.

The Devil's Bargain

These continued crises, as well as the lack of connection to presidential elections that people in so many non–swing states feel every four years, are a direct result of the framers' conservative philosophy that elites, rather than the majority of Americans, should control the government. But the framers' worst act was their devil's bargain with "slave power"—the term that Northerners frequently used to refer to the power that slave owners had over American politics.

Given the political tenor of the times, when slavery wasn't abolished even in most Northern states, let alone in the South, it is no surprise that slavery was not eliminated in the United States at the Constitutional Convention. But it is equally true that Northern and moderate Southern delegates who knew better were so desperate for a stronger centralized government that they were willing to cut deals with slave power that they knew in their hearts were wrong, deals that would come back to haunt the country time and time again in future years. As Garrett Epps wrote in *Democracy Reborn*, "Southerners vowed they would risk disunion rather than give up the protections they sought. Northerners believed them; and so, link by link, they forged the multiple chains that would tie slavery to the federal government."

Among the concessions granted to the strongly pro-slavery delegates were:

- The notorious and shameful three-fifths rule in determining congressional and Electoral College apportionment, wherein pro-slavery forces demanded that their slaves be counted toward their population, with each slave being equal to three-fifths of a human (this was actually a compromise with the North, as slave owners originally demanded that the slave population be counted in a state's population), even though their slaves had no voting or legal rights whatsoever.

- Congress was allowed the ability to tax imports, which was far more important to the Northern economy, but not exports, which was much more essential for the slave economy.

- Congress would not be allowed to regulate the importation of slaves until 1808.

- Northern states would be required to return all runaway slaves to their masters.

- If slave owners were faced with a slave revolt, the federal government would be required to help defeat it.

Southern conservatives also proposed and coalesced around the Electoral College idea, since they figured that the three-fifths rule would give them extra leverage in those elections.

Even conservatives in the North and moderate Southerners recoiled at these concessions. As described in the notes James Madison took at the Constitutional Convention, Gouverneur Morris—the pro-aristocracy, conservative enemy of Tom Paine mentioned in chapter 2—said about the three-fifths rule that the proposal "comes to this: that an inhabitant of Georgia and [South Carolina] who goes to the Coast of Africa, and in defiance of the most sacred laws of humanity tears away his fellow creatures from their dearest connections & damns them to the most cruel bondages, shall have more votes in a Gov[ernment] instituted for protection of the rights of mankind, than the Citizen of P[ennsyl-vania] or N[ew] Jersey who views with a laudable horror, so nefarious a practice."

This was a fool's bargain, Morris warned. "What is the proposed compensation to the Northern States for a sacrifice of every principle of right, of every impulse of humanity[?] They are to bind themselves to march their militia for the defence of the S[outhern] States; for their defence ag[ainst] those very slaves of who they complain."

The Virginian George Mason, a progressive worthy of far more notice than has generally been given him, also vehemently objected. He was one of only three delegates to oppose the Constitution, partly on the grounds of the slavery provisions, and partly on the grounds that there was no Bill of Rights.

In the end, though, the pro-slavery Southern conservatives bullied their way to all these concessions. The wealthy, mostly conservative delegates of the North were far more concerned with the specter of Shays' Rebellion–style outbreaks happening again (poor farmers and workers arming themselves and rebelling against their creditors), than with the plight of the slaves or even the future long-term implications for the country if the slave-owning planters of the South were given so much power.

Was a different path possible had Northern delegates taken a tougher approach to the threats from Southern conservatives? It is always hard to know how history might have been different, but I suspect the answer is yes. The wealthy Southern planters needed a stronger union just as much as the Northerners did. And even slaveholders had put forth a variety of proposals for gradual emancipation. Jefferson, for example, had suggested freeing slaves who had been born after the current generation, so that slave owners would not suffer immediate financial losses but slavery would gradually wither away. Other proposals being floated included prohibiting slavery in any new states that were admitted to the Union or immediately stopping the slave trade. The three-fifths rule should have been summarily rejected, as should have any federal role in putting down slave rebellions.

But it was not to be. The wealthy Northern conservatives cared far more about their own political power and economic security. The poison of slavery entered our Constitution and festered and grew there for more than seventy years, until the Civil War almost brought the entire Union down.

The Debate over the Bill of Rights

The fight over the Bill of Rights was not led by the politicians; it was led by the people. If it had been left to the politicians, nothing would have happened, since both the framers and the anti-Federalists were lukewarm or downright opposed to having a Bill of Rights in the new Constitution. The anti-Federalists ended up using the idea of the Bill of Rights for their own purposes, rather than trying to actually get it passed. But what the debate did show was how powerful and important public opinion was in determining policy, even in the earliest days of the country. The Constitution as it was originally drafted, despite being supported by George Washington and many other prominent and revered people, was almost defeated, and the most effective argument that was used to try to defeat it was that it did not contain a Bill of Rights. In fact, without Madison and other Federalist leaders promising a Bill of Rights, the Constitution we have today would very likely never have been adopted.

The Bill of Rights was not much of a subject of discussion at all at the Constitutional Convention. Very close to the end, after the long and exhausting debate in the hot, humid summer weather, and the extensive deal making in regard to the Constitution's structure, George Mason rose and suggested adding a Bill of Rights. The conservative delegates just weren't interested because they didn't think a Bill of Rights was a priority, and they overwhelmingly voted Mason's proposal down. That was a huge political mistake because from the moment the Constitution went to the public without a Bill of Rights, there was an outcry.

Neither the anti-Federalist leaders, who wanted to defeat the Constitution entirely, nor the framers, who were committed to its adoption, were initially enthusiastic about a Bill of Rights. In fairness, one of the reasons the framers didn't consider it particularly important was that most of the states already had their own Bills of Rights. But the framers were further opposed to the Bill of Rights for at least two major reasons:

First, they thought of themselves as being pro-freedom. The idea that there was a need for the Bill of Rights didn't occur to many of them because they didn't believe that responsible citizens such as themselves would ever have a government that would abridge people's rights. Like many politicians, they deluded themselves over their own essential goodness.

Second, Alexander Hamilton and other framers posited that a Bill of Rights would be dangerous, as well as unnecessary, because it would inevitably not list all freedoms and would therefore make more likely the future restricting of liberties that were not listed. They argued that the federal government would have no rights to restrict liberty anyway, so why list specific freedoms? Why, they asked, declare that things shall not be done when there is no power to do so? Why, for instance, should it be said that liberty of the press shall not be restrained when no powers were given to the federal government to restrict them?

Leonard Leavey, in his book *Origins of the Bill of Rights*, argues convincingly that excluding a Bill of Rights from the Constitution was actually fundamental to the constitutional theory of the framers. Pennsylvanian James Wilson, who many historians think was second only to Madison in influence at the Constitutional Convention, led the ratification fight in Pennsylvania and was hard-pressed by the strong contingent of progressive delegates represented in its legislature to explain why there was no Bill of Rights. Wilson's defensive answer, as described by Leavey, was that the people of the states had vested in their government all powers and rights that they did not, in explicit terms, reserve, but the case was different as to the federal government, whose authority rested on positive grants of power expressed in the Constitution. For the federal government, the reverse of the proposition prevails, and everything that is not given is reserved to the people of the states. That distinction, Wilson argued, answered those who believed that the omission of the Bill of Rights was a defect; its inclusion would have been absurd because the Bill of Rights stipulated the reserved rights for the people, whereas the function of the Constitution was to provide for the existence of the federal government, rather than enumerate rights not divested.

These were clearly convoluted arguments, and the framers' assumption that all rights would be assured if not spelled out proved very wrong. Only eleven years later, in John Adams's term as president, Congress passed the Alien and Sedition Acts, which violated the very freedoms that the framers had promised would always be there. Ironically, Hamilton was one of the strongest proponents of these laws.

The folks who were against the new Constitution, the anti-Federalists, were against it for a whole range of reasons. They didn't want as much of a central authority. They were concerned about the new powers that the Constitution granted the federal government. They were concerned that states had less power and fewer rights. They were worried about the federal government imposing taxes. But none of those arguments gained much traction. What did gain traction with the people was the omission of a Bill of Rights. This became a flashpoint because it was what really worried the citizenry. As states were electing legislatures and debating the issue, the Bill of Rights became the major issue that drove the debate, and the anti-Federalists got behind it in the hopes of defeating the Constitution altogether.

The Federalists were clearly losing the battle of public opinion, and they knew it. They kept throwing arguments out, in addition to the ones I've already mentioned. They said, inconsistently, that some states had no Bill of Rights but were as free as the ones that did. They were as free because the Federalists' view of personal liberty didn't depend on what Hamilton called "parchment provisions," which he called inadequate in a struggle with public necessity. He stated that it depended, rather, on public opinion and on a pluralistic republic of competing interests in a limited government structured to prevent any interests from becoming an overbearing majority. Basically, he was making a case for the Constitution itself, as written by the framers. All of the Federalists' arguments, however, fell flat because in fact they had enumerated certain rights in the Constitution already, and since they had done that, people did not accept their basic premises. The longer the debate went on, the weaker the pro-Constitution forces' position got.

As the Federalists' position became more exposed, they grew ever more defensive. Governor Randolph of Virginia said that Virginia's declaration of rights had never protected its citizens from any danger: "It has been repeatedly disregarded and violated." He added, "Our situation is radically different from that of the people of England. What have we to do with Bills of Rights? A Bill of Rights, therefore, accurately speaking, is quite useless, if not dangerous to a Republic."

The anti-Federalists continued to gain steam by promoting a Bill of Rights because the public was so much on their side. If a Bill of Rights was so unnecessary, the anti-Federalists asked, why did the Constitution protect some rights and not others? This was clearly a problem for the Federalists to answer, and they ended up starting to attack their opponents in harsher and harsher language. Alexander Hamilton alleged, "It is the plan of men of this stamp to frighten the people with ideal bug bearers in order to mold them to their own purposes. The unceasing cry of these designing croakers is, my friends, 'your liberty is invaded.'" Anti-Federalists capitalized on this Federalist rhetoric, hoping to defeat the Constitution or hamstring it, in order to get a second chance at a national government.

Fortunately, more thoughtful people, some of whom had not been at the Constitutional Convention, carried the day. Thomas Jefferson, who was the minister to France in 1787 and had not been at the Constitutional Convention, wrote to Madison that he liked the idea of the Constitution but had some reservations. First, he said what he did not like: the omission of the Bill of Rights. After listing rights that he thought deserved special protection, starting with freedom of religion and of the press, he added, "Let me add that a Bill of Rights are what the people are entitled to against every government on Earth, general or particular, and what no just government should refuse or rest on inference." An argument for the Bill of Rights, wrote Jefferson to Madison, was the legal check that puts it into the hands of the judiciary. Jefferson believed that an independent court could withstand oppressive majority impulses by holding unconstitutional any acts that violated the Bill of Rights. As to the point that the Bill of

Rights could not be perfect and might leave out some rights, Jefferson replied that half a loaf is better than none. Even if all rights could not be secured, let us secure what we can, he argued.

The ratification of the Constitution was a very, very close thing. Several states balked, and only through a great deal of political skill and maneuvering was the Constitution approved at all. It was ratified only in Virginia, at the time the biggest and most powerful of the states, when Madison promised that a Bill of Rights would be added to the new Constitution.

In the end, James Madison was persuaded by both the raw politics of the situation and by his friend Thomas Jefferson. He ended up becoming the single strongest proponent of the Bill of Rights and used his conviction and position as the first Speaker of the House to win its adoption. The politics of the fight was very dicey. Madison was caught between Federalists like Hamilton, who were totally dismissive of a Bill of Rights, and anti-Federalists, who didn't want to take away their strongest argument for rewriting the Constitution as a whole. (The anti-Federalists became more lukewarm about the idea once Madison started to campaign for it because they realized that if a Bill of Rights were adopted, they would lose their most powerful political critique of the Constitution.) But he successfully guided the amendments through. The anti-Federalists were stuck with their own arguments in advance of the Constitution, so they had to end up voting for it, and Madison convinced enough of the Federalists to win the day. It is extraordinarily fortunate for us that these freedoms were written into the Constitution because without them, this country would have gone down a far more antidemocratic, far less free, track.

The Battle Is Joined over Defining the Bill of Rights

As important as it was to win the battle over putting the Bill of Rights into the Constitution, this hardly resolved the issue of whether all Americans would forever have the rights listed in those ten amendments.

A central issue early on revolved around what the politicians of the 1790s meant by freedom of speech and freedom of the press. When the more conservative Federalists were in power, they didn't understand those freedoms the same way we do today. They felt that if newspapers or other citizens were saying negative things about the government, any negative things, they could be prosecuted for "libeling" the government or the elected official in question. Jeffersonians argued for an interpretation of the 1st Amendment that was much broader in definition, a view of the freedom of the press and of speech much closer to the modern view today. This debate over the definition of freedom of speech and of the press came to a head in 1798 at a time when there was a fierce debate in the United States over how much to get involved with the disputes between France and England. Federalists were more pro-England; Jefferson's Democratic-Republican party was more pro-France. In the midst of this debate, the Federalists worked themselves into a frenzy, convincing themselves that the Democratic-Republicans were in treasonous league with the French, and they passed the Alien and Sedition Acts. This legislation said that Federalists could arrest hostile newspaper publishers and other pro-Jeffersonian leaders on the grounds that they were consorting with French "aliens" and engaging in sedition against the government.

As in most times of war or foreign policy threats, the public initially rallied around the government, and the Federalists won the 1798 congressional elections in big numbers. But as they continued to arrest individuals who spoke out against them, more and more people realized that Adams, Hamilton, and the Federalists were overreaching and were in fact a threat to the very freedoms that people had fought for in the Revolution. Democratic-Republicans won the 1800 elections, and the Jeffersonian interpretation of our civil liberties embedded in the Bill of Rights came to be the widely accepted version.

Even with that being the case, a much bigger threat to the freedoms of American citizens was the idea that while the Bill of Rights kept the federal government from curtailing our fundamental liberties, the states were still perfectly free to do so. This view of states' rights, as we shall see in the next chapter, became the dominant philosophy of Southern conservatives and would be a major impediment to the liberties of American citizens living in the South. The Southern philosophy of states' rights continues to this day.

The Separation of Church and State, and the Freethinkers

Conservatives today like to vehemently point out that the phrase about a "wall" between church and state does not exist anywhere in the Constitution, but Jefferson's use of that phrase to describe the separation of church and state was neither accidental nor out of keeping with the founders' opinion on the matter. Although there had been many conservative clerics who supported the idea of state sponsorship of religion, and many states and localities still had government sponsorship of religion in their laws, a broad and strong majority of the founders were vehemently opposed to church and state intermingling. This opinion was due in great part to the recent history of England and the rest of Europe, which was full of examples as to why this mixing was a bad idea. Ironically, the idea of a wall between church and state was most aggressively pushed by the Baptists and people of other evangelical churches, who were very tired of the government getting in their way every time they tried to convert people.

One of the little-known facts about the Founding Fathers is how strongly they were influenced by a philosophy called Deism. Deism propounds the theory that God exists and created the universe but does not in any way intervene in human affairs. While most of the political leaders of the American Revolution were understandably quite discreet about any questioning of conventional religious beliefs, there is a great deal of evidence, especially in their private correspondence, that to one extent or another Jefferson, Madison, Washington, Adams, and Franklin all tended toward a Deistic philosophy. The most open of the founders about his religious beliefs, as we saw in the last chapter, was Tom Paine, and he was attacked viciously by conservatives for his views. He was called a freethinker. It is strange to think of now, but in those days the word *freethinker*—like the word *democracy*—was a curse. Conservative clerics hated the people they called freethinkers and denounced them for their irreverence at every opportunity.

Fortunately, outside of the South (whose citizens didn't believe that the Bill of Rights applied to Southerners), the new freedoms that were delineated in the American Constitution liberated freethinkers to say and write whatever they wanted about religion and God. The freethinker movement certainly wasn't all or even mostly atheistic or agnostic, but most freethinkers aggressively challenged conventional church hierarchies and theology.

In addition to Paine and some of the other Founding Fathers, the freethinking movement had a big influence on many important leaders in the 1800s and early 1900s. Lincoln, although deeply religious in his own way, was particularly shaped by the philosophy. Other leaders who were greatly influenced by the movement included:

- Early feminist leaders such as Elizabeth Cady Stanton, Susan B. Anthony, and Lucretia Mott;
- Civil rights leaders, including Frederick Douglass and W. E. B. DuBois;
- The most influential progressive lawyer in history, Clarence Darrow;
- The important reformer Robert Dale Owens, who, among many other things, helped Congress write perhaps the most important post–Bill of Rights constitutional amendment, the 14th Amendment;
- The prominent labor leader Eugene Debs;
- Some of America's greatest writers, including Mark Twain and Walt Whitman; and
- ACLU founder Roger Baldwin

All of these "freethinkers" contributed enormously to our nation. Their ideas and values helped bring about profound change for the better in this country's history and added immeasurably to America's culture and character. Ironically, given the hatred assigned to them by conservative religious leaders, they did more to help "the least of these" whom Jesus cared so deeply about in his ministry than any conservative leader has.

I mention the Deistic and freethinking influences of some of our most important writers and activists in this chapter on the Constitution because of the fundamental way the Bill of Rights influenced American thought and culture. Where freedom of thought and speech and press and religion was crushed, either by the state or by local violence, as in the slave/Jim Crow South, the culture of progressive thinking and politics did not develop. In those parts of the country that honored the Bill of Rights, progressives competed vigorously and quite often successfully with conservatives.

The drafters of our Constitution gave us truly important gifts. The kind of stability that took root in our country and that has been unique over the last two-plus centuries is a wonderful thing. Not having too much power centralized in any one institution of government is profoundly important as well.

But the drafters also failed us, by not including the progressive voices of Paine or Jefferson or the shopkeepers, the mechanics, and the small farmers of the 1780s. The framers' antidemocratic tendencies, as exemplified by the Electoral College, put us in danger of enduring political crises time and time again. Their initial omission of a Bill of Rights almost caused the whole project to go down in flames, and their failure to give the federal government the power to enforce these rights in the states meant a lack of basic liberties and civil rights in many states for far too long. Finally, their deal with the slavery devil not only almost destroyed us in the Civil War but has poisoned our society in countless ways ever since. When conservative ideas carried the day at the Constitutional Convention, the country suffered as a result. When progressive ideas broke through, as in the fight for the Bill of Rights, the freedoms we love most took root.

4

Civil Rights, States' Rights, and the Re-Creation of the American Idea

There is great nobility to the idea of American democracy— a society where we are all created equal and where government is of, by, and for the people. We should be proud of these ideals, which have inspired so many around the world, and proud of the great good that this country has achieved in its history.

But as a nation, we have also been plagued historically with some great evils. None has been more profound, none has gone deeper into the very marrow of our national soul, than the scourge of racism. From the time British colonists landed on these shores and started to kill off Native peoples and bring over slaves from Africa (which began in 1619, a year before the Pilgrims landed at Plymouth Rock), we have been neck deep in the curse of racial inequality and its ill consequences. The political fights we have had and continue to have over the issues of race are still deeply affecting us today.

One of the saddest things about the history of American racism is that it stains the legacy of some of our otherwise strongly progressive politicians. Jefferson made an incredibly important contribution to progressive thought, as discussed in chapter 2, but was a slave owner and a firm supporter of slavery in his final years.

Andrew Jackson helped expand suffrage to working-class white men and was a big advocate in general for progressive economic and political measures to help working people, but he was also a staunch supporter of slavery and one of the worst offenders in history in terms of his policies toward Native Americans. Woodrow Wilson helped pass a progressive income tax and other great reforms but was one of the most extreme racist presidents in U.S. history: among other things, he hosted a viewing of a movie that praised the Ku Klux Klan. FDR pushed through the greatest economic reforms in American history but was silent on Jim Crow and imprisoned Japanese Americans during World War II, along with refusing to let large numbers of Jewish immigrants into the United States to escape the Nazis.

This historical record reminds us that many factors have allowed racism to flourish throughout the years of our country's history. In terms of the history of race inequity, you can divide the players who have held back progress into the following three categories (though there is, of course, some overlap and bleeding of roles):

1. The stone-cold racists. Along with leaders such as Andrew Jackson and Woodrow Wilson, this group also includes John C. Calhoun, Stephen Douglas, Richard Russell, Jesse Helms, Tom Tancredo, and many, many other politicians over the years; the hate groups such as the Ku Klux Klan and the White Citizens Council; and vicious lawmen like Bull Connor and J. Edgar Hoover, who were supposed to be protecting people and the rule of law but instead used their power to maintain the status quo.

I think it is important to understand the depths of racism from some of these revered "statesmen," including those in our recent history. Here's a sampling: John C. Calhoun said, "The difficulty is in the diversity of the Races. . . . No power on earth can overcome the difficulty. The causes lie too deep in the principles of our nature to be surmounted. Slaves cannot be separated from whites, and cannot live together in peace, or harmony, or to their mutual advantage, except in their present relation."

Bull Connor said, "We want them [African Americans] to go parallel and side by side, but not intermixed, intermarried and integrated. Segregation will keep our nation from becoming another Brazil, where the intermingling of the races, I am told, has produced a hapless, helpless nation."

Jesse Helms, in his weekly TV program *Viewpoint* for WRAL in North Carolina, said, "The Negro cannot count forever on the kind of restraint that's thus far left him free to clog the streets, disrupt traffic, and interfere with other men's rights." He referred to civil rights activists as "communists" and "sexual perverts." He called the Civil Rights Act of 1964 "the most dangerous piece of legislation ever introduced in Congress." Seventeen years later, Helms said, "Crime rates and irresponsibility among Negroes are a fact of life which must be faced."

2. Those who knew better. The greatest failure of the writers of the Constitution was leaving slavery firmly in place, and many of them knew better: their debates are full of acknowledgments that slavery was wrong and would curse future generations. As noted in chapter 3, the otherwise conservative Gouverneur Morris gave an eloquent speech at the Constitutional Convention against slavery but then never said a word thereafter and happily went along with all of the deals that were made with Southern slave owners.

These Founding Fathers, like many in the years since, accepted racial injustice (in this case, slavery) either for economic reasons (Jefferson, for example, depended on his slaves for economic survival) or for political ones.

3. Those who did nothing. FDR knew that Jim Crow and the internment of Japanese Americans were wrong, but he stayed silent to keep his political coalition together. In the 1876 election, Rutherford B. Hayes knew that ending the role of federal troops protecting black civil rights in the South was wrong, but he did it anyway so that he would win the disputed presidential election. Today many politicians of both parties know that comprehensive immigration reform is desperately needed but play political games with the issue to win short-term political points. History is full of examples of politicians lacking courage when it comes to doing the right thing on race.

In the face of these three types of politicians blocking progress on the issue and the other factors that stand in the way, why has our country made advances? There is a combination of reasons, to be sure. One is simply the march of history, through better education and science and more modern views. Another is international relations, as our political leaders have realized over time that the oppression of people of color on American soil has hurt our ability to influence other countries around the globe. That view is part of what motivated an otherwise reluctant JFK to push for more civil rights. White progressives have certainly played an important role in both the abolitionist and the modern civil rights movements. But I believe the bulk of the credit throughout history goes to the leaders and the activists of the oppressed communities.

The great Frederick Douglass, the former slave who became the single most important abolitionist leader, summed up movement politics best in what is perhaps my favorite quote of all time:

> If there is no struggle, there is no progress. Those who profess to favor freedom, and yet deprecate agitation, are men who want crops without plowing up the ground. They want rain without thunder and lightning. They want the ocean without the awful roar of its many waters. This struggle may be a moral one; or it may be a physical one; or it may be both moral and physical; but it must be a struggle. Power concedes nothing without a demand. It never did and it never will . . . men may not get all they pay for in this world; but they must certainly pay for all they get.

Power concedes nothing without a demand. That fundamental principle has been at the heart of the strategy for social progress in this country, but nowhere more so than in the great battles over racial justice. And that demand has been powered by the oppressed themselves; otherwise, it never would have succeeded. As important as William Lloyd Garrison and Harriet Beecher Stowe were to the abolitionist movement, it never would have blossomed without Douglass's and Sojourner Truth's brilliant leadership abilities. As important as the white students coming to the South for Freedom Rides and Mississippi Summer were, they wouldn't have had any reason to go without the remarkable courage of the black leaders of the civil rights movement in the South. As important as white politicians such as Abe Lincoln and Earl Warren and Bobby Kennedy and LBJ were to changing the laws for the better, they never would have succeeded without the African American–led political movements that created the moment for change.

If racism is the great curse of American history, the philosophical battles over what to do about it are our history's fundamental flashpoints. This battle over race has resulted in:

- Many of Congress's most intense and bitter debates
- Numerous pieces of historic landmark legislation (among them, the Missouri Compromise of 1820; the Compromise of 1850; the Kansas-Nebraska Act of 1854; the Reconstruction-era legislation; the Civil Rights Act of 1964; the Voting Rights Act of 1965; the Civil Rights Act of 1968, including the Fair Housing Act; and the Martin Luther King Jr. holiday)
- Arguably the three most famous and far-reaching Supreme Court decisions of all time (the Dred Scott decision, *Plessy v. Ferguson*, and *Brown v. Board of Education*)
- Three incredibly important constitutional amendments (the 13th, the 14th, and the 15th)
- The formation of the modern-day Republican Party and several third-party movements (including the Liberty and Free Soil pre–Civil War abolitionist parties, the Southern Democrat Party of 1860, Strom Thurmond's States' Rights Party in 1948, and George Wallace's American Independent Party of 1968)

- The biggest and fastest regional political realignment in American history, when the South went from being a one-party region that always voted overwhelmingly Democratic to a region that has voted strongly Republican in every presidential election since 1980

- The Civil War, the most horrific and costly war ever fought in the Western Hemisphere

- The two most important and influential speeches in American history: Lincoln's Gettysburg Address and King's "I Have a Dream" speech

That's a lot of big-time action over one issue.

The Emergence of States' Rights as a Conservative Principle

From the 1830s on, the central rhetorical and philosophical pivot in the race debate has been "states' rights." Before the 1830s, the debate over the role of the federal government versus the role of the states was far more nuanced and far less ideologically driven—and racism-related—than the debate became at that point. After independence from Britain was declared in 1776, the Articles of Confederation vested a vast amount of power in the states. Once the Revolutionary War was won and the new country began to drift both economically and politically, the debate over the size and the strength of the federal government began to be played out, and that debate factored into the intricate compromises written into the new Constitution. The practical and philosophical debates over the next few decades as the new nation was being established weren't really along ideological lines but tended to be about more pragmatic things: the differing economic interests of various regions, the worries by small states of being dominated by the big states, the many ways that economic development and territorial expansion were playing out, and so on. It should also be noted that there were many early debates over slavery, including at the Constitutional

Convention, and over the extremely important Missouri Compromise, which established the famous Mason-Dixon Line, below which slavery would be allowed as new states came into the Union. In those early debates, rhetoric around states' rights was not central to the arguments.

That all began to change in the 1830s, in part because some of those earlier issues had been pretty well resolved, but mostly because of John C. Calhoun and the rise of growing tensions over the slavery issue—tensions fueled by the abolitionist movement.

If Edmund Burke is the intellectual founder of modern conservatism, John Calhoun is its political founder. In his long career, Calhoun's résumé included being a congressman and a senator from South Carolina, a secretary of state under two different presidents, and a vice president under two different presidents (John Quincy Adams and Andrew Jackson, who were bitter opponents and rivals in the 1824 and 1828 elections—Calhoun switched sides when he saw that Jackson was going to win). But Calhoun's main claim to fame was the development of the states' rights doctrine: that states are sovereign political entities that join the Union of their own free will and have the right at any time to ignore or nullify federal law and/or to secede from the Union.

Ironically, given the centrality of the states' rights doctrine to all of the subsequent debates about slavery, Reconstruction, and Jim Crow, the first major battle that Calhoun launched on behalf of his new philosophy was about a tariff bill that disadvantaged South Carolina's economy. Calhoun, who was Jackson's vice president at that time, led the fight against the tariff and began a bitter personal war with Jackson over the issue. The conflict famously provoked an exchange of toasts at, ironically, a Jefferson Day dinner in 1830. Jackson, staring directly at Calhoun, toasted to "Our Union: it must be preserved." Calhoun's reply was "Our Union, next to our liberty, most dear."

The boiling point of the crisis came in 1832, when South Carolina declared the tariff "null and void" within the borders of South Carolina, and Jackson issued a proclamation saying that nullification would not be allowed and secession was not the right of any state. Calhoun resigned as vice president and was quickly appointed a senator from South Carolina, where he kept the fight going. Finally, a compromise tariff was passed, and the crisis was averted. But that battle created the states' rights movement, whose advocates would soon push the country to civil war over the slavery issue.

States' rights would quickly become the center point of a rapidly growing debate over slavery. Although there had always been opposition to slavery, the abolitionist movement really started to gather steam in the 1820s. A black man named David Walker, who was born free in North Carolina, had moved to Boston, saying, "If I remain in this bloody land, I will not live long. As true as God reigns, I will be avenged for the sorrows my people have suffered." In 1829, he published "Walker's Appeal," one of the greatest abolitionist pamphlets of all time, and his dramatic words stirred people up on both sides of the slavery debate. When Nat Turner led his courageous slave revolt two years later, and William Lloyd Garrison published the first issue of his *Liberator* magazine the same year (1831), the South was truly afraid and enraged.

It was the moral tone of the abolitionists that drove Southerners crazy. In Garrison's first editorial, he wrote his famous lines that have become a clarion call for idealist moral crusaders ever since:

> I will be as harsh as truth, and as uncompromising as justice. On this subject [slavery] I do not wish to think, to speak, or write, with moderation. No! No! Tell a man whose house is on fire to give a moderate alarm; tell him to moderately rescue his wife from the hands of the ravisher; tell the mother to gradually extricate her babe from the fire into which it has fallen; but urge me not to use moderation in a cause like the present! I am in earnest—I will not equivocate—I will not excuse—I will not retreat a single inch—AND I WILL BE HEARD.

The combination of moral indignation and the potential for violent slave rebellion totally outraged Calhoun and the arrogant Southerners whom he led. They started fulminating and threatening. Jefferson's anguished fears about slavery destroying the nation that he helped create were becoming true.

One of the ironies of an institution like slavery is that it sabotaged the very fabric of freedom for everyone in society, slave and freeman alike. Fearful of its slaves being "stirred up," the South became an utterly repressive society and did not allow free speech or the publication of anything that was even mildly critical of slavery. Entrepreneurs who needed laborers and wanted to pay them were discouraged from coming into the South. Religions that encouraged anything remotely akin to "free thinking" were driven out. Even farmers who wanted to pay their help to work for them were vilified and boycotted.

In 1859, Carl Schurz, the brilliant German immigrant who became one of the major leaders of the antislavery movement, both before and after the Civil War, talked about this dynamic in his influential speech titled "True Americanism." In the speech, Schurz said that the whites of the South were no freer than their slaves: "Where is their liberty of the press? Where is their liberty of speech? Where is the man among them who dares to advocate open principles not in strict accordance with the ruling system? They speak of a republican form of government, they speak of democracy, but the despotic spirit of slavery and mastership combined pervades their whole political life like a liquid poison."

Besides this kind of repression, Southerners needed to construct a political theory that justified slavery and answered the moral arguments of the other side. That theory was, of course, part pure racism but was also one part Burke's worship of tradition and at least two or three parts Calhoun's new states' rights theory.

Calhoun posited, more than a little ironically, that states' rights was the only remedy against minorities' rights being trampled on by the majority, that is, that the poor trampled-on Southern white slave owner's minority rights would be overrun by those nasty Northern abolitionists. His *South Carolina Exposition*, published in 1828 (before the major tariff crisis with Jackson), said that any state could annul any federal law and mentioned both tariffs and slavery as examples of issues where the rights of Southerners might need to be protected. In subsequent writings and speeches over the next two decades, Calhoun denounced both abolitionists and democracy. He wrote that rule by a majority was "but government of the strongest interests . . . [which] when not efficiently checked is the most tyrannical and oppressive that can be devised."

Aware that the North's economy and population were growing much faster than those of the stagnant South, Calhoun became virulently opposed to democracy itself: "The will of the majority is the will of a rabble. Progressive democracy is incompatible with liberty." The only solution to the growing numerical power of the North, he said, was that states should have the "right of self-protection," that is, nullification and secession.

Calhoun's political theories became the basis for Southern resistance regarding slavery, the Civil War, Reconstruction, and Jim Crow. And he became a hero to conservatives for all time.

While the states' rights doctrine as articulated by Calhoun would become the central narrative in the South's continuing to hang on to the struggle of its racist society, Southern leaders' political perspective was also predicated on a kind of paternalistic tradition. Needing to rationalize the evil of slavery and later Jim Crow, they made the claim that because of blacks' inherent inferiority, white people needed to take care of them. Again, no one explains the philosophy better than Calhoun himself: "But I take it to a higher ground. I hold that in the present state of civilization, where two races of different origin, and distinguished by color, and other physical differences, as well as intellectual, are brought together, the relation now existing in the slaveholding states between the two, is, instead of an evil, a good—a positive good."

As we shall see, Calhoun's philosophy founded an enduring conservative political movement that would rear its ugly head over and over again throughout American history and into today's battles. But perhaps more intellectual conservative movement leaders have chosen to shy away from Calhoun because of his blatant racism? Not so much.

The dean of twentieth-century intellectual conservatism, Russell Kirk, is positively rhapsodic about Calhoun:

Bold and fertile opinions, these. Calhoun's Disquisition is open to many of the objections that commonly apply to detailed projects for political reform. He slides quickly over formidable objections, he evades any very precise description of how the principle may be applied, and he really has small hope of any immediate practical consequence from these ideas. Yet these flaws yawn more conspicuously in the great popular reform-schemes of our era—Marxism, Fabian Socialism, distributism, syndicalism, production-planning. Calhoun is not playing Lycurgus; he is describing a political principle, and it is one of the most sagacious and vigorous suggestions ever advanced by American conservatism. The concurrent majority itself; representation of citizens by section and interest, rather than by pure numbers; the insight that liberty is a product of civilization and a reward of virtue, not an abstract right; the acute distinction between moral equality and equality of condition; the linking of liberty and progress; the strong protest against domination by class or region, under the guise of numerical majority—these concepts, provocative of thought and capable of modern application, give Calhoun a place beside John Adams as one of the two most eminent American political writers. Calhoun demonstrated that conservatism can project as well as complain.

While modern-day conservatives have thankfully given up their overtly racist rhetoric, they are still happy to embrace the philosophy underlying the old Southern slave system.

The Boiling Pot Leading to the Civil War

As Southerners grew ever more offended and threatened by the spreading abolitionist movement in the North, Northerners grew more and more tired of the arrogance of slave power. Despite the Northern states having three times as many people as the slave states, these less populous states continued to be able to block any progressive reforms on any issue suggested by

Northerners, in part because of their power in the Senate and in part because of the notorious three-fifths rule embedded into the Constitution in 1787. And one event after another ratcheted up the anger on both sides:

- The Compromise of 1850, which was widely seen in the North as no compromise at all but a piece of legislation heavily skewed to slave power. Among other things, it criminalized doing anything in any way to help slaves escape, even in the states that had outlawed slavery, and it forced Northerners to help locate runaway slaves. (This provision has a lot in common with modern attempts by conservatives to stop churches from providing sanctuary to undocumented immigrants.)

- The publication of *Uncle Tom's Cabin* by Harriet Beecher Stowe, which inflamed Northern opinion against slave states and outraged Southerners.

- The passage of the Kansas-Nebraska Act, which overrode past compromises and allowed slavery above the Mason-Dixon Line as long as the "people" of those states wanted it. This set off the worst American-on-American violence before the Civil War, as pro- and antislavery advocates rushed into those territories and started killing one another in an attempt to win the issue.

- The formation of the openly antislavery Republican Party.

- The vicious caning of abolitionist senator Charles Sumner on the floor of the Senate by an offended Southern member of Congress, Preston Brooks. Brooks received great acclaim in the South for this violent act.

- The notorious Dred Scott decision, which ruled that people of African descent, whether free or slave, were not citizens of the United States, and that Congress had no authority to prohibit slavery in federal territories.

- The raid by John Brown on Harper's Ferry. Brown's goal was to start a massive slave revolt by supplying slaves with rifles.

Every incident raised the anger on each side to new heights. The house divided against itself, as Lincoln had put it, could not stand. Jefferson's nightmare was coming true.

When Abraham Lincoln was elected president, the Southern states, starting with Calhoun's home state of South Carolina, used Calhoun's states' rights doctrine as their justification to secede. The great irony is that conservative historians in the years since have also used the states' rights theory as a way to gloss over the idea that the Civil War was really about slavery. Almost all of the textbooks I read while growing up, which were mostly written by Southerners, talked about how the Civil War was more a battle over the philosophy and political theory, about whether states had the right to go their own way. Because of Calhoun's high-minded rhetoric—adapted, of course, by the next generation of Southerners to justify their decision to secede—conservative historians have since tried to argue that slavery wasn't the main issue at all.

Although states' rights was the exalted reason sometimes given for the Civil War, there is no justification whatsoever in the historical record for any other conclusion than that the war was first, last, and totally about the slavery issue. For one thing, all of the incidents leading up to the war—the Missouri Compromise, Nat Turner's revolt, the Compromise of 1850, *Uncle Tom's Cabin*, the Kansas-Nebraska Act, the Dred Scott decision, Sumner's caning, John Brown's raid, an openly antislavery party winning the White House in 1860—were 100 percent about slavery. Second, if you go back and read about the state legislative debates over secession, the pro-secessionists argued that even poorer, non-slaveholding white people should still be in favor of secession because, as the governor of Georgia at that time put it, slavery was "the poor man's best government. . . . Among us the poor white laborer does not belong to the menial class. The negro is in no sense his equal. . . . He belongs to the only true aristocracy, the race of white men." Poor farmers, he went on to say, "will never consent to abolition rule" because they know "that in the event of abolition of slavery, they would be greater sufferers than the rich, who would be able to protect themselves."

In addition, a leading Alabama newspaper argued that poor whites should join slaveholding planters in the seceding states because most Southern whites could agree that "democratic liberty exists solely because we have black slaves" whose presence "promotes equality among the free. . . . Freedom is not possible without slavery."

But even if that rather compelling, not to mention ironic, point wasn't enough to convince you, consider some of these statements from Confederate leaders. President of the Confederacy Jefferson Davis said that the Southern states left the Union "to save ourselves from a revolution" that threatened to make "property in slaves so insecure as to be comparatively worthless." In 1861, the secretary of state of the Confederacy told foreign governments that the Confederacy was formed to preserve their old institutions—namely, slavery. Confederate vice president Alexander Stephens was very clear about slavery being at the heart of the reason for the Confederacy's existence. He postulated that if the signers of the Declaration had meant to include African Americans among the all men who were created equal, that they were just wrong, adding, "Our new government is founded upon exactly the opposite idea; its foundations are laid, its cornerstone rests upon the great truth that the negro is not equal to the white man; that slavery . . . is his natural and normal condition. This, our new government, is the first in the history of the world based upon this great physical, philosophical, and moral truth."

Good to know. And so much for being high-minded.

The Progressive Agenda of Lincoln and the Radical Republicans

One of the most overlooked aspects of American political history in that intense period was that with Southern conservatives out of Congress, the progressive reformers who came into power with Abraham Lincoln had the chance to pass some of the most far-reaching and significant progressive legislation in the history of the country. Abe Lincoln was no saint, though—he sometimes moved to the right on the issue of black equality, to save himself from the prevailing racist attitudes in the country; he moved more slowly on abolition at times than he should have; and he made some serious mistakes. But what he achieved was stunning.

In the midst of the worst crisis in American history, even while focused on winning the Civil War, Lincoln worked with Congress to pass four major bills. This legislation created a domestic agenda that moved millions of poor people into the middle class for generations to come and set the stage for progressive achievements over the next century:

1. The progressive income tax. The first progressive income tax, a tax where the wealthy paid more than the poor, in American history was passed under Lincoln. It was a modest tax to help pay for the Civil War and was bitterly opposed by conservatives, who complained of paying a tax to help the slaves.

This income tax was later repealed, but Lincoln's strong commitment to the concept that those who can afford to pay more in taxes should pay more was an idea kept alive by progressives for years. Finally enacted for good by Woodrow Wilson, the idea of progressive taxation has continued to be a battle fought year in and year out between progressives and conservatives.

2. The Pacific Railroad Act. One of the two most important infrastructure projects in American history (the other being Eisenhower's interstate highway system), this bill set the stage for linking the country's transportation and commerce from coast to coast. As with Eisenhower's interstate system, which created substantial pollution problems, this bill definitely had a downside: crooked politicians and railroad executives in the 1880s and 1890s used the railway system to exploit farmers and Native Americans. But the overall impact in terms of connecting different parts of the country and building a modern economic base for the nation was a lasting boon for a stronger American economy and helped create a modern economic powerhouse.

Whenever the federal government has taken on massive infrastructure projects like this, it has always run into opposition from conservatives who are afraid of higher taxes and "big government."

This legislation had languished for years in Congress, due to the opposition of Southern conservatives. But investing in these kinds of infrastructure projects—as in this case—almost always pays off economically because it helps to build and strengthen the middle class.

3. The land-grant university system. Three major government initiatives in American history have allowed large numbers of low-income and middle-class kids to go to college: the modern student loan-grant programs, the GI bill in 1945, and Lincoln's land-grant university system.

The land-grant university system was an initiative with enormous implications. Consider these statistics: only 6 percent of young people in the 1850s graduated from high school and only 4 percent graduated from college. Today 85 percent of students graduate from high school and close to 30 percent graduate from college. Major universities such as the University of Nebraska, Washington State, Clemson, and Cornell were chartered as land-grant schools. State colleges like the University of Michigan and the University of North Carolina at Chapel Hill brought higher education within the reach of millions of students. Given the relative lack of college scholarships and loan programs compared to today, the establishment of much less expensive public universities literally opened up college education for the middle class and for some poor students. With the possible exception of the GI bill, which was passed after World War II, creating the land-grant university system was the single greatest contribution to expanding college education opportunities in U.S. history.

4. The Homestead Act. Giving away 160 acres of free land to anyone who wanted to apply for it was the largest government grant program to lower- and middle-income Americans in the country's history. This program was the equivalent of giving away nearly $60,000 per person in today's dollars. But, as with the best of progressive programs, it wasn't just a giveaway program; it was an investment in people. It made a deal with the people who were willing to take it: the U.S. government will give you land you couldn't afford to buy any other way, and if you work the land and make something of it, you will have a ticket to the middle class.

With this law, Lincoln kept the American West from sliding into a kind of Third World economic structure, where a few wealthy barons bought up land at a cheap price and used it to dominate the agricultural economy and drive out families who were trying to make a living on smaller farms. The Homestead Act was somewhat like the massive land redistribution practiced in certain Third World countries, but in reverse. With so much land so widely dispersed, the family farm system of agriculture was able to establish itself and survive, even through the Great Depression, into the 1980s, when Reagan's farm policies finally destroyed most of what remained of smaller family farms.

Think about the achievement of passing all of this remarkable legislation—probably America's most progressive and ambitious package of domestic legislation outside of the New Deal—in the middle of the most destructive war and the biggest crisis in U.S. history. Lincoln was the most amazing political leader this country has ever seen, and he stood clearly in the great progressive tradition of this nation.

The Role of Lincoln in the Great Progressive versus Conservative Debate

Another truly remarkable thing about Lincoln was that in the midst of the worst crisis in the nation's history since independence was declared from Britain, he sought to redefine the terms of the American political debate for all time. And, stunningly, he succeeded.

Lincoln went back to that founding moment in 1776, to Jefferson's Declaration, to make his case for a national government, governed by its people, that would protect the equal rights of all its citizens. And he did it in just 272 words in the Gettysburg Address. I think it's worth reprinting that remarkable speech here in its entirety:

Fourscore and seven years ago our fathers brought forth on this continent a new nation, conceived in liberty and dedicated to the proposition that all men are created equal. Now we are engaged in a great civil war, testing whether that nation or any nation so conceived and so dedicated can long endure. We are met on a great battlefield of that war. We have come to dedicate a portion of that field as a final resting-place for those who here gave their lives that that nation might live. It is altogether fitting and proper that we should do this. But in a larger sense, we cannot dedicate, we cannot consecrate, we cannot hallow this ground. The brave men, living and dead who struggled here have consecrated it far above our poor power to add or detract. The world will little note nor long remember what we say here, but it can never forget what they did here. It is for us the living rather to be dedicated here to the unfinished work which they who fought here have thus far so nobly advanced. It is rather for us to be here dedicated to the great task remaining before us—that from these honored dead we take increased devotion to that cause for which they gave the last full measure of devotion—that we here highly resolve that these dead shall not have died in vain, that this nation under God shall have a new birth of freedom, and that government of the people, by the people, for the people shall not perish from the earth.

Lincoln's Gettysburg Address was hardly uncontroversial at the time. In Garry Wills's brilliant Pulitzer Prize–winning book *Lincoln at Gettysburg: The Words That Remade America*, he wrote about how conservative contemporaries of Lincoln argued vehemently against the president's words at Gettysburg. He noted that the *Chicago Times*, a leading conservative newspaper, stated that the Constitution said nothing of equality and was tolerant of slavery. The *Times* editorialized, "It was to uphold this Constitution and the Union created by it, that our officers and soldiers gave their lives at Gettysburg. How dare he, then, standing on their graves, misstate the cause for which they died and libel the statesmen who founded the government?"

Lincoln's words have now taken on iconic status, but conservatives have directly, or much more often indirectly, argued ever since against the vision enunciated in the Gettysburg Address. That simple speech fundamentally reshaped American political thinking for good. Listen to the words of Wilmore Kendall, a leading conservative writer from the mid-1900s: "Abraham Lincoln . . . attempted a new act of founding, involving concretely a startling new interpretation of that principle of the founders which declared that 'all men are created equal.'"

Kendall wrote in another place: "We should not allow him [Lincoln]—not at least without some probing inquiry—to 'steal' the game, that is to accept his interpretation of the Declaration, its place in our history, and its meaning as 'true,' 'correct' or 'binding.'"

Here are the ideas in the Gettysburg Address that conservatives have found so hard to overcome:

- That the American nation was founded on the central "proposition that all men are created equal." Modern conservatives such as Supreme Court nominee Robert Bork, Ronald Reagan, and Attorney General Ed Meese, in Wills's words, think that "equality as a national commitment has been snuck into the Constitution."

- That America is governed by a single people, rather than by a collection of elites in the states. The Gettysburg Address is a clear answer to Calhoun and his fellow conservatives. Simple yet incredibly compelling, it provided an answer to the states' rights doctrine laid out by Calhoun and supported by conservatives in Lincoln's time and ever since. Lincoln's argument, and that of progressives today, is that the American people are one people, all due the same rights and liberties, no matter where we live or what the local power structure says.

- That our government is to be a government "of the people, by the people, for the people." Conservatives have always wanted the elites to rule. That's why they have opposed universal suffrage and even today want to make it harder for poor people to register and vote. That's why conservatives pushed so hard (unfortunately, successfully) for an Electoral College, rather than a straight popular vote for president. That's why it wasn't until the second decade of the 1900s that U.S. senators were elected by popular vote, rather than by state legislators. That's why, today, so many elites are terrified of blogs and other new forms of political organizing through the Internet. Lincoln's definition of American government as "of, by and for the people" is the clearest rebuke ever given to this kind of conservative philosophy.

To again quote Wills:

The Gettysburg Address has become an authoritative expression of the American spirit—as authoritative as the Declaration itself, and perhaps even more influential, since it determines how we read the Declaration. For most people now, the Declaration means what Lincoln told us it means, as a way of correcting the Constitution itself without overthrowing it. It is this correction of the spirit, this intellectual revolution, which makes attempts to go back beyond Lincoln to some earlier version so feckless. The proponents of states' rights may have arguments, but they have lost their force, in courts as well as in the popular mind. By accepting the Gettysburg Address, its concept of a single people dedicated to a proposition, we have been changed. Because of it, we live in a different America.

There were three transformative intellectual moments in the history of the United Sates and in the history of progressive thought in this country. The first was Jefferson's Declaration of Independence. The last was Martin Luther King Jr.'s "I Have a Dream" speech. In between the two, at perhaps the most critical moment in our nation's history, with the country on the verge of breaking apart, came the Gettysburg Address. The sweeping power of its central ideas re-created and renewed Jefferson's and Paine's original idea of America and made it even stronger and more progressive.

Lincoln's transformative speech, relatively unnoticed and undiscussed in the news coverage of the Gettysburg ceremony, has echoed through the American political and intellectual canyon and has helped build a foundation of progressive thinking ever since.

The Radical Republicans and Reconstruction

One would think that after betraying their country, launching a horrendously bloody Civil War, and being thoroughly defeated militarily, Southern conservatives would show some humility, and that Calhoun's theory of states' rights would go into history's dustbin. No such luck.

In fact, with Lincoln's death and Southerner Andrew Johnson's ascension to the presidency, Southern elites actually expected that all would return to the way things were before the war: that they would still have the catbird's seat in terms of congressional power, and that they would still have the right to control the lives of their former slaves, despite emancipation. If President Andrew Johnson had gotten his way, that is exactly what would have happened. Fortunately, the "Radical" Republicans—as historians have always referred to them—had other ideas. Although they lost their epic struggle with Southern conservatives in the post-Reconstruction Jim Crow era, their early successes in giving African Americans political power were a model for civil rights–era progressives to build on, and the constitutional amendments they passed set the foundational cornerstones for most of the important progressive advances of the twentieth century.

For all his brilliance, Lincoln made two enormous mistakes in the course of his otherwise truly extraordinary presidency. The first was to trust General George McClellan for too long—McClellan's weakness as a general prolonged the war for years and cost hundreds of thousands of lives. The other mistake, though, was politically far more important: making Andrew Johnson his running mate in 1864. Johnson was a Jacksonian Democrat and had earned Lincoln's notice as a Southerner (Tennessee) who had stayed strongly loyal to the Union. Lincoln thought it was a good idea politically to pick a Southern Democrat as his running mate to demonstrate that his overriding goal was national unity. He also wanted to send a signal to Southerners that they would be welcomed back if they left the rebel cause.

Given Lincoln's death, Johnson turned out to be a terrible choice. He was a megalomaniac whose gigantic ego was fed by Southern gentlemen coming and kissing his presidential ring to ask for forgiveness. He had no concern for the rights of the newly freed slaves and considered any disagreement on such matters to be a personal betrayal. Quickly allying himself with the old Southern elite whom he had condemned during the war, Johnson was on a collision course with the Republican reformers Lincoln had been working with.

Garrett Epps, in his superb book *Democracy Reborn*, described white Southern attitudes immediately after the Civil War: "The Constitution as they had known it guaranteed the sovereignty of every state, and made it in all but a few spheres superior to the Union. The battles of the past few years had changed the military facts . . . [but] had not changed the Constitution or the power of the individual state." Epps quoted Sidney Andrews, a reporter for the *Chicago Tribune* who traveled to the South in post-Appomattox 1865: "The states' rights heresy was as dominant in this [Georgia] convention, almost as in [the secession convention] of 1861." Andrews went on to note that among Southern elites, there was "not merely a broad assertion of the rights of the states, but an open enunciation of the supremacy of the state over the federal government."

Northern Republicans, for very good reason, feared the return of "slave power." They feared that Southern conservatives would merely stop freed slaves from having the vote or any civil or economic rights and then would come back to Congress in the same kind of dominating political position they had been in before the war, when they had blocked not only abolition but the many progressive reforms that had been passed under Lincoln with the Southerners gone. If the South kept African Americans from having the vote or any other power and preserved the lack of freedom to dissent that existed before the war, nothing would be changed politically.

Because Johnson was impossible to work with and the Radical Republicans had big majorities in a Congress that still had not accepted the Confederate states back, the Radical Republicans developed a new strategy: before allowing the old rebel states back into Congress under the unfair political rules devised by the Southern elites, Congress would pass a series of constitutional amendments that essentially remade the Constitution in terms of civil rights and states' rights and would overrule Johnson by adapting a strong Reconstruction policy that empowered freed slaves to vote and hold office.

The first of these amendments was the 13th, which put into the Constitution what had already happened with Lincoln's Emancipation Proclamation and the winning of the war. Of huge importance, there was a provision in it that went to the core of the states' rights debate: it granted Congress the power to enforce its provisions. It is noteworthy that while Southerners realized they had no hope after the war of getting slavery back and so begrudgingly accepted the part of the amendment outlawing slavery, they bitterly objected to the provision about Congress's right of enforcement. They knew that this provision eroded the power of states in general and set a terrible precedent as far as they were concerned.

The final amendment of the three (the 15th) was passed in 1870. It stated that "the right of citizens of the United States to vote shall not be denied or abridged by the United States or by any state on account of race, color, or previous condition of servitude." It again had a provision allowing Congress to enforce the law. This amendment was truly radical because in the past, states had always had full responsibility for determining voter qualifications. And it meant that future immigrants of any race, as long as they became citizens, could vote.

As huge and profound as those two amendments were over the long run, the 14th Amendment went even deeper than the other two toward changing the nature of American society. Certainly, the debate it provoked went to the core of the difference between the progressive vision of America and the conservative one.

The 14th Amendment was passed at the height of the Radical Republican frustration at Johnson's alliance with Southern conservatives on Reconstruction. Section 1 asserted that the federal government, not the states, decided who U.S. citizens were and gave that citizenship to all those born in the United States or naturalized by the federal government. The states were prohibited from denying those citizens their civil rights and "the equal protection of the law." It was the first time the Constitution created a definition of national citizenship as opposed to just leaving it to the states. Section 2 stated that any state denying the right to vote to any of its (male) citizens was to proportionally lose seats in Congress and the Electoral College. Sections 3 and 4 denied Southerners who had held federal office before the war and then served the rebel cause the right to run for federal office again, and ensured that debts that the Confederacy had incurred would never be paid by either federal or state governments.

The 14th Amendment was designed by progressives to be a long-term stake in the heart of states' rights and slave power by asserting that the federal government, not the states, had the right to guarantee American citizens their civil and political rights under the law. It literally extended the Bill of Rights to all American citizens, no matter what state they lived in, and gave the federal government the power to enforce those rights. The third provision was designed to stop Southern political leaders who had led their states to war from ever participating in the federal government again. The fourth provision would prevent the wealthy planters and bankers who had subsidized the Confederacy by loaning it money from making a profit for their betrayal.

Both Northern and Southern conservatives screamed bloody murder. Since Southerners were still mostly excluded from the debate because they hadn't been readmitted to Congress, Northern conservatives made their arguments for them. Some of these arguments were blatant appeals to racism (all quotes are taken from *Democracy Reborn*):

Sir, I trust I am as liberal as anybody toward the rights of all people, but I am unwilling, on the part of my State to give up the right that she claims, and that she may exercise, and exercise before very long of expelling a certain number of people who invade her borders; who owe to her no allegiance; who pretend to owe none; who recognize no authority in her government; who have a distinct, independent government of their own, an imperium in imperio; who pay no taxes; who never perform military service; who do nothing, in fact, which becomes the citizen, and perform none of the duties which devolve upon him, but, on the other hand, have no homes, pretend to own no land, live nowhere, settle as trespassers wherever they go, and whose sole merit is a universal swindle; who delight in it, who boast of it, and whose adroitness and cunning is of such a transcendent character that no skills can serve to correct it or punish it; I mean the Gypsies.—Edgar Cowan, Pennsylvania

I want it distinctly understood that the American people believe that this government was made for white men and white women. God save the people of the South from the degradation by which they would be obliged to go to the polls and vote side by side with the negro!—Andrew Rogers, New Jersey

But all of their arguments were also couched in the states' rights philosophy of Calhoun:

Thomas Hendricks (of Indiana, who later became vice president under Grover Cleveland): [But] during this session there has been claimed for them such force and scope of meaning as that Congress might invade the jurisdiction of the States, rob them of their reserved rights, and crown the Federal Government with absolute and despotic power.

Cowan: What conceivable difference can it make to a citizen of Pennsylvania as to how Ohio distributes her political power? . . . [To] touch, to venture upon that ground is to revolutionize the whole frame and texture of the system of our Government.

Rogers: The right to marry is a privilege. The right to be a judge or President of the United States is a privilege. I hold if [Section 1] ever becomes a part of the fundamental law of the land it will prevent any State from refusing to allow anything to anybody embraced under this term of privileges and immunities. That, sir, will be an introduction to the time when despotism and tyranny will march forward undisturbed and unbroken, in silence and in darkness, in this land which was once the land of freedom.

The Sundering of the Abolitionist and Feminist Movements

Although the 14th Amendment was a great step forward for progressives overall, the debate over it would have one tragic consequence: the long-term sundering of what had been a strong alliance between the abolitionist and the feminist movements. Both social justice movements had been growing in strength since the 1830s, and from the beginning had been closely united in solidarity with each other. The leaders of the abolitionist movement, such as Frederick Douglass and William Lloyd Garrison, had been strong supporters of equal rights and voting rights for women; the leaders of the feminist movement, Elizabeth Cady Stanton and Susan B. Anthony, had been fervent supporters of abolition; and the incredibly eloquent Sojourner Truth had stood at the intersection of both movements and been an inspirational leader of both. As Epps put it, "Since the abolition movement had begun, women had been its heart and soul—the shock troops that had brought antislavery from the fringes of political discourse in the 1840s to the very center of national politics in 1866. Until the spring of that year, antislavery and feminism were not allied; they were the very same movement, springing from a common core of passion and looking forward to a common future of racial and sexual equality."

Conservatives loved mocking both the abolitionist and the feminist causes, as we've already seen with some of the racist statements on the African American side. A *New York Herald* reporter covering a women's rights meeting wrote that the attendees were mostly women "from the interior of New England, where the mental and physical culture of females is attended to more closely than the art of adornment in dress." A New York legislative committee, when presented with a petition for women's rights by Susan B. Anthony, responded by saying that if there was inequality between male and female, "the gentlemen are the sufferers."

When the debate over civil and voting rights for the freed slaves was joined after the Civil War in the 14th Amendment, that mockery of feminism took its toll. The Radical Republicans had the votes to pass the 14th Amendment if women were excluded, and because African Americans and male abolitionists were desperate to get some legal rights written into law due to the massive violence already being committed against freed slaves by the Ku Klux Klan and other racist terrorists, they took the deal.

Feminists felt betrayed, and the two movements that had been so closely aligned from their earliest days were split asunder. The bitterness was reflected in the years to come, as many women's movement leaders stopped working for civil rights for blacks, and black leaders did little to help in the fight for women's suffrage. That estrangement finally began to ease in the modern civil rights movement, as the two movements increasingly began to work together on issues, but even then it wasn't always easy. When the topic of women's rights came up at a Student Nonviolent Coordinating Committee (SNCC) conference in 1964, Stokely Carmichael cut off discussion of the issue by proclaiming that "the only position for women in SNCC is prone."

The Continuing Battle over Civil Rights and States' Rights and the South's Alliance with the Republican Party

The language of the 13th, 14th, and 15th amendments was as clear as can be, and the Radical Republicans won important temporary victories in the administration of Reconstruction, which allowed freed slaves real political power in the South for about ten years.

But Southern conservatives were determined. The Ku Klux Klan was founded, and terrorism against both blacks and their white supporters remained high. That first generation of progressive Republicans gave way to a second generation that became corrupted by the Northeast industrialist robber barons, and concern about black civil and voting rights faded. As noted in chapter 3, Southern Democrats and the Republican Party cut an evil deal in the disputed 1876 election, giving the electoral votes of three Southern states to the Republican candidate, Rutherford B. Hayes, in exchange for his withdrawal of the last remaining federal troops in the South that were safeguarding African American rights. Conservative-dominated Supreme Courts ignored the language and intent of the 13th, 14th and 15th amendments in rulings such as the notorious *Plessy v. Ferguson*, which allowed "separate but equal" schools, and in earlier rulings that completely disregarded those amendments. In an 1873 case, the majority even said that the intent of the 14th Amendment couldn't possibly have been "to bring within the power of Congress the entire domain of civil rights heretofore belonging exclusively to the States," when it was incredibly obvious from the language of the amendment and the congressional debate just three years before that that was the exact intent of the 14th Amendment. As a result, Jim Crow became embedded into the culture and the law of Southern states.

But the seeds had been planted, in the words of the Constitution, in the hopes and dreams of African Americans, and in the aspirations of the broader progressive movement. Eventually, more progressive justices on the Supreme Court started to respect those amendments and the fundamental changes they had made in the Constitution. In 1925, the Court said that "freedom of speech and of the press . . . are among the fundamental personal rights and liberties protected by the due process clause from impairment by the states." One by one, the Court ruled that the due process clause protected the freedoms laid out in the Bill of Rights: freedom of the press, of speech, of assembly and petition, and of religion. And finally, in 1954, the Warren Court delivered *Brown v. Board of Education*.

Meanwhile, African American leaders kept organizing, all through those bleak and ugly years. Frederick Douglass, W. E. B. DuBois, A. Philip Randolph, and a host of other national and local leaders kept up their courageous struggle. They literally put their lives and careers on the line repeatedly in those lonely years, sometimes joined by white progressives such as Eleanor Roosevelt and Clarence Darrow.

The Southern conservative states' rights movement never went away, though, and was able to block any reform for long decades. But slowly, the tide started to turn. When Harry Truman desegregated the armed forces after World War II and Hubert Humphrey won a floor fight to put a civil rights provision in the 1948 Democratic platform, Southern conservatives bolted and formed Strom Thurmond's States' Rights Party. When the civil rights movement began to rise up in the 1950s, these conservatives again used the states' rights and Southern tradition arguments they had borrowed from Calhoun and Jefferson Davis.

Of course, some of the people taking this position were the stereotypical Southerners doing their faux populist redneck shtick, such as George Wallace railing against the federal government's "pointy-headed bureaucrats." But they also came from more "respectable" Southern intellectuals, such as Senator Richard Russell of Georgia, a man so revered by his colleagues that they named one of the main Senate office buildings for him. Russell had come to the Senate in 1933 as a Roosevelt Democrat, voting for every measure of Roosevelt's New Deal program. Russell was even considered a moderate on race issues by people in D.C. But when Roosevelt pushed for an antilynching bill in 1935 and 1937, Russell opposed it on the basis of states' rights. And in the 1940s, he attacked Truman's civil rights legislation, calling it an "uncalled-for attack on our Southern civilization."

By the time of the epic civil rights battles of the 1950s and 1960s, Russell's seniority and prominence in Congress made him the leader of the Southern conservatives. When *Brown v. Board of Education* came down, Russell and Thurmond led the drive to get signatures from Southerners on a fiery rebuttal to that Court decision titled "The Southern Manifesto" (one of the signatories was Senator Willis Robertson of Virginia, the father of televangelist Pat Robertson). In it, they said:

> We regard the decision of the Supreme Court in the school case as a clear abuse of judicial power. It climaxes a trend in the Federal Judiciary undertaking to legislate, in abrogation of the authority of Congress, and to encroach upon the reserved rights of the States and the people. . . . We decry the Supreme Court's encroachments on rights reserved to the States and to the people, contrary to established law, and to the Constitution. We commend the motives of those States which have declared the intention to resist forced integration.

Southern conservatives weren't the only ones who supported states' rights over civil rights. Senator Barry Goldwater opposed civil rights legislation on the basis of the states' rights doctrine and was rewarded with the electoral votes of several states in the Deep South (South Carolina, Georgia, Alabama, Mississippi, and Louisiana) in his landslide loss to Lyndon Johnson in 1964, the only states he won outside of his home state of Arizona. While Republican moderates supported civil rights legislation, conservative Republicans increasingly joined the segregationists from the South.

The Kennedys' and LBJ's embrace of civil rights forever broke apart the coalition of Northern New Deal progressives with the South, and Republicans and conservatives seized on the opportunity to build a new national conservative majority based on an alliance with the South. Richard Nixon made his "Southern strategy" central to his electoral base-building. He used direct appeals to Southerners like Strom Thurmond, and made catchphrases like "states' rights" and "law and order" central to his message. The old confederacy moved virtually overnight from being the "solid South" for Democrats to being a mostly Republican region. Before 1964, Mississippi, Alabama, and South Carolina had never voted for the Republican nominee for president; since 1964, they have voted Democratic only once (when the Southern favorite son Jimmy Carter won in 1976).

The most symbolically weighted moment of the new partnership between the South and the conservatives in the Republican Party occurred on August 3, 1980. Ronald Reagan, in the official kickoff of his general election campaign, went to a little town called Philadelphia, Mississippi. Philadelphia was an odd choice in a whole lot of ways: it was a small town, kind of hard to get to, and not close to any major media markets. Mississippi was a small state with only seven electoral votes, and it certainly wasn't a swing state in the general election, as Reagan was expected to carry it easily. And he sure wasn't there to hearken back to Bobby Kennedy's famous tour of destitute homes in the poor African American region of the Mississippi Delta.

The only thing Philadelphia, Mississippi, was noteworthy for in its history was that it was the town where the civil rights workers James Chaney, Andrew Goodman, and Michael Schwerner had been murdered during Freedom Summer, fifteen years prior.

Reagan wasn't there to talk about Chaney, Goodman, and Schwerner's deaths—he didn't mention them at all. What he did do was talk about states' rights: "I believe in states' rights; I believe in people doing as much as they can for themselves at the community level and at the private level. And I believe that we've distorted the balance of our government today by giving powers that were never intended in the Constitution to that federal establishment."

Reagan was there to seal the deal between the modern conservative movement and the old South. Going to the town where these courageous civil rights activists had been murdered in cold blood and talking about states' rights was one of the most shameful symbolic political acts in modern American history, but it was effective. The South has become a Republican stronghold, with most of modern Republicanism's leadership coming from that region: Jesse Helms, Newt Gingrich, Karl Rove, Lee Atwater, Tom DeLay, Dick Armey, Trent Lott, Bill Frist, Mitch McConnell, and, of course, the two Presidents Bush. In addition, a wide array of conservative movement leaders have hailed from the old slaveholding states as well, including Pat Robertson, the late Jerry Falwell, Ralph Reed, Oliver North, Rush Limbaugh, and American Family Association founder Don Wildmon.

Old-line Southern conservatives, driven by racism and dressed up in the veneer of Calhoun's traditionalism and states' rights doctrine, dominate today's conservative movement. John C. Calhoun would be proud.

5

The Battle over Democracy

I n 1972, when I was still in junior high school, George McGovern was the Democratic nominee for president. Being the
precocious little twerp that I was, I loved to argue about politics with my conservative teachers, and that year's campaign gave
me plenty of fodder. In one memorable encounter, I was going on
and on about how the nasty things Nixon had done, such as supporting dictatorships in Vietnam and elsewhere, were not worthy of
a democracy. My Republican teacher very haughtily informed me
that the point was irrelevant because America was a republic, not
a democracy, and we were lucky that was the case. It was the first
direct attack on the idea of democracy as a good thing that I had
ever heard, but it would not be the last. Conservatives have always
disliked democracy because they want elites, rather than regular
people, to run things. All during my life as a political organizer, I've
fought against conservatives who were trying to raise, rather than
lower, barriers to voting; who wanted to make government more
secretive, rather than providing more access to information about
its workings; who attempted to enhance the power of big-moneyed
special interests, rather than lessen it; and who were horrified at
the idea that elected officials would be forced to actually be responsive to activists and voters, rather than to the wise elites. The conservative philosophy that the private good takes precedence over
the public interest, that the free market will cure all things, and

that government should just get out of the way has led to a corruption of government itself, time and time again in our history.

The battle over how much democracy to have in this country and what kind of democracy we would have was joined in 1776 and has been fought in all the years since. Lincoln's "government of the people, by the people, for the people" is still a highly controversial idea to the conservative movement.

Voting Rights

There is a comforting myth about American democracy, one with a grain of truth in it, that says that although we started out giving the vote only to white male property owners, the franchise has gradually expanded until now everyone has an equal right to vote, and the democratic process now works just fine for everybody. The grain of truth is that America did begin its national history with very limited voting rights and that they have expanded dramatically since. The myth is that it has been a steady uphill climb, that everyone today has the same voting rights as everyone else, and that the battle for voting rights is over.

One of the most vigorous points of debate between the Jefferson-Paine progressives and the Adams-Hamilton conservatives was over how much to open up voting to nonelites. Hamilton's aversion to democracy and "the people" has been noted earlier in chapter 2. Adams, on the specific topic of voting, had this to say:

> The same reasoning which will induce you to admit all men who have no property, to vote, with those who have, . . . will prove that you ought to admit women and children; for, generally speaking, women and children have as good judgments, and as independent minds, as those men who are wholly destitute of property; these last being to all intents and purposes as much dependent upon others, who will please to feed, clothe, and employ them, as women [are] upon their husbands, or children on their parents. . . . Depend upon it, Sir, it is dangerous to open so fruitful a source of controversy and

altercation as would be opened by attempting to alter the qualifications of voters; there will be no end of it. New claims will arise; women will demand the vote; lads from twelve to twenty-one will think their rights not enough attended to; and every man who has not a farthing, will demand an equal voice with any other, in all acts of state. It tends to confound and destroy all distinctions, and prostrate all ranks to one common level.

Adams, unfortunately, did not represent an anachronistic sentiment that was around only in the first few years of America's emerging new form of government. Throughout the last part of the 1700s, the entire 1800s, and well into the 1900s, such views were regularly voiced and in fact won the day much of the time in many parts of the country.

One of the problems was that those conservative framers, who were scared enough of democracy to create tortuous institutions like the Electoral College, also decided to punt on the issue of suffrage and leave the matter up to the states. As a result, wildly diverse laws were developed on who was allowed to vote and who wasn't, and as one political faction or another would gain power in a given state, restrictions were added or loosened up. The property requirement did begin to fade in most places as the Jeffersonian and Jacksonian Democrats gained power politically, but new restrictions were frequently put into place when more conservative people gained seats in legislatures, or as compromises emerged to satisfy fears about certain classes of people having the right to vote. Among the new classes of people who were disenfranchised through legislation in various places between 1800 and 1850 were the following:

- **Paupers.** People who received any kind of public assistance and/or lived in alms houses were denied the right to vote in a dozen states between the 1790s and the late 1800s. "The theory of our Constitution is that extreme poverty . . . is inconsistent with independence," said conservative Josiah Quincy in pushing for this legislation.

- **Felons.** Before the Civil War, people convicted of crimes were denied the right to vote in twenty-five states. Many of these kinds of restrictions still exist today.

- **Migrants.** Some states started to impose or, in some cases, lengthen residency requirements. As Alexander Keyssar noted in his book *The Right to Vote: The Contested History of Democracy in the United States*, "Those who favored lengthy residency requirements were generally seeking to prevent 'vagrants and strangers,' 'sojourners,' or transients of any type from voting. . . . Most of these floating men were manual workers."

- **Immigrants.** Although immigrants were welcomed with open arms in the early parts of the country's history, and in some states and regions (especially in the West) for most of the 1800s, particularly if they came with enough money to buy farms or start businesses, class and ethnic bigotries began to create fierce anti-immigrant backlashes beginning in the 1830s. Working-class immigrants, especially Irish Catholics, and Chinese immigrants out West, began to be denied citizenship and the right to vote in many cities in the 1850s, as the "Know-Nothing" movement reared its ugly head.

- **Freed blacks.** Every new state that entered the Union between 1819 and the Civil War prohibited free blacks from voting, and some other Northern states added those exclusions in this period. New York even put a set of property requirements for blacks into the same Constitution that eliminated property requirements for white men.

The arguments for more voting restrictions in all of these cases were almost always class-based, along with some mix of other bigotries thrown in, depending on the people involved.

With the elimination of property requirements in most states during the first half of the 1800s, the trend was toward more voting rights, rather than fewer, at least for white men. And with the rise of the Radical Republicans, fueled by the abolitionist movement and the Civil War, the drive to extend the vote to African Americans reached its pre-1960s apex in the 1860s with the passage of the 14th and 15th amendments to the Constitution. Although neither of those amendments was as far-reaching as their proponents originally hoped for, they both were giant steps toward expanding democratic voting rights. This was obviously true for the newly freed African Americans toward whom they were targeted, but the amendments also had two other major implications: (1) unlike the Constitution as originally written in 1787, they clearly established that the federal government had a role in determining voting rights and the power to enforce those voting rights in the states; and (2) they established in the Constitution the principle that discrimination along racial lines was illegal.

These amendments might have gone even further. Proposals were debated that would have kept states from denying voting rights to any adult male of sound mind, except for those who had engaged in rebellion or other "infamous" crimes. Although compromise language was eventually adopted, the fact that these kinds of measures were being seriously debated signaled the depth of the Radical Republicans' democratic impulses.

As we saw in chapter 4, while these amendments were great steps forward, the progressive impulse faded, Republicans were corrupted by the robber barons and Social Darwinism (more on that in chapter 6), and conservative impulses took over regarding democracy and voting rights, as well as economic policy. In the latter half of the nineteenth century, conservatives made a serious counterattack on voting rights. This assault extended beyond the Jim Crow South, but it was at its height there, as the rise of the Ku Klux Klan, the most violent and powerful terrorist threat the country has ever seen, began to forcefully deny blacks the vote. By the 1890s, Jim Crow was firmly in place everywhere in the South, legally and by threat of force.

In the North, voting rights were under attack less by race than by class and immigrant status, although race was certainly thrown into the mix in political debates in the North as well. Charles Francis Adams Jr., the great-grandson of John Adams and no less of an elitist than his ancestor, was typical of the conservatives at the time when he wrote, "Universal suffrage can only mean in plain English, the government of ignorance and vice—it means a European, and especially Celtic, proletariat on the Atlantic Coast; an African proletariat on the shores of the Gulf, and a Chinese proletariat on the Pacific." Another influential writer, Francis Parkman, wrote an article titled "The Failure of Universal Suffrage," where he expressed his horror that "There is probably no sweeter experience in the world than that of a penniless laborer . . . when he learns that by casting his vote in the right way, he can strip the rich merchant . . . of a portion of his gains."

From Alexander Keyssar's brilliant book on the history of voting rights in America (from whom I drew much of this history): "The laws governing elections in most states were revised often between the Civil War and World War I. Many states, new and old, held constitutional conventions that defined or redefined the shape of the electorate as well as the outlines of the electoral process. State legislatures drew up increasingly detailed statutes that spelled out electoral procedures of all types, including the timing of elections, the location of polling places, the hours that polls would be open, the configuration of ballots, and the counting of votes."

In that period, the conservative drive to eliminate voting rights was countermanded by two major forces. The first of these was the growing population of immigrants coming to both the big cities of the East and the vast stretches of the Midwest and West. Eventually, the raw numbers of these immigrants, combined with the success of unions in organizing them politically, began to break through these voting barriers.

In fact, one of the big battles over voting involved conservatives trying to keep working-class voters, immigrants and nonimmigrants alike, from having a voice in the political process. But the labor movement and immigrants' rights groups fought hard against these voting restrictions. Regarding such an effort in Massachusetts, the Knights of Labor spoke out strongly in their *Journal of United Labor* in 1889:

If the law of Massachusetts had been purposely framed with the object of keeping workingmen away from the polls it could hardly have accomplished that object more effectually than it does. It probably was drawn up with just that sinister purpose in view. In order to register it is necessary for the workingman to lose a day or at least half a day in presenting himself personally to substantiate his right to vote—no small sacrifice in the case of the hardly driven and badly paid workers in the cotton mills and other poorly remunerated industries. Then again, the payment of the poll tax of $2 is a prerequisite to voting. . . .

The registration and poll-tax law of Massachusetts is essentially unjust and un-American. It virtually debases the right of suffrage to a part of the tax collecting machinery, and instead of making it really, as it is in theory, the birthright of every American citizen renders it a privilege to be secured by a money-payment.

The other movement that was slowly and steadily chipping away at the status quo to win voting rights throughout the late 1800s and the early 1900s was the feminist movement. No movement in history, voting rights or otherwise, had a harder road than this one. The seventy-one-year gap from the first feminist meeting at Seneca Falls, New York, in 1848 to the passage of the women's suffrage amendment in 1919 was a period of courageous and painful struggle, during which women suffered derision and mockery, arrest for civil disobedience, disappointment, and betrayal by people who should have been allies. Although sometimes aided by men along the way, this fight, like the battle for black civil rights, was overwhelmingly led by the oppressed whose rights were at stake. And in the end, the movement would not be denied. On June 4, 1919, women won the vote with the passage of the 19th Amendment to the Constitution.

From the beginning of the feminist movement, as I have noted in chapter 4, conservatives dealt with the demands for equal rights as they have and still do: with scorn. But sadly, sometimes even erstwhile allies in the early days suggested that while certain civil and property rights might be okay, women shouldn't have the right to vote or have certain other rights because they needed to be protected. At a women's rights meeting in Akron, Ohio, supposedly allied men were rising to speak against voting rights and other rights on that basis, when the remarkable Sojourner Truth, a former slave who was a key leader in both the abolitionist and the feminist movements, responded with her soon-to-be worldfamous answer:

Well, children, where there is so much racket there must be something out of kilter. I think that 'twixt the negroes of the South and the women at the North, all talking about rights, the white men will be in a fix pretty soon. But what's all this here talking about?

That man over there says that women need to be helped into carriages, and lifted over ditches, and to have the best place everywhere. Nobody ever helps me into carriages, or over mud-puddles, or gives me any best place! And ain't I a woman? Look at me! Look at my arm! I have ploughed and planted, and gathered into barns, and no man could head me! And ain't I a woman? I could work as much and eat as much as a man—when I could get it—and bear the lash as well! And ain't I a woman? I have borne thirteen children, and seen most all sold off to slavery, and when I cried out with my mother's grief, none but Jesus heard me! And ain't I a woman?

Then they talk about this thing in the head; what's this they call it? [a member of audience whispers, "intellect"] That's it, honey. What's that got to do with women's rights or negroes' rights? If my cup won't hold but a pint, and yours holds a quart, wouldn't you be mean not to let me have my little half measure full?

Then that little man in black there, he says women can't have as much rights as men, 'cause Christ wasn't a woman! Where did your Christ come from? Where did your Christ come from? From God and a woman! Man had nothing to do with Him.

If the first woman God ever made was strong enough to turn the world upside down all alone, these women together ought to be able to turn it back, and get it right side up again! And now they is asking to do it, the men better let them.

Conservatives who opposed voting rights for women made precisely the same arguments then as antifeminists do now. Here is an excerpt from a speech by a delegate to the California constitutional convention in 1879: "The demand is for the abolition of all distinctions between men and women, proceeding upon the hypothesis that men and women are all the same. . . . Gentlemen ought to know what is the great and inevitable tendency of this modern heresy, this lunacy, which of all lunacies is the most mischievous and most destructive. It attacks the integrity of the family; it attacks the eternal degrees of God Almighty; it denies and repudiates the obligations of motherhood." A Pennsylvania politician of the same era, W. H. Smith, said that if women could vote, "the family . . . would be utterly destroyed."

Slowly but surely, though, feminists made progress on winning the right to vote. Employing Jeffersonian arguments about equal rights for all and building important alliances with labor unions in the East and the populist movement in the West, they kept making more and more political inroads. Western states were the first to give women the right to vote, and eventually progressive-era politicians of both parties agreed to the constitutional amendment. When it was finally ratified, the number of citizens who were eligible to vote almost doubled overnight.

The last great widely known struggle was the battle for voting rights for African Americans in the South. Many people assumed that with the end of Jim Crow, the struggle over voting rights was essentially over. But most states throughout the mid-1900s had a variety of restrictions on voting, and many states had and still have barriers designed to lessen participation. The push for black voting rights in the South helped decrease these kinds of obstacles nationwide by raising the general awareness of the voting issue. But barriers persisted, and conservatives to this day continue to argue for voting restrictions, making the same argument time after time: the need to protect against fraud. The ironic thing about these arguments is not only how little fraud has ever been documented in efforts to get more minorities, poor people, and young people to the polls, but also the fact that most electoral fraud in our nation's history and in the present day is perpetuated by the governing party, such as the Katherine Harris fiasco in Florida in 2000 that illegally denied the right to vote to thousands of African Americans.

I have done a great deal of work in the field of voter registration, getting out the vote, and protecting voting rights. I have found many different ways that conservatives and Republicans try to stop poor people, black people, and young people from voting. Among the techniques that have been used in my experience over the last thirty years are the following:

- Mailings to black voters threatening them with arrest if they show up to vote without "proper documentation," as was used by Jesse Helms in his 1990 race against Harvey Gantt, an African American former mayor of Charlotte, North Carolina.

- Forcing voters to show photo ID, even though many poor, urban, and older voters don't have driver's licenses. In Georgia, Republicans passed a photo ID law, then imposed a $10 fee to get a photo ID if you didn't have a license, and finally set up the offices to get these special photo IDs deep in the outer suburbs of Atlanta, hours away from the inner city where most African Americans without drivers' licenses lived.

- Voter registration purges by Republican database firms, such as the one Katherine Harris hired in Florida that eliminated from the rolls far more African American voters than people in any other demographic category, including thousands of voters who were legally eligible to vote.

- Limiting precincts in black and/or Hispanic neighborhoods to only two or three voting machines, while giving similar-size precincts in heavily white precincts ten or twelve machines. This tactic is what created ten-hour lines in black neighborhoods in the 2004 election in Ohio. Poll workers in that state repeatedly requested more machines, which were not delivered even though there were available voting machines sitting in a warehouse.

- Training Republican Election Day volunteers to challenge the right to vote of all or most voters who come to the polls in poor neighborhoods, to try to get them placed in the "provisional vote" category. Provisional votes, which the law defines as votes that have a question as to their eligibility, are almost always counted late or not at all unless there is a recount. This technique was even written into the state Republican Party training manual for Election Day workers in Maryland in 2004.

- Republican county sheriffs in recent elections in Virginia and Florida have set up road blockades on the main roads going to the polling places on Election Day in heavily black precincts for no discernible law-enforcement reason.

- Republicans have hired off-duty police officers in black and Hispanic precincts to stand outside polling places and ask aggressive questions of people who come to vote.

- In many counties with Republican election officials, lawsuits have had to be filed because new registrants from poor, black, and/or Hispanic neighborhoods simply were not being processed.

- The notorious Kenneth Blackwell, the far-right-wing Ohio secretary of state who was part of the voting machine fiasco in 2004, found an obscure 1800s provision of state law to declare that people conducting voter registration had not been using the right kind of paper stock, and he tried to invalidate hundreds of thousands of mostly African American registrations. He was forced to back down by the courts.

- Polling places in black neighborhoods and on college campuses (or, in one documented case in Florida, both—a precinct in a historically black college) have been shut down and padlocked on the morning of the election with no explanation.

- In 1988, during one get-out-the-vote operation that I was involved with in New Jersey, we got word that Republicans were paying gang members to show up at polling places in black neighborhoods with their gang colors showing and threatening anybody who walked in to vote. We were able to get them to back down.

- George W. Bush's administration has dramatically slowed the naturalization process for legal immigrants, knowing that once they are naturalized, the immigrants who tend to register to vote will vote Democratic.

The battle over who gets to vote is not a historical relic; it is a struggle in every election. Conservatives try to keep blacks, Hispanics, poor people, and students from voting simply because they know those voters are more likely to vote for progressive candidates and causes. They also do whatever they can to spotlight any problem with voter registration drives. Out of the millions of new voters registered in the last couple of elections, there have been less than a dozen cases found with legal problems, but each of those cases has been, of course, trumpeted to the high heavens by Republicans and their allies in the media, such as Rush Limbaugh.

Progressives like Michael Waldman at the Brennan Center have been doing some great work in creating a broad pro-democracy agenda that will not only curb the kinds of abuses I've described but build a stronger democracy in our country overall. Waldman's new book, *A Return to Common Sense: 7 Steps to Save Our Democracy*, argues compellingly for sweeping reform in the areas of voting rights and campaign finance reform. Like me, he wants to abolish the Electoral College and eliminate gerrymandering of congressional districts as well. He also discusses restoring checks and balances, including rolling back the abuses of government secrecy.

Government Secrecy

Another major debate about the nature of American democracy has been the argument over government secrecy, with conservatives pressing for ever more secrecy on the grounds of national security and progressives claiming that secrecy erodes a healthy democracy. Government secrecy was not a major political issue for the first 150 years of U.S. history, but that began to change with the beginning of J. Edgar Hoover's reign as head of the FBI. Like Calhoun before him and Jesse Helms after, Hoover was one of those far-right conservatives who established an unbeatable power base and was a major figure in American politics for half a century. He was able to keep his job as head of the FBI despite a string of presidents who really didn't like him very much through building close ties to reporters who gave him great publicity and by threatening black-mail of government officials on whom he kept secret files of their personal lives.

Hoover's obsession with secrecy (perhaps exacerbated by his penchant for cross-dressing while at home with his top aide and roommate, Clyde Tolson) dovetailed conveniently with the development after World War II of the Cold War and the Red Scare. In Joe McCarthy's and J. Edgar Hoover's postwar America, communist spies were around every corner. And in that environment, the need for government secrecy became one of the guiding principles of American conservative dogma. With the addition of the CIA and the National Security Council, and with the postwar military build-up, the military-industrial complex against which Eisenhower warned became one of the biggest political power bases in the country and one of the most conservative. Secrecy was at the heart of its culture.

Throughout the 1950s, 1960s, and early 1970s, the military-industrial infrastructure was used to further conservative ends, frequently in disregard of the presidents its members were supposed to be working for. Hoover used the FBI apparatus to spy on Martin Luther King Jr., even sending pictures of King's liaisons with women to Coretta Scott King in an effort to get King to back off on his civil rights movement activities. Far-right John Birch Society members were a major presence in the armed forces and the spy agencies and were doing enough recruiting and proselytizing inside the military to alarm the Kennedys about the chances of an American military coup. Kennedy ended up firing Major General Edwin Walker for openly recruiting soldiers to join the John Birch Society, and Walker helped organize the riot that shut down the University of Mississippi when James Meredith registered there as a student. Curtis LeMay, another top general, who alarmed Kennedy with his warmongering during the Cuban missile crisis and elsewhere, ran with George Wallace as his vice presidential pick in 1968. As Arthur Schlesinger Jr. put it in his biography of Bobby Kennedy: "The military leaders [of the time] were Cold War zealots. They had sedulously cultivated relations with powerful conservative legislators—John Stennis, Mendel Rivers, Strom Thurmond, Barry Goldwater. They hunted and fished with right-wing politicians, supplied them aircraft for trips home and showed up at their receptions. The alliance between the military and right disturbed the Kennedys." JFK was sufficiently worried about a military coup that he encouraged John Frankenheimer to make *Seven Days in May*, a thriller about a military coup in the United States, as a way of warning the public about what might happen.

Secrecy became a political tool for conservatives in times of scandal as well. Nixon invoked national security, the need for secrecy, and "executive privilege" constantly during the investigation of the Watergate scandal, until court orders forced him to reveal the fact that the only security he was safeguarding with those claims was his own. The documents and the tapes he was compelled to turn over proved conclusively that he had been at the center of the conspiracy to cover up Watergate. The Reagan administration invoked executive privilege and national security constantly as well, but especially during the Iran-Contra affair, a blatantly illegal secret operation to sell arms to the Iranian government and use the money to support right-wing military forces in Central America.

One of the most frightening glimpses into the U.S. government's use of secrecy during the height of the Cold War era was uncovered by the Church Committee. Chaired by a great progressive, Senator Frank Church of Idaho, this committee shined a light in 1975–1976 on the truly antidemocratic secret activities carried out by the FBI and the CIA. Documenting the assassinations and attempted assassinations of several foreign leaders, the numerous coups carried out, and the spying on literally hundreds of thousands of Americans, the Church Committee revealed the FBI and the CIA to be agencies that were completely unaccountable to the American public and at times even to presidents of the United States. The committee's work helped bring needed reforms to safeguard American liberties.

But no president, not even Nixon at the height of Watergate, has relied more on government secrecy than George W. Bush. From refusing to give any information about the membership of Dick Cheney's energy task force, to rejecting all attempts by Congress to investigate mounting scandals, to destroying millions of White House e-mails in blatant violation of the law, no administration has ever stretched the limits on government secrecy further than Bush's. The Bush administration has even claimed that Vice President Cheney is a branch of the government unto himself, part of neither the executive nor the legislative branches and thereby subject to no scrutiny of his records. Bush and Cheney have refused media requests for information based on the fact that a judicial investigation was under way, then ignored questions once the investigation was over.

Even conservative journalists and activists, normally staunch allies of the Bush administration, have been alarmed at the Bush-Cheney secrecy obsession. Robert Novak called it a "passion for secrecy" and suggested that they have only themselves to blame for people being upset with them. Phyllis Schlafly, a proud McCarthy soldier fifty years earlier, said, "The American people do not and should not tolerate government by secrecy." And the conservative legal group Judicial Watch sued the Bush administration multiple times over the secrecy issue.

Among its pro-secrecy policies and practices, the Bush administration has done the following:

- Dramatically widened the range of classified and confidential
  materials.
- Expanded its ability to criminally prosecute government whis-
  tleblowers.
- Aggressively gone after reporters who publish leaks.
- Used new "material support" statutes that do end runs around
  1st Amendment liberties.
- Removed thousands of unclassified documents from govern-
  ment Web sites.
- Created secret deportation hearings of immigrants.
- Instructed agencies to withhold information on Freedom of
  Information requests whenever possible and created an un-
  defined "sensitive but unclassified" category that made it easier
  for them to do so.
- Limited access to presidential records through a presidential
  executive order.

Justifying all of these actions as necessary in an age of terrorism,
the Bush administration has gone much further to promote secrecy
than has any administration in history. Perhaps, as I discuss in the
next section, it is because they have so much to hide.

Big Money and Corruption in Conservative Politics

Conservatives from Hamilton's time until today have always viewed
government as best used as an instrument to benefit business and
wealthy elites. Unfortunately, this philosophy has bled over all too
often into private interests using government for personal enrich-
ment. Keeping our democracy from being overrun by corruption
is always a challenge, but it has been made more difficult by the
conservative Social Darwinist philosophy that views government
as a tool to assist the already wealthy.

Humanity being imperfect as it is, political leaders from the inception of our republic, starting with profiteers in the Revolutionary War, have been guilty of corruption. But in the first hundred years of America's history, these scandals tended to be more idiosyncratic, more related to the weaknesses of the individuals involved. Partly, this was because the country was so close to the razor's edge in those early days. There was such doubt as to whether we would make it that American leaders had to focus more on survival than on feathering their own nests. Another factor, even more fundamental, was that there simply wasn't that much money in the American economy yet. The wealthy were not yet super-wealthy, businesses were not yet vast corporate empires, and the federal government had fewer resources to work with. In that kind of environment, there was simply less money to steal, and the margins tended to be narrow enough that people usually noticed pretty fast when graft occurred.

All of this changed dramatically in the years following the Civil War, as capitalism emerged in its modern form. The American economy was growing exponentially, and a few corporations were rapidly becoming behemoths whose size and wealth made even the most successful of earlier businesses seem tiny in comparison. With this economic and corporate expansion, a new level of corruption emerged. A new pattern related to the philosophy around that corruption emerged as well, a pattern that has stayed with us to the present day.

In the post–Civil War Gilded Age, Social Darwinism (which I discuss at more length in chapter 6) supported the notion that corruption might even be a force for good: the dominant and wealthy would advance society and force the weak out of the way. Some politicians became remarkably blunt in their adherence to this kind of Social Darwinism. A late-1800s senator from Kansas, John Ingalls, had this to say about reformers: "The purification of politics is an iridescent dream. Government is force. Politics is a battle for supremacy. . . . To defeat the antagonist and expel the party in power is the purpose. . . . The modern cant about the corruption of politics is fatiguing in the extreme. It proceeds from the tea-custard and syllabub dilettantism, the frivolous and desultory sentimentalism of epicenes."

Corporations were relatively open about their practice of bribing politicians. According to Jack Beatty's book *Age of Betrayal*, Union Pacific spent $400,000 on bribes between 1866 and 1872, while Central Pacific actually budgeted $500,000 a year for bribes between 1875 and 1885—and that was in 1870s-era dollars. Widespread and well-documented stories told of congressional members receiving $5,000 for every important vote, stocks in companies, and free services like railroad tickets at any time upon request. Republican presidential candidate James Garfield took a $150,000 contribution from robber baron Jay Gould and, in exchange, promised to appoint whomever Gould wanted to the Supreme Court.

And that was just the everyday run-of-the-mill corruption. Between 1869 and 1880 alone, there were nine major headline-making scandals involving bribery, market manipulation, and other kinds of graft. The Radical Republicans had given way to the corporate Republicans, and they justified their actions, just as the pro-slavery Southerners had, with a conservative philosophy. Social Darwinism allowed conservatives of that era, in both parties—at the federal, state, and local levels—to intellectually rationalize their corrupt actions by saying, "Might makes right."

The pressure of populist and then progressive-era reformers brought this heyday of bribery and graft to an end, and the first two decades of the 1900s were relatively free of new federal government scandals. But then the next great wave of corruption hit in the 1920s.

Warren G. Harding, the hapless conservative who was known to tell visitors to the White House that the job was too much for him and to break down weeping when administration officials came to meet with him, brought in a bunch of cronies who were intimately connected to big business. His administration was a disaster from the start. The head of the Veterans' Bureau was imprisoned for taking kickbacks, as was the head of the Office of Alien Property. One administration official committed suicide over some of the scandals, and another either committed suicide or was murdered to cover up the evidence. Harding's attorney general was kept informed of all the various incidents of graft and got kickbacks himself. And Harding's interior secretary received six-figure bribes for oil leases in the notorious Teapot Dome Scandal, which was widely considered by historians to be one of the worst scandals in all of American history.

After Harding died (somewhat mysteriously), Coolidge took over. As Will Rogers put it at the time, the scandals had gotten so horrific that there was "the great morality panic of 1924," as Republicans scurried to pronounce themselves outraged by all this corruption. Coolidge, and later Hoover, did at least start to appoint some competent people to key cabinet posts. But with no questioning of, or change in, the prevailing business philosophy, the 1920s remained a time of wild corporate corruption, as stock speculation, "creative accounting," and other financial shenanigans flourished with no government oversight whatsoever. These types of private corruption, utterly unsupervised by the federal government, led directly to the 1929 stock market crash and the worst depression the country had ever seen.

One final thing that should be noted on conservatism and corruption in the 1920s: the unintentional yet clear link between the traditional, Protestant church–based conservatism of that era and the rise of organized crime. The 1920s were the only full decade of prohibitionism. Protestant church–based moralists had succeeded in passing a constitutional amendment outlawing the sale of alcohol, the only time that kind of "traditional morality"–style amendment has ever been successfully added to our Constitution (although these sorts of amendments, such as ones prohibiting abortion, same-sex marriage, and flag-burning, have certainly been proposed many, many times in recent decades). Prohibition was a terrible failure because most of the people who had always consumed liquor continued to drink but merely turned to illegal sources for their booze. Prohibition was quickly repealed when FDR's progressive Democrats swept into power in 1933, but it did leave our country with one lasting consequence: the dramatically strengthened power of organized crime.

Like the cleansing effect of the Progressive Era from 1900 to 1920, the New Deal brought forth a time of relatively low levels of government and corporate corruption. There were occasional scandals, but more aggressive government oversight kept these problems at a modest level. One example: when then senator Harry Truman went after war profiteers with a vengeance during World War II, corporations that were trying to make money off the war effort were forced to be far more careful.

By no means were things in America a nirvana in that era, as organized crime had gained serious power, big-city machines allowed too much graft, and wealthy political figures and those connected to wealth continued to spend money freely to win elections. But in terms of major political corruption, the 1930s through the 1970s were a relatively clean period at the federal level.

The Nixon years were the next big period of scandal in government. The Watergate scandal, which was mostly about raw political power rather than greed, forced Nixon to resign and also compelled the resignations and/or imprisonment of Nixon's chief of staff, deputy chief of staff, chief counsel, attorney general, and several other longtime political aides. A separate scandal—this one involving old-fashioned bribery—forced the resignation of Vice President Spiro Agnew. A major financier of Nixon's campaigns, Bebe Rebozo, also got into legal trouble.

The happy result of all of this corruption was the passage of the most comprehensive campaign finance reform bill in history. And, of course, Nixon was out the door. The next six years were relatively peaceful on the scandal front. Then Reagan, closely aligned with big business, came into power and brought another wave of corruption, both corporate and governmental, with him.

The most well-known of the Reagan-era scandals was the infamous Iran-Contra affair, when the Reagan administration developed a rogue plan for helping right-wing paramilitary groups in Central American (the contras) by illegally selling arms to Iran, an avowed enemy of the United States. But Iran-Contra was just the tip of the iceberg and was, in fact, atypical of the scandals of the Reagan era: most of the rest had to do with pure greed.

Like the Gilded Age a century earlier, the dominant philosophy of the era was, in the words of Wall Street financier Michael Milken (and then *Wall Street* character tycoon Gordon Gekko), "Greed is good." With Reagan helping big business weaken the unions and regulators turning a blind eye to corruption, it was a wonderful time to be a corporate CEO and a Wall Street financier, as many of them started raking in hundreds of millions of dollars a year.

The most costly and significant scandal of the decade, in fact, was not Iran-Contra, but the savings and loan bailout that ended up costing taxpayers more than $160 billion. The Reagan administration dramatically weakened the oversight regulations for savings and loans, and then the pro-corporate regulators whom Reagan appointed pretty much ignored even those rules. Politicians such as John McCain helped sleazy CEOs rake in tens of millions of dollars illegally (McCain was one of the five senators, known as the Keating 5, who pressured regulators to go easy on the Lincoln Savings & Loan Association, which had given major contributions to McCain and four other senators). Soon, greedy operators were turning federally guaranteed deposits in savings and loans into their own little playground, ripping off billions. It was the biggest financial scandal in history, in terms of the costs to taxpayers.

Iran-Contra and the savings and loan crisis were the two worst scandals of the 1980s but certainly not the only ones. A truly remarkable total of 225 people who served in the Reagan administration either quit or were fired, arrested, indicted, and/or convicted for breaking the law or violating the ethics code. Attorney General Ed Meese was investigated by three different special prosecutors. Interior secretary James Watt, a far-right-wing zealot who believed that since Jesus was coming back soon, we should just go ahead and exploit the hell out of the environment, was indicted on twenty-four felony counts. The Department of Housing and Urban Development had four different senior officials indicted or convicted. Two former White House senior staffers, Michael Deaver and Lyn Nofziger, were convicted of various influence peddling–related crimes. The Environmental Protection Agency was involved in a huge scandal, with staffers forced out and convicted of lying to Congress.

When Democrat Bill Clinton took office, Republicans were still angry at all of the investigations of the Reagan administration and vowed to do worse to Clinton. Between Ken Starr's $61 million investigation of Clinton and numerous Republican-led investigations of every aspect of the Clinton administration, Republicans were able to exploit a couple of sex scandals (Clinton himself, of course, and HUD secretary Henry Cisneros), some fund-raising problems in the 1996 reelection campaign, and a whole series of other investigations in which administration officials were never indicted or reprimanded for any activity. The only administration official actually indicted on any kind of criminal corruption charge was agriculture secretary Mike Espy, and he was found innocent by a jury on all counts. The Clinton administration was hardly perfect on the scandal front, but there wasn't much fire for all the smoke the Republicans tried to create.

The Bush Administration:
The Most Corrupt in History

When George W. Bush came into office in 2001, the investigatory zeal shown by the Republican Congress vanished in a heartbeat. This was especially remarkable given the depth of corruption we were to see over the next eight years. But hearings were not called, congressional ethics committees stopped holding investigations, and oversight into any kind of ethics issues evaporated.

Any interest in investigating potential corruption in the corporate sector disappeared as well, and the country would soon pay the price in the early and frightening wave of business scandals that hurt an already weak economy. In the fall of 2001, Bush appointed a chair of the Federal Energy Regulatory Commission (FERC) who was a close ally and a former lawyer of a company called Enron. Enron had been the single biggest corporate contributor to Bush's election campaign in 2000, and Bush and Enron CEO Ken Lay were extremely close friends. But Enron was a company built on a house of cards. "Enron-style accounting" would soon become a frequently used phrase in American culture, signifying the worst kind of corporate corruption, and not only would Enron go down—the seventh-biggest company in the United States before its collapse—but it would take down with it Arthur Andersen, one of the largest, oldest, and most prestigious accounting firms in the world. The astonishingly rapid downfall of Enron and Arthur Andersen sent shockwaves throughout the economy, as pension funds, along with corporate and foundation portfolios with large investments in Enron's stock, were decimated. With Enron-style accounting exposed to the harsh glare of light, other companies (i.e., WorldCom, Adelphia Communications, Bristol-Myers Squibb, and ImClone) with shaky accounting and underregulated financial dealings were soon to be in trouble as well.

The Enron scandal and all of the similar problems of companies sinking under the weight of their own fraud have to be laid at the doorstep of American conservatism. Bush, in his brief turn as president, helped get Enron's top choice for regulator installed at FERC and had already, by the time of the company's collapse in late 2001, given it assistance by helping it acquire investment deals in India and screw California consumers in the great energy crisis of the summer of 2001, as well as in numerous other ways, big and small. But it wasn't only the Bush administration that played a role in the Enron fiasco. Senator Phil Gramm, whose wife was on the board of Enron, got a key regulatory change passed that allowed some of the worst of Enron's creative accounting. And the Republican Congress forced a bill through in the 1990s, over Clinton's veto, that took away the rights of stockholders to sue companies to force a higher standard of accountability for Enron's management team.

The corporate scandals that emerged in the first two years of the Bush administration would hardly be the only outrages of its reign. It almost seemed at times that it was intentionally trying to outdo the Grant, Harding, Nixon, and Reagan administrations, competing to be the most corrupt administration in history. And if that was the goal, the Bush administration probably succeeded.

There are way too many Bush administration scandals to list in this modest-size book, and readers are likely all too familiar with their gory details. Many of them involved greed, including the Abramoff bribery scandals, when Jack Abramoff built a money-laundering and bribery network that involved House majority leader Tom DeLay's top aides and several members of Congress and Bush administration officials, including Steven Griles, the number-two person at the Department of the Interior, the head of procurement at the Office of Management and Budget, and one of Karl Rove's top lieutenants. Other scandals included the no-bid, nonaudited abuses of military contractors such as Halliburton and contractors who got lucrative deals to clean up New Orleans and did little in return; the literally hundreds of millions of dollars that disappeared, unaccounted for, in Iraqi reconstruction; the head of the General Services Administration, Lurita Doan, who resigned after trying to award contracting work to a political friend; the abuse of power, such as the torture at Abu Ghraib, at Guantánamo, and in secret CIA locations; the outing of an under-cover CIA agent as an act of political revenge; giving White House credentials to phony journalists, government payments to colum-nists touting the administration line, and phony "news reports" to local TV stations; the firing of U.S. attorneys for not being "team players"; bringing trumped-up charges against political opponents such as Alabama governor Don Siegelman; or the invention of facts to hype the war in Iraq or accomplish other ends, such as the uranium in Niger that Saddam Hussein was supposedly trying to buy.

Sometimes it was a mix of greed, abuse of power, and a variety of other corruptions. White House press secretaries were given false information by their superiors. Incompetent cronies were given important jobs such as heading up FEMA. Evidence was covered up by destroying e-mails in direct violation of the law. Senior White House staff members perjured themselves and then saw their sen-tences commuted. The independent scientists and legal experts who worked for government agencies were routinely overruled to benefit administration contributors.

It was a veritable bacchanalia for the Bush administration's allies: if you paid, you got to play. It's no wonder that the White House counsel in the Nixon administration and Watergate veteran John Dean called the Bush administration's scandals worse than Watergate.

The corruption in this period was hardly limited to the executive branch. In this atmosphere of open abuse of the law, the Republicans in Congress got into the act as well. The level of indictments and serious investigations broke all former records in terms of corruption, even in the worst days of the Gilded Age.

The Republican majority leader during this period, Tom DeLay, was a festival of corruption unto himself. After the House Ethics Committee admonished him for three separate ethics-related incidents, DeLay got the chair of the committee replaced by someone less independent. DeLay was then indicted on an illegal corporate money–raising scheme and was forced to resign. Meanwhile, two of his top former aides were convicted in the Abramoff scandal, with Abramoff himself well known to be one of DeLay's best friends.

DeLay was hardly alone. Overshadowed by DeLay's indictment, Abramoff, the Foley sex scandal, and all the rest, Speaker Dennis Hastert bought a piece of land and then secured a $207 million earmark that enhanced the value of the land by more than $2 million. Another Republican member of Congress, Bob Ney of Ohio, served prison time in connection with the Abramoff scandal. Representative Duke Cunningham (R-CA), in a separate scandal, actually put in writing the amount of bribe money he wanted for each vote or committee earmark, and he went to prison as well. Representative Rick Renzi (R-AZ) was indicted in a land deal. Senate majority leader Bill Frist (R-TN) was investigated for insider trading, while Senator Conrad Burns (R-MT) was another player investigated in the Abramoff scandal. House Appropriations chairman Jerry Lewis (R-LA) was investigated by the Department of Justice for trading earmarks directly for contributions. Representative Curt Weldon of Pennsylvania, another Republican, had his house and office raided by the FBI in a bribery scandal. Republican congressmen John Doolittle, Jerry Pombo, Ken Calvert, Tom Feeney, Jeff Miller, Jeff Sessions, and Charles Taylor were all, or are still, under investigation by the Department of Justice for various bribery and kickback schemes. And then there is the infamous Mark Foley scandal, which I normally wouldn't even mention because sex scandals to me are pretty unimportant compared to public corruption, but this one was especially rotten because of the abuse of power involved: several Republican leaders knew that Foley was soliciting underage minors—high school congressional pages—and not only did nothing about it but encouraged him to run for reelection.

I can already hear my Republican friends complaining, "But there are crooked Democrats, too." Yes, there are. Democratic members of Congress sometimes take bribes and Democratic administrations have sometimes abused their power. Democratic big-city machines have had serious problems with corruption. Labor unions have occasionally been corrupted by organized crime or crooked leaders. But my point in listing all of these examples of conservative corruption is to make a point about the overall way that events have played out in our democracy: the ideology of private interest over the public good has led to a historical pattern such that when conservatives have been in power, much more corruption tends to happen.

As Arthur Schlesinger Jr. put it, "Private interest eras rest on the principle that the individual in promoting his own interests promotes the general interest. . . . This priority of wealth over common-wealth naturally nourishes a propensity to corruption in government. When public purpose dominates, government tends to be idealistic. Idealists have many faults, but they rarely steal. . . . When private interest dominates, public morals are very different."

It's also important to note that the big-city machines and corrupt unions were generally not progressive in nature. Richard Daley, the man who sent his police force into the streets of Chicago to beat up protesters and who yelled at Senator Abraham Ribicoff at the 1968 convention, "Fuck you, you Jew son of a bitch, you lousy mother-fucker, go home," was hardly a progressive leader. And the most mob-ridden union in America, the Teamsters from the 1950s to the 1990s, regularly endorsed Republicans, including Reagan.

When you look back at the trends in our nation's history, it is simply a fact that since the Gilded Age ushered big money and Social Darwinist ethics into our governmental system, when conservatives have dominated our government, corruption has also been at its peak. Conservatives have believed, as the conservative philosopher Bernard Mandeville put it, that private vices yield public benefits. But that kind of philosophy leads to stealing from the public coffers. And as the Bush-era conservatives have just shown us, that kind of avarice, combined with a blatant willingness to abuse power, leads to a level of corruption that is truly historic.

From the beginning of our nation's history, conservatives have been more than a little uncomfortable with the idea of true democracy. They have preferred to have a country run by the elites to one run by the "mob" and "rabble" of a true democracy. Hamilton's theory of mercantilism, where elite upper-class government officials would work in direct partnership with wealthy businessmen and bankers to manage the affairs of the nation, gave way in the middle of the 1800s to government just letting big business do whatever it wanted whenever it wanted. Because, after all, private vices yield public benefits. It was to be government of the elite, by the elite, and for the elite.

It is no surprise, given this philosophy, that conservatives have always believed in more, rather than fewer, barriers to voting; that they have had no problem with the elites doing the business of government in secret; and that they found it acceptable for the rich to get richer at the public's expense.

Progressives have always stood in opposition to that philosophy. They have pushed for more voting rights for working-class and poor whites, for women, and for people regardless of their race. They have worked to open up government and air out secrets that didn't have a legitimate national security basis. They have looked to clean up corruption, both public and private, and bring idealism to government.

They have pushed for government "of the people, by the people, for the people." Just as Lincoln was opposed by the conservatives of his own day and by conservatives now, for advocating such a radical concept, modern-day progressivism has had to go toe-to-toe in the fight for what is at the heart of the American ideal.

6

Trickle-Down vs. Bottom-Up

From the earliest days of the republic, an ongoing debate has raged between democrats and aristocrats, populists and the wealthy, debtors and bankers, the working class and big business, the advocates of a "free" money supply and those of a "tight" money supply, the "levelers" versus the elitists, and people who wanted government to invest in and be a guarantor of equal opportunity for all and those who worshipped the free market above all else. Whatever the era, whatever form the battle took, and whatever the specific rhetoric or issues, this divide has been intrinsic to American history.

Modern conservatives actually understand this very well; they just don't like to openly admit it. Behind the scenes, though, they are very clear about whose heirs they are in the historic debate. There are two examples that illustrate my point:

1. When Ronald Reagan became president, he very quietly took down Jefferson's portrait from his office and put up that of Calvin Coolidge. It seemed like an odd choice. Jefferson was a revered Founding Father with his own glorious monument on the National Mall in Washington, while Coolidge was one of the most obscure and little-known presidents. He was mainly known to historians as "Silent Cal" and had no signature accomplishments. His conservative, antiregulation policies had led to the stock market crash of 1929 and the Great Depression, which happened just a few months

after he left office. The choice of Coolidge struck people as highly quirky. But Coolidge was a conservative's conservative, a strike-breaking antilabor ideologue who cut taxes and opposed any regulation on business or banking. He was the last president before the Great Depression swept FDR and a progressive Democratic majority into a forty-year dominance of American politics. Reagan's fondest hope was to go back to that time, when government was small, regulations on business were nonexistent, taxes were low, and unions were weak.

2. Karl Rove wanted to go back even further in history. He didn't like either the New Deal or the Progressive Era, when Teddy Roosevelt and Woodrow Wilson busted corporate trusts, eliminated child labor, created a national parks system, instituted a progressive income tax, and gave women the right to vote. Rove's political hero was William McKinley. Again, a pretty obscure president who didn't really have any astable accomplishments to his presidency besides a trumped-up war with Spain that allowed us to have colonies in the Philippines. But McKinley was the ultimate pro–big business corporate president, and he had defeated the most economically progressive and populist major party presidential candidate of all time, William Jennings Bryan—twice. McKinley put Teddy Roosevelt on the ticket as vice president to end Roosevelt's reign as governor of New York, where he had really started to annoy big business. He would have been appalled at his successor's reforms. But while McKinley lived, big business reigned supreme. For Rove, this otherwise lackluster president's pro–big business credentials and his willingness to make up reasons to go to war made him and his administration a perfect prototype for the second Bush presidency.

In the earlier chapters, I described the debates and the discussions of the early days of the United States, as progressives such as Paine and Jefferson pushed for more economic rights for the working class and the poor, and conservatives like Hamilton, Adams, and Gouverneur Morris argued for government policies that benefited the aristocracy. I will not, in this chapter, go deeply into the debates of those early years, other than to note again that they were just as intense, or more so, as the toughest and most forceful debates of today.

What is important to note at this juncture, though, is that economic change benefiting poor and working-class Americans, like the other types of change cycles I have noted, tended to happen in spurts. The conservative framers of the Constitution succeeded well enough in stacking the deck against change, and the power of money is always strong, so economic change has been an uphill struggle except in certain distinct periods of history. There have been long periods of conservatism, or in some cases just inertia, in which nearly insurmountable barriers and hurdles were established to impede the working class and the poor. These eras included:

- The first dozen years after the adoption of the Constitution, when more conservative men such as Washington, Adams, and Hamilton dominated the government.
- The late 1830s through 1860, when a succession of weak and cautious presidents—none of them reelected —did nothing progressive, and the increasingly bitter debate about slavery tended to drown out discussion of other issues.
- The early 1870s through 1901, the Gilded Age, when the post–Civil War government was controlled and thoroughly corrupted by the wealth of the robber barons.
- The 1920s, the post-Progressive, pre–New Deal era that was as dominated by conservative policies as any in the nation's history.
- The 1980s through today, the era of Reagan, the two Bushes, and the likes of Newt Gingrich and Tom DeLay, who held sway over Congress from 1995 through 2006. Our most recent history has been thoroughly subjugated by conservative, pro–big business policies, and the economic standing of working-class and poor people has slipped badly.

At the other end of the spectrum, the Jefferson, Jackson, and Lincoln presidencies all contributed significantly toward investing in progressive economics. In the twentieth century, the Progressive Era of Teddy Roosevelt and Woodrow Wilson, the New Deal of FDR, and the major advances of the 1960s and the early 1970s were the high-water marks.

The Changing Roles of Government and Corporations

Theories about the government's role in the economy began to shift in the Jacksonian era of the 1830s, a shift that accelerated rapidly after the Civil War. When Jefferson and Hamilton were having their great debates about the common man versus the business interests of the 1790s, the economy was structured so fundamentally differently as to make the argument over the role of government seem strange to modern ears.

Hamilton favored a strong central government in direct alliance with financiers and manufacturers. An advocate of a political philosophy called mercantilism, Hamilton wanted the federal government to guarantee debt and enforce its collection, to charter corporations to undertake specific tasks in service to government, and to charter a national bank, controlled in part by the federal government and in part by investors, that could be a source of capital for business interests.

Jefferson, on the other hand, was appalled at the idea that the federal government would align itself so closely to wealthy business interests, and he decried the strong role government was playing in partnership with economic elites.

These alignment theories began to be reversed in the 1830s, because of both Andrew Jackson and new economic conditions.

Corporations were free of government charters and sponsorship and did not need as much capital investment from government. As a result, these businesses and their allies began to oppose "big government." Free from direct ties to government sponsorship, corporations began to be far more wary of government in general, especially when Jackson and his allies were so activist and aggressive in pushing for policies that would help the "common man," in contrast to the rich and powerful business interests that Jackson failed to assist.

The Modern Corporation and Social Darwinism

While the economy and the role that government played began to shift in the 1830s, the divide over slavery so dominated American politics from the 1830s to the 1860s that it slowed down the economic and political transformations that newly independent corporations were making in the economy, so it makes sense at this point to pick up the story of our country's great economic debates in the 1860s. The combination of the Civil War's decimation of the old Southern slave economy, the economic reforms passed by Lincoln and the Radical Republicans (especially the Homestead Act, the land-grant university system, and the Pacific Railroad Act), and the coming age of industrialization created a totally different kind of economic system in America, one that was completely foreign to the system that Hamilton, Jefferson, Jackson, and our country's other early leaders had experienced. The emergence of the modern major corporation was by far the most profound change and would reshape every single thing about the way the economy worked.

Lincoln, with his customary insight, recognized this change and feared it greatly. In a letter to Colonel William Elkins, Lincoln made this observation, which was stunning in its nature, given the trauma that he and the country had just been through:

> We may congratulate ourselves that this cruel war is nearing its end. It has cost a vast amount of treasure and blood. . . . It has indeed been a trying hour for the Republic; but I see in the near future a crisis approaching that unnerves me and causes me to tremble for the safety of my country. As a result of the war, corporations have been enthroned and an era of corruption in high places will follow, and the money power of the country will endeavor to prolong its reign by working upon the prejudices of the people until all wealth is aggregated in a

few hands and the Republic is destroyed. I feel at this moment more anxiety for the safety of my country than ever before, even in the midst of war. God grant that my suspicions may prove groundless.

Tragically, though, Lincoln was killed. In addition to his undoubtedly being a far greater friend to African Americans than Andrew Johnson was, we will never know whether Lincoln's postwar presidency might have included some new progressive measures to counter the growing power of big business. Following the 1860s, a generation of both Republican and Democratic politicians got in bed with the new behemoths of finance, oil, railroads, and manufacturing. That era is widely considered to be the most thoroughly corrupt in American history (although, as I discussed in the last chapter, the last few years have been making historians question whether that is still true), with many members of Congress openly taking direct bribes from these businesses, and little being done about it by the courts or the Department of Justice. For two decades, the robber barons ran the country from top to bottom and got everything they wanted, while workers and farmers got virtually nothing from their government.

One of the things that happens when this kind of evil walks the land so openly is that its perpetrators need a lofty philosophy to justify it. As we have seen, in slavery's and Jim Crow's case that need was met by Calhoun's states' rights philosophy. In our own era, the theory of "supply-side economics" has provided the justification for massive tax cuts for millionaires, while giving little or no help to the poor and the middle class. In the Gilded Age, the philosophical veneer was supplied by something called Social Darwinism.

The father of Social Darwinism was an Englishman named Herbert Spencer. Spencer was a conservative before Darwin's evolutionary theory was published, but Spencer used Darwin's theories to create a justification for the robber barons that fit their needs perfectly. According to Spencer, society, like nature, worked best when it was organized around survival of the fittest. If the strongest in society overran and exploited the weak, that was not only okay, it was actually a good thing because it would lead to a strong society. "Society exists for the benefit of its members, not the members for the benefit of society," he said.

Like modern-day conservatives, Spencer hated government ("Government is essentially immoral," he said), taxes ("We do not commonly see in a tax a diminution of freedom, and yet it clearly is one"), and the idea that a jury of "twelve people of average ignorance" would ever sit in judgment of great corporations or wealthy individuals. Like conservatives of earlier years, Spencer had no problems defending the rights of kings to do what they will ("Divine right of kings means the divine right of anyone who can get uppermost," he said approvingly) or attacking the practicality of a more democratic form of government, saying that it required "the highest type of human nature, a type nowhere at present existing."

In America, the robber barons and their disciples in academia were thrilled to import Spencer's ideas. The most influential American Social Darwinist was a stunningly blunt Yale professor named William Graham Sumner. Sumner hated the idea of equating liberty with a share of political power and thought that freedom meant accepting inequality as the natural and better state of society. He believed that every society faced only two alternatives: "liberty, inequality, survival of the fittest" or "liberty, equality, survival of the unfittest." Sumner published a book in 1883 titled *What Social Classes Owe to Each Other*. In his view, government had only one purpose, which was to protect "the property of men and the honor of women."

Although the blatant nastiness of the Social Darwinists' "might makes right" philosophy made its rhetoric less popular over time, there was no question that the basic ideas of Social Darwinism fit modern pro-corporate conservatism like a glove. The main tenets of that philosophy—laissez-faire economics, small government, worship of the free market above all other things, aggressive individuality, low taxes, little regulation, and an assumption that if you weren't making it economically, it was your own fault—are the foundation stones for modern-day economic conservatism.

The problem with conservative philosophy, though, is that in the final analysis it doesn't work for most people. The reason that the reforms of the Progressive Era, the New Deal, and the 1960s and the early 1970s have stayed firmly in place in the American system is that they worked, and people liked them. The Social Darwinist system of giving all advantages to the wealthy and the powerful caused terrible economic burdens for farmers and workers, and the result in the 1880s and 1890s was the growing populist movement.

Populists and Progressives

The populist movement, whose core constituency was the farmers who had taken advantage of Lincoln's Homestead Act, had a broadly progressive agenda, in addition to the pro-silver position it is most famous for. The preamble to the populist movement's political party, the People's Party, in its 1892 platform explains the core importance of democracy: "when corruption dominates the ballot box . . . public opinion is silenced." Although mostly agrarian based, the People's Party decried the fact that "the urban workmen are denied the right to organize," and its members said that "the interests of rural and civil labor are the same."

Their goal, they said, was to "seek to restore the government of the Republic to the hands of the 'plain people.'"

The People's Party supported a progressive income tax; nationalizing the railroads, the telegraph, and telephone companies; a secret ballot (which was still not in existence in many states); a shorter workday; liberal pensions to veterans; and direct election of senators, who at the time were still elected by state legislatures. It opposed "any subsidy of national land to private corporations for any purpose," the maintenance of a large standing army, and the corporate ownership of land for speculative purposes.

A progressive populist movement found no home with the Republican Party of the time, which was dominated by politicians aligned with Northern industrialists, or with the Democratic Party, which was controlled by conservative Southern segregationists, but it started to grow dramatically as a third party. The People's Party got more than a million votes out of the less than twelve million cast in the 1892 election, and the movement kept growing over the next few years.

In 1896, a major turning point in history occurred. Readers of this book may be curious as to why, in the first chapter, I listed William Jennings Bryan's 1896 Democratic Convention speech as one of only three speeches that I consider to be a big change moment in American history. Given that Bryan did not go on to win the presidency and that most of what he advocated did not become law until many years later, it might have seemed an odd choice. But Bryan's nomination that year, like Barry Goldwater's 1964 nomination, began the process of a movement that would take over and transform a political party. Bryan's speech, without which he would not have gotten the nomination, started the transformation of the Democratic Party. Previously, it had been the home of Southern segregationists and conservative Northerners such as President Grover Cleveland (who as president at the time had just called out federal troops to crush the labor movement in Chicago), and, in great part due to Bryan, it would become the home of economic progressives like FDR, Truman, and LBJ.

Bryan was an unlikely man to be a presidential nominee. He had served only one term in the U.S. House, in 1893–1894, and was defeated when he ran in the 1894 election for the Senate. He was only thirty-six years old, the youngest man ever to make a serious run for president. He was from a tiny rural state, Nebraska, far away from the big states that were at the center of political power. And he was diametrically opposed in every way—policy, rhetoric, style, region, political base—to the incumbent president of his own party, the fifty-nine-year-old pro-corporate conservative from New York, Grover Cleveland.

But Cleveland's conservative policies had driven the economy ever deeper into the ditch, and the populist tide kept rising. With the deeply conservative, strongly pro-big business William McKinley firmly in control of the Republican Party, populist organizers focused their attention on the Democratic Party.

The key symbolic issue that became the focal point of populist organizing was the supply of money in the economy. Although the money-supply issue still gets talked about in our political debates, as politicians criticize or support Federal Reserve policies that increase or lower interest rates and money circulation, for people living today the issue has lost most of its intensity and passion. But in the pre–Federal Reserve years, the political debates over the amount of money in circulation and how it was controlled quite frequently provoked the biggest and bitterest fights in American politics. The money supply was the issue that Jefferson and Hamilton had their most intense conflict over; it was the issue that Andrew Jackson made the main cause of his presidency. And it was the symbolic issue around which American politics revolved in the mid-1890s.

The issue was fundamental because it pitted large financial interests, mostly based in New York and other populous cities in the East, against struggling farmers who were barely making a living in the Midwest, the West, and the South. The leading bankers wanted the money supply tight, interest rates high, and inflation extremely low because they made a lot more money that way. Farmers had to borrow every spring as they planted their crops, and if commodity prices stayed low, they weren't always able to pay everything off on time, which meant that their debts continued to grow. They wanted lower interest rates and more money in circulation.

Tying the dollar supply to gold, a far rarer commodity than silver, thus helped the bankers and hurt the farmers, which is why eliminating the gold standard became such a central cause for populist organizers. And by allying themselves with labor and other progressives, the populists had great success in organizing a nationwide movement. By the time the Democratic convention opened in Chicago in the summer of 1896, the "silver" Democrats had done such a good job of organizing that they had a clear majority of delegates to the convention. Delegates adopted a platform that was the clearest repudiation ever of an incumbent president from their own party. It was far from clear, though, how the convention would play out in terms of the presidential nominee.

There were thirteen candidates whose names were placed in nomination, with none of them even close to having the votes they needed (which was made even more complicated by a rule that said you had to get two-thirds of the delegates, rather than 50 percent plus one). Some of the thirteen were even pro–gold standard, hoping to somehow slip in as a compromise choice or at least block a strong pro-silver candidate from getting the nomination. Southern planters were pro-silver but far more conservative on every other topic.

Bryan's speech came before the voting was to start, as part of a planned debate on the gold vs. silver money-supply issue. Bryan was a superb performer and gave the greatest, clearest rendition of common people's populism ever given. In a brilliant passage summarizing the progressive populist economic philosophy, Bryan said:

> You come before us and tell us that we are about to disturb your business interests. . . . We say to you that you have made the definition of a business man too limited in its application. . . . The man who is employed for wages is as much a business man as his employer; the attorney in a country town is as much a business man as the corporation counsel in a great metropolis; the merchant at the crossroads store is as much a business man as the merchant of New York; the farmer who goes forth in the morning and toils all day . . . and who by the application of brain and muscle to the natural resources of the country creates wealth, is as much a business man as the man who goes upon the board of trade and bets upon the price of grain; the miners who go down a thousand feet into the earth, or climb two thousand feet upon the cliffs, and bring forth from their hiding places the precious metals to be poured into the channels of trade are as much business men as the few financial magnates who, in a back room, corner the money of the world.

Concluding with his famous lines "We will answer their demand for a gold standard by saying to them: You shall not press down upon the brow of labor this crown of thorns, you shall not crucify mankind upon a cross of gold," Bryan then stepped back and extended his arms out like Jesus on the cross. It was pure melodrama, pure theater, but it won the hearts of the crowd like no speech in history. Michael Kazin, in his biography of Bryan, described the scene this way:

> For several "painful" moments, the Coliseum was silent, as if thousands of people were all holding their breath. Bryan left the stage and walked slowly toward his delegation. Then it exploded. "The floor of the convention seemed to heave up," marveled the *New York World.* "Everybody seemed to go mad at once. . . . The whole face of the convention was broken by the tumult—hills and valleys of shrieking men and women."
>
> The joyful riot produced a wealth of distinct memories. Willis J. Abbot, a pro-Bryan reporter from New York City, saw two southern delegates "of advanced years" embrace while "crying bitterly, great tears rolling from their eyes into their bearded cheeks." A young editor from Nebraska recalled that both women and men stood on their chairs and flung off their hats, "never caring where they should come down." A farmer in the gallery who before the speech had called Bryan "that crazy Populist" banged his coat against a gallery seat and yelled, "My God! My God! My God!"

Bryan went from being one of the most obscure and least likely of the thirteen candidates to being the man everyone was talking about. He did not lead on the first ballot, but the crowd's reaction to the speech in the convention hall had made a big impression on the delegates, and Bryan picked up more votes on every ballot, going over the two-thirds mark on the fifth.

McKinley raised huge amounts of money and outspent Bryan by at least 10–1 and very probably quite a bit more. McKinley's campaign was led by the brilliant strategist Mark Hanna, who was as central to McKinley's success as Karl Rove was to George

W. Bush's. Hanna was clear: he, according to historian Margaret Leech, "wanted to place the corporations in the saddle and make them pay in advance for the ride." He raised millions from Wall Street financiers and got a $250,000 (more than $3 million in today's dollars) contribution from John D. Rockefeller. Hanna essentially invented the modern political campaign, creating a model that Republicans would use for decades to come. He hired fourteen hundred organizers to work in targeted states and printed up 120 million pieces of literature. McKinley's campaign was even the first in history to put the candidate on film.

Bryan lost that campaign, but as in Goldwater's victory in the Republican primary almost seventy years later, Bryan captured the hearts of his political party and put together an organizational structure that would come to dominate the Democratic Party in the decade ahead. By bringing the People's Party into the Democratic fold, he further solidified progressive populists' hold on the Democrats. Although conservative Democrats in the South and the Northeast would continue to battle for the soul of the party, they would lose more and more often before being thoroughly swept away by FDR. After Republican president Teddy Roosevelt captured the imagination of progressives during his term upon succeeding McKinley in 1901, conservative Democrats came back in 1904 and nominated a New York corporate lawyer who then got destroyed by Roosevelt in the general election. But Bryan captured the nomination in 1900 and 1908, and in 1912 he still dominated the party enough that Woodrow Wilson moved substantially to the left so that he could get Bryan's blessing and thereby win the nomination. Bryan became Wilson's secretary of state but resigned over Wilson's decision to go to war in 1917.

Besides the populists, the other great progressive movement of that era was, well, the progressive movement. Writers today, myself included, use the term *progressive* more broadly, as a way of describing those who advocate for equal rights and opportunity, more democracy, and investment in bottom-up economic strategies, rather than trickle-up. But in the language of the early 1900s, the progressive movement referred to reformers who were advocating for a set of policies that would clean up government corruption and rein in the power of big corporate trusts.

Although the progressive movement shared a great many policy goals with the populist movement led by Bryan, it had a more urban and middle-to-upper-middle-class constituency. Its members were more leery of labor unions and less supportive of some of the populists' more radical economic goals, like nationalizing the railroads and the telephone companies. But they were also less inclined to veer toward the anti-immigration and pro-segregation tendencies of the working-class populists who had ties to Southerners, such as Tom Watson of Georgia (a People's Party vice presidential candidate with great economic instincts who, at times in his career, sadly pandered to the racism of the South).

The presidents who were most closely identified with the progressive movement were Teddy Roosevelt and Woodrow Wilson; the great Robert La Follette of Wisconsin was their other most important political leader. But other great progressive movement leaders included the feminists, who finally achieved women's suffrage in 1919; Margaret Sanger, who started Planned Parenthood; Upton Sinclair, whose book titled *The Jungle* convinced Roosevelt of the dangers of unsanitary conditions in the food-production business; Gifford Pinchot and Sierra Club founder John Muir, who helped Roosevelt create the national parks system; the great muckraking journalists Ida Tarbell and Lincoln Steffens; and hugely influential intellectuals such as John Dewey and Thorstein Veblen. As always in American history, these movement leaders were at least as important, if not more so, than the progressive political leaders who acted on their ideas.

From a policy point of view, the progressive movement was an extraordinary success. It made the policy goals of the populists, such as the progressive income tax, direct election of senators, and breaking up the corporate trusts, a reality. And progressives brought in the first wave of environmental laws with the national parks system, ensured better food safety, improved the quality of public education, pushed for the elimination of child labor, and, most important, finally won women the right to vote. None of these reforms have ever been repealed, although conservatives have continued to hack away at many of them.

The progressive movement built a bridge between the wild-ass rural and working-class populists and the more urban and intellectual followers of progressivism. This alliance, although sometimes rough around the edges, has lasted until modern times in the Democratic Party. Urbane politicians like FDR and JFK have coexisted with the rougher-hewn politicians of middle America, such as Harry Truman and LBJ. Politicians like Barack Obama, who appeal more to higher-income, better-educated constituencies, can comfortably coexist with modern-day populists like John Edwards and the late Paul Wellstone. The blend of the two constituencies and the two styles has produced the Democratic Party's greatest political achievements over the last century.

Conservative Policy and the Great Depression

The conservatives fought back, as they always do. After all of the big changes of those first twenty years of the 1900s and after the trauma of World War I, conservatives pushed for, in the words of Warren G. Harding's successful 1920 presidential campaign, a "return to normalcy." The next three presidents of the 1920s, all Republicans, were three of the most conservative presidents in history, rivaling only Ronald Reagan and George W. Bush in the modern era.

Harding is on most historians' list of the all-around worst presidents in history, right at the top, along with pre–Civil War president Buchanan and, increasingly, in recent years, George W. Bush. Harding was probably the dumbest president in history. He let his corrupt lieutenants loot the government store, resulting in some of the biggest scandals of all time (the Veterans' Bureau Scandal, the Justice Department Scandal, the Alien Property Custodian Scandal, and the most famous, the Teapot Dome Scandal). Harding died of food poisoning in 1923, although some historians have speculated as to whether he wasn't intentionally killed to cover up even worse scandals.

Harding had named Calvin Coolidge as his vice president. Coolidge ascended to the presidency upon Harding's death and then was elected to a full term in 1924. Coolidge had come to the attention of national Republicans when, as governor of Massachusetts in 1918, he broke a police union strike by calling out the National Guard.

There was a good reason Coolidge was so admired by Reagan: he was truly a conservative's conservative. His most famous quote was "The chief business of the American people is business." He made big tax cuts for corporations and the wealthy a central feature of his economic policy, kept spending low, did nothing to help farmers as a farm crisis spread, and did not regulate the wildly escalating speculation of the financial markets. He was a firm believer in trickle-down economics and no regulation, as well as a big believer in traditional Christian piety. He was a classic modern-day conservative.

Although Hoover, in desperation, did make some modest-size efforts to use government to soften the blow of the Depression, his fundamental conservatism kept those efforts from being either bold enough or big enough to matter. He honestly didn't believe government should actually help people in trouble. In the depths of the Depression in 1931, he was remarkably blunt: "The sole function of government is to bring about a condition of affairs favorable to the beneficial development of private enterprise."

He categorically rejected helping the 25-plus percent of Americans who found themselves unemployed. He dabbled in public works but never invested in them significantly. He did little to stabilize or regulate the banking system, even though it edged closer and closer to a complete breakdown.

Conservative economics had utterly failed the American people, and the desperation caused by the Great Depression was beginning to be palpable.

The New Deal

A decade of laissez-faire capitalism in the 1920s, with virtually no regulation of the financial sector, low wages for workers, low incomes for farmers, and corruption rampant in government and business, led directly to our nation's worst economic crisis of all time. The policies of Harding and Coolidge set the stage for an excess of overspeculation in the stock market, and Hoover's conservatism made him totally ineffectual in dealing with the Depression when it came. Conservative policies had led to periodic depressions before—about once every twenty years in the previous century— but none had compared to this one. America was teetering on the edge of total financial collapse.

But the United States has been a lucky country to date. In its first twenty-five years, from 1776 to 1801, it had been very lucky to survive at all, winning the revolution against great odds, going through the traumas and uncertainty of trying to create a new style of government, and making it through early crises like the Alien and Sedition Acts and the Electoral College fiasco of 1800. With the presidency of Jefferson, things had stabilized until sixty years later, when that great poison slavery had almost destroyed us again. Fortunately, after a series of weak and ineffectual presidents, at the height of our greatest crisis, Abraham Lincoln emerged to not only hold the country together, but move us forward.

History repeated itself, as another great president came to power at the apex of our country's other great crisis. Following the disastrous presidencies of Harding, Coolidge, and Hoover, Franklin Roosevelt both calmed a terrified country and started to put the foundation pieces in place for a revitalized economy. And just as Lincoln and his party had used the cauldron of the Civil War not merely to hold the country together, but to free the slaves, give new political rights to all Americans, and allow millions more to obtain college educations, FDR used the cauldron of the Great Depression to change America for the better for all time.

Roosevelt's New Deal sought to do five things at once:

1. Calm the country's collective panic, especially the run on the banks that had forced a bank "holiday" at the beginning of Roosevelt's term.

2. Provide immediate relief to the unemployed, the starving, and the destitute (which was at least a quarter of the country by that point).

3. Stimulate the country's overall economy so that it started to move forward again, instead of being totally frozen.

4. Put in place a degree of long-term economic security for most of the country's population.

5. Establish long-term regulatory agencies so that this kind of economic collapse would not happen in the future.

The fact that FDR ended up being successful at all of these things was remarkable.

He did it with a bottom-up strategy that invested in ordinary people, a stark contrast to the trickle-down "What's good for business is good for America" strategy. Here are some examples:

- **Banking regulation.** One of FDR's key banking reforms was to guarantee Americans that their bank holdings would be insured, so that if a bank closed its doors, people would not lose their life savings. This gave average customers confidence in the banking system again and also encouraged people to start saving money.

- **Higher wages.** FDR believed that if most people had higher wages, they would have more to spend, and that would help the economy. He pushed through a minimum wage for workers and worked closely with progressive labor leaders such as John L. Lewis and Walter Reuther to pass legislation that made it easier for workers to organize labor unions.

- **Supporting family farmers.** With 25 percent of the nation still living on family farms, FDR invested heavily in rebuilding the agricultural economy. One of the first bills passed was the Agricultural Adjustment Act (AAA), which helped farmers get better prices for their crops. Although the original AAA was ruled unconstitutional, it provided more than $100 million to cotton farmers. FDR also worked with the great Senator George Norris from Nebraska (the only Republican to work consistently with FDR in a serious way on New Deal legislation) to pass the Rural Electrification Act (REA), which brought electricity to farmers who had been ignored by private utilities because there was no profit in getting electricity to rural areas. The government aided farmers by granting cooperatives low-cost loans. By the end of 1938, just two years after its inception, 350 cooperative projects in 45 states were delivering electricity to more than 1.5 million farms. By 1950, 90 percent of American farmers had electricity. Other measures included mortgage and credit relief; university extension programs that provided education, research, and technical assistance; and investment in transportation infrastructure to reduce the cost of transporting crops to market.

- **Social Security.** In 1930, only about one-third of men and about one-twelfth of women over the age of sixty-five had gainful employment. Industrial retirement plans covered only about 15 percent of the aged, and only 10 percent of these plans required employers to keep their commitment to those retired. Only eighteen states had old-age assistance laws, paying just $1 a day, on average, to the few who qualified. As such, most senior citizens lived in dire poverty, and American family incomes were stretched to the breaking point as families were taking care of their elderly parents. Social Security ended that terrible pattern, once and for all, and again helped the economy by giving the elderly (and now disabled individuals and their dependents) an income stream that allowed them to spend money that boosted the local economy. Social Security will become even more important as the baby boomer generation starts to retire.

- **Safety net.** FDR created the first-ever long-term federal government safety net for the poor and the unemployed. With so many people out of work for so long, he knew there would be mass starvation if nothing was done to provide relief.

And he understood that relief checks would mean more people buying food and other essentials, which would help farmers and local merchants.

- **Public works programs.** The New Deal invested heavily in public works programs, again under the theory that getting people to work helped the economy, since people with jobs were far more likely to buy products. His Work Projects Administration (WPA) alone provided jobs for 8.5 million people, as many as 3 million at a time. The other great advantage of these public works programs was that they created greatly needed infrastructure: 78,000 bridges were constructed; 46,000 more were improved; and 572,000 miles of rural roads were built, along with 67,000 miles of urban streets. More than 39,000 schools, 2,500 hospitals, and 12,800 playgrounds were either built or improved. During this time, the WPA was responsible for major projects such as the Bay Bridge in San Francisco; the Triborough Bridge in New York City; the Hoover Dam in Nevada; the Skyline Drive in Shenandoah Valley, Virginia; and the National Airport in Washington, D.C.

Conservatives protested mightily against these policies. Every single Republican in the House voted against Social Security, for example, and the leading Republicans on the Ways and Means Committee argued that "business and industry are already operating under very heavy burdens." They contended that Social Security and other forms of social insurance would cause more unemployment. (Sound familar? It should—these are the arguments conservatives have used, and still use, every time a progressive economic program is proposed.) The debate verged on hysteria: "Never in the history of the world has any measure brought here so insidiously designed as to prevent business recovery, to enslave workers, and to prevent any possibility of the employers providing work for the people" and "the lash of the dictator will be felt and 25 million free American citizens will, for the first time, submit themselves to the fingerprint test" (the fingerprint test being a rather odd way of describing the GOP's fear of big government). One Republican protested, "This bill opens the door and invites the entrance into the political field of a power so vast, so powerful as to threaten the integrity of our institutions and to pull the pillars of the temple down upon the hands of our descendants."

Unlike conservatives such as his predecessors, Hoover and Coolidge, and conservatives throughout history from Hamilton to George W. Bush, FDR saw government's role as investing in regular people, instead of in wealthy businesses. And it paid off. Modern-day conservatives are fond of saying that the New Deal didn't really work, that it was only World War II that got the economy humming again. But that's simply untrue. The banking panic faded because people knew that their deposits were guaranteed. The farm sector got steadily stronger throughout the 1930s. Unemployment started at a peak of 24.9 percent in 1933 and went down every year except one in the period prior to World War II, ending at less than 10 percent in 1941, the last year before the war.

Another key aspect of the New Deal was to bring regulation and a sense of stability to banking and the stock market. The most important and long-lasting of these reforms was the creation of the Securities and Exchange Commission (SEC), which finally brought some oversight to the wild gyrations and speculation of the stock market and closed the door on some of the most fraudulent corporate practices, such as manipulating stock prices. Reagan and the two Bush presidencies began to loosen these regulations, resulting in the worst corporate fraud in our country since the 1920s.

Another key reform was the Glass-Steagall Act of 1935, which founded the Federal Deposit Insurance Corporation (or FDIC, which was the law that guaranteed bank deposits) and prohibited banks from owning insurance companies and other kinds of financial institutions. These measures were essential in reducing the financial risks that had caused not only the Great Depression but many of the other depressions of the previous hundred years. And again, Republicans rolled back the Glass-Steagall Act in 1999, exposing our economic system to more risk.

The regulatory framework set up by the New Deal was remarkably successful for the next sixty years. In most of American history, severe depressions hit almost like clockwork approximately every twenty years as traditional unregulated business cycles produced them: 1819, 1837, 1857, 1873, 1893, 1907, and 1929. After the New Deal regulatory reforms, we have not had a serious depression since because our downturns have turned into recessions or even merely slower growth. FDR dealt with a recession in 1937, but the economy started to pick up again the very next year. Ironically, that 1937 recession was caused when FDR's budget advisers convinced him to cut the federal budget, one of the few times that FDR agreed to go in a more conservative direction. It is worth noting, by the way, that the worst of the recessions since the New Deal occurred in 1957, 1973, 1982, 1991, and 2007—all of them under the watch of Republican presidents. And the most sustained periods of economic growth after the New Deal were in the 1960s and 1990s, two decades governed primarily by Democratic presidents. Another economic pattern worth noting is this simple fact: every Republican president since Eisenhower has presided over increasing economic inequality. The only Democrat who has is Jimmy Carter, and he was easily also the most conservative Democratic president of modern times on economic issues.

FDR was a big believer in experimentation, innovation, and trying a wide variety of new policies to get us out of the Depression, and occasionally, that led to some confusing or even mildly contradictory policies. He has been accused by opponents at the time and ever since of not having an underlying core philosophy. But again, the evidence contradicts this idea. FDR was not a radical, and he was overly cautious sometimes, but he was deeply influenced by progressive thinkers and progressive ideas, and his speeches reflect that progressive orientation.

In his first campaign, FDR spoke in direct opposition to Hoover's notion that the sole function of government is to help private enterprise. FDR said that "Modern society, acting through its Government, owes the definite obligation to prevent starvation or the dire want of any of its fellow men and women who try to maintain themselves but cannot." In another speech, he spoke of the laissez-faire philosophy, which, when juxtaposed with human suffering, required "not only greater stoicism, but greater faith in immutable economic law . . . than I, for one, have."

The idea of America as a community whose members needed to work together and look out for one another was essential to his thinking. He asked that "there be a real community of interest, not only among the sections of this great country, but among its economic units. . . . Each unit must think of itself as a part of a great whole; one piece in a larger design."

One of FDR's most influential discourses was his Four Freedoms speech. Like many other great orations, including the Gettysburg Address, the Four Freedoms speech was remarkably short. But it laid out a vision of freedom that was not only concerned with the traditional negative freedoms of the Bill of Rights (e.g., government shouldn't repress its citizens' freedom of speech, religion, and so on) but also with economic freedom and freedom from the scourge of war. It is worth quoting in its entirety:

> In the future days, which we seek to make secure, we look forward to a world founded upon four essential human freedoms.
>
> The first is freedom of speech and expression—everywhere in the world.
>
> The second is freedom of every person to worship God in his own way—everywhere in the world.
>
> The third is freedom from want—which, translated into world terms, means economic understandings which will secure to every nation a healthy peacetime life for its inhabitants—everywhere in the world.
>
> The fourth is freedom from fear—which, translated into world terms, means a world-wide reduction of armaments to such a point and in such a thorough fashion that no nation will be in a position to commit an act of physical aggression against any neighbor—anywhere in the world.

That is no vision of a distant millennium. It is a definite basis for a kind of world attainable in our own time and generation. That kind of world is the very antithesis of the so-called new order of tyranny which the dictators seek to create with the crash of a bomb.

To that new order we oppose the greater conception— the moral order. A good society is able to face schemes of world domination and foreign revolutions alike without fear.

Since the beginning of our American history, we have been engaged in change—in a perpetual peaceful revolution—a revolution which goes on steadily, quietly adjusting itself to changing conditions—without the concentration camp or the quick-lime in the ditch. The world order which we seek is the cooperation of free countries, working together in a friendly, civilized society.

This nation has placed its destiny in the hands and heads and hearts of its millions of free men and women; and its faith in freedom under the guidance of God. Freedom means the supremacy of human rights everywhere. Our support goes to those who struggle to gain those rights or keep them. Our strength is our unity of purpose.

To that high concept there can be no end save victory.

The Four Freedoms speech, the strong value that FDR placed in a sense of American community, his rejection of laissez-faire and trickle-down economics, his belief that the economy required a regulatory framework to keep economic downturns from turning into disasters, and his conviction of the need for a bottom-up approach to economics all made for a clear and compelling philosophy. That philosophy was a brilliant blend of 1890s Bryanesque populism with Teddy Roosevelt's and Woodrow Wilson's progressivism. When FDR railed against the "economy royalists," raised taxes on the wealthy, helped the farm economy so dramatically, and supported labor, he sounded like William Jennings Bryan on the stump. When he pushed through the Securities and Exchange Act, hired the unemployed to work in the national park system, and kept banks from owning insurance companies, he reflected the progressive movement.

The New Deal was easily the most progressive economic program in history and also the most successful, in terms of both its economic impact and its political power. The economy-killing depressions that were endemic to the previous 125 years of American history immediately ceased, to be replaced by milder downturns. Increasing wages created the largest and most prosperous middle class in history. Social Security and the safety net cushioned families from the desperation of poverty. The GI Bill and other student aid programs allowed more poor and working-class kids to go to college than at any other time in history, adding strength to the expanding middle class and giving more entrepreneurs the tools to succeed at business. By 1956, 7.8 million World War II veterans (51 percent of those eligible) had received an education under the program.

But for all its success, the New Deal's progressive reforms almost didn't happen. Although FDR had strong progressive instincts, he had not been a terribly bold governor of New York or run a particularly strong progressive campaign in 1932. He had many old friends from his wealthy economic background who counseled him to be cautious and slower. And in a sobering account of FDR's first hundred days, *The Defining Moment*, Jonathan Alter described the strong advice FDR was getting from many people to declare martial law to deal with the economic crisis and increasing panic that had reached a frightening peak in early 1933.

Fortunately, FDR did not listen to the advice to be too cautious or to become a dictator. He went with his better instincts and responded instead to the growing progressive movement that had emerged in the country, a movement led by the revitalized labor movement but also built on the ideas of the populist and progressive movements that flourished as FDR had come of age. In partnership with progressive thinkers and activists, FDR created the greatest run of success for progressivism and the country in our history.

Because the New Deal worked so well as policy, it was also incredibly successful politically. FDR was elected president four times, all by landslides, and his vice president Harry Truman, who took office upon his death, won in his own right in 1948. The only Republican to win the presidency between 1932 and 1968 was war hero Dwight Eisenhower, and he governed as a moderate, never challenging the basic tenets of the New Deal policy. Democrats controlled the House of Representatives for all but two terms after FDR's election in 1932, until 1994, an astounding and unprecedented sixty-two-year run, and they controlled both houses of Congress for fifty-two of those years.

Truman's Populism

Modern-day conservatives enjoy quoting Truman, and George W. Bush especially likes to compare himself to Truman. Bush mentions how Truman was unpopular while in office but that he was redeemed by the judgment of history. Harry Truman, being the blunt-spoken populist that he was, would have been likely to use swear words if he heard this.

It is true that Truman stood up strongly to communists. But his signature foreign policy achievement, the Marshall Plan, countered communist aggression with foreign aid and consistent diplomacy, not with bluster or leaping to war. And his economic policy was pure populism.

Truman first drew the attention of Roosevelt by going aggressively after war profiteers and corrupt defense contractors during World War II. He was a Midwestern son of the soil, having grown up poor on a Missouri farm. If you have any doubt about whether he was a "centrist" Democrat or even a closet conservative, I suggest you check out these passages from his stump speeches in 1948 while he was on his famous whistle-stop campaign tour:

> The Democratic Party represents the people. It is pledged to work for agriculture. . . . The Democratic Party puts human rights and human welfare first. . . . These Republican gluttons of privilege are cold men. They are cunning men. . . . They want a return of the Wall Street economic dictatorship.

Something happens to Republican leaders when they get control of the Government. . . . Republicans in Washington have a habit of becoming curiously deaf to the voice of the people. They have a hard time hearing what the ordinary people of the country are saying. But they have no trouble at all hearing what Wall Street is saying. They are able to catch the slightest whisper from big business and the special interests.

Republican candidates are apparently trying to sing the American voters to sleep with a lullaby about unity. . . . They want the kind of unity that benefits the National Association of Manufacturers . . . the real estate trusts . . . [the] selfish interests. . . . They don't want unity. They want surrender. And I am here to tell you people that I will not surrender.

Some things are worth fighting for. . . . We must fight isolationists and reactionaries, the profiteers and the privileged class. . . . Our primary concern is for the little fellow. We think the big boys have always done very well, taking care of themselves. . . . It is the business of government to see that the little fellow gets a square deal.

Conservative elites today frequently insist that populist rhetoric has never been successful in American politics, and I have to laugh when I look at the words of Jefferson and Jackson and both of the Roosevelts. But I especially have to chuckle thinking of Truman, the man all the pundits and the elitists wrote off in 1948. He barnstormed the country with that kind of rhetoric and shocked the elites out of their socks.

The Economic Successes of the 1960s

By practically any measure you want to name, the most prosperous decade in this country's history, especially for the middle class but also in general, was the 1960s. Following the economic doldrums of Eisenhower's final years, the remarkable prosperity of the 1960s was stunning. Unemployment was at record lows, but so was inflation. Average wages for workers were climbing steadily, as was their net worth, due to home values and generous pensions. Despite all the tumult of those years, the economy hummed along like a fine-tuned machine. And it was no accident that the 1960s were also the time of the most broadly progressive economic policies in our history. LBJ took the New Deal framework and kept building on it. The best example? Despite the advance of Social Security, older Americans were still at risk financially due to rising health-care costs. LBJ solved that problem with Medicare and also brought health-care coverage to poor people through Medicaid.

Conservatives now love to mock and dismiss LBJ's War on Poverty. It was quickly abandoned once Nixon took office, and Reagan completed the dismantling. But the plain fact is that it actually worked. In 1963, the year LBJ became president, 19.5 percent of Americans lived in poverty. He announced his War on Poverty in January 1964, and by the time he left office in 1969, the poverty rate was 12.1 percent, an incredible success story (by the Reagan years, it had drifted back up to more than 20 percent). Especially impressive was the nine-point drop in poverty among children. LBJ's policy wasn't merely increased welfare payments, either: he invested money in inner-city jobs and job training, education, and health care—Medicaid alone helped millions climb out of poverty. And he helped community organizers mobilize poor people on their own behalf, a politically gutsy move that made local elected officials irate. War on Poverty programs included Head Start, Legal Services, Community Action Agencies, Job Corps, and community service programs such as VISTA—all of them highly successful programs that addressed critical needs of low-income people.

The economic policies of the 1960s were an incredible policy success, but, sadly, they did not carry with them the political success of the New Deal. The progressive coalition broke apart because of the Vietnam War, and because race-related issues and social upheaval provided conservatives with an opportunity to build an alliance with working-class whites.

The massive movement organizing of the 1960s carried over to the early 1970s, giving progressives some great victories in those first few years, including the Clean Air Act, the Clean Water Act, the EPA (Environmental Protection Agency), OSHA (Occupational Safety and Health Administration), and the *Roe v. Wade* decision. But the center-right economic policies of Nixon, Ford, and Carter (yes, Carter—he was good on environmental, consumer, and human rights issues but was pretty conservative on economic ones and started the deregulation trend that Reagan was happy to continue), combined with the energy price shocks of those years, stopped the economic progress of middle-class and poor Americans. But it was Reagan's right-wing ideology that did the most to take away from the middle class and the poor and give to the rich.

The Reagan Era

Reagan loved to tell the story in stump speeches during his presidential elections, as well as in office, of a "welfare queen" from Chicago who had eighty names, thirty addresses, and twelve Social Security cards and collected benefits from four different deceased husbands, none of whom actually existed. Reagan said she bilked the government out of more than $150,000 and drove a Cadillac. He used her as an example of why welfare benefits should be eliminated or drastically scaled back and how government in general was wasting way too much money.

The fact that Reagan based his story on one African American woman who was convicted of using two aliases to collect $8,000 didn't matter to him at all. For years after reporters pointed out that his facts were wrong, he kept using the story in his speeches, with all of the false details listed in the previous paragraph. Reagan held on to his original version because it was a perfect story to help drive working-class whites away from progressive economic policies.

Reagan helped popularize the term *supply-side economics* in the American political debate. He said that an analysis of tax rates by an economist named Arthur Laffer proved that cutting taxes for the wealthy would stimulate economic activity as rich people invested, thus actually generating increased tax revenues. The fact that Reagan's big tax cut instead created the biggest deficit in American history (until his disciple George W. Bush won the same kind of tax cut twenty years later, creating his own yawning deficit) did not matter to Reagan, either. He was all about returning to the free-market fundamentalism that the Social Darwinists in the 1880s and Coolidge in the 1920s championed. Here are its tenets:

- Lower taxes, especially for the wealthy. Reagan's tax cut, passed in 1981, lowered income taxes by 5 percent in the first budget year and 10 by percent in each of the next two years. Low-income Americans received 16 percent of the dollar savings, with top income earners saving 84 percent.

- Have minimal regulation, especially for big business.

- Weaken unions.

- Weaken family farms. Reagan's farm policies caused the worst depression in the agriculture sector since the 1920s and early 1930s.

- Cut money for domestic programs of all kinds.

- Return power to the states (except when they tried to regulate big business; then Reagan wanted to preempt those powers).

- Shred the safety net. Reagan orchestrated a 12 percent decrease in the number of elderly and disabled people on Medicaid. In 1980, the last full year of Carter's term, over 2.8 million people were receiving Social Security Disability Insurance (SSDI). The rate of recipients had grown exponentially since the introduction of SSDI, at the rate of about 100,000 per year since 1960. Nearly a million people alone received benefits between 1970 and 1975. Yet by 1985, the number of recipients was actually *down*, to 2.6 million, victims of Reagan's cuts. More than a million children were eliminated from school lunch programs. Approximately half a million families were removed from Aid to Families with Dependent Children rolls.

- Assume the free market is always right.

Reagan's ideology was one the Social Darwinists of a hundred years earlier would have loved, and it had the desired effect: the rich got a lot richer, and the middle- and lower-income folks got poorer.

George H. W. Bush, Reagan's vice president and successor, continued Reagan's policies and his politics, although a deal with Democrats in Congress to close the deficit by raising taxes (including on the wealthy) made the conservative movement angry. Bush got elected the first time in part by race-baiting his opponent with the infamous Willie Horton ads and tried to get reelected against Bill Clinton by fearmongering and even red-baiting Clinton. But the second tough recession of the Reagan-Bush years convinced Americans that the time had come to try a Democrat.

The Clinton Era

Although Bill Clinton portrayed himself (and governed) as a centrist and sent some signals to inoculate himself on issues where Democrats had been hurt (calling, for example, to "end welfare as we know it"), his "Putting People First" platform had a lot of old-fashioned progressive populist rhetoric in it. He announced his plan by harkening back to FDR's era, saying, "My strategy puts people first by investing more than $50 billion each year over the next four years to put America back to work—the most dramatic economic growth program since World War II." Clinton described his plan as being for the forgotten Americans, "who work hard and play by the rules" but weren't getting the rewards from the economy that CEOs and the wealthy were. The plan would be paid for primarily by "forcing the very wealthy to pay their fair share of taxes, closing corporate tax loopholes, and implementing rigorous health care cost controls." The plan called for putting America back to work by revitalizing cities, by converting from a defense economy to a peacetime economy, and by "rebuilding our country." It called for universal health care and sweeping campaign finance reform to limit the power of big money and lobbyists.

Although there were some more conservative-sounding proposals in "Putting People First"—opening up trade barriers, cutting a hundred thousand unnecessary federal government jobs, and welfare reform—all in all, it was a pretty progressive and populist platform.

Once Clinton got into office, his record was mixed. The 1993 budget and economic plan that was passed was the most progressive since LBJ's heyday. It gave a major cut to the poor through the Earned Income Tax Credit, boosted taxes substantially on the wealthy, funded a hundred thousand cops in community-policing programs, funded thousands of national service volunteers to help the poor, reformed student loan programs and put money into scholarships so hundreds of thousands of kids could go to college, and increased money for Head Start and hundreds of other deserving domestic programs. Typical of the hysterical Republican arguments against the economic plan was the one from Newt Gingrich, when he said, "The tax increase . . . will lead to a recession . . . and actually increase the deficit." Dick Armey, the then House Republican conference chairman, said that the "impact on job creation will be devastating." And Senator Bob Packwood even said he would bet his mortgage that the deficit, unemployment, and inflation would all go up as a result of Clinton's economic plan. If Packwood had bet his mortgage on that, he would have lost his house: all of those Republican predictions turned out to be 100 percent wrong.

Clinton also passed a Family and Medical Leave bill, the Violence Against Women Act, a major increase in children's health coverage (through the S-CHIP legislation), the only raise in the minimum wage from 1989 to 2007, and a variety of increases in funding for good programs in the federal budget. He stood up to Newt Gingrich and the Republican onslaught when they attempted to slash Medicare, Medicaid, education funding, and environmental programs in the 1995 budget fight, beating them so thoroughly politically that they mostly gave in to him on budget battles for the rest of his presidency. He appointed progressive people to environmental, labor, judicial, civil rights, and consumer positions. His economic policies produced prosperity throughout his time in office and helped lower the poverty rate for the first time since LBJ's administration. The poverty rate declined from 15.1 percent in 1993 to 11.3 percent in 2000—the largest six-year drop in poverty since the War on Poverty. The poverty rates for single mothers, African Americans, and the elderly dropped to their lowest levels on record, and Hispanic poverty dropped to its lowest level since 1979. Home ownership reached record levels. The Clinton years saw the creation of more than 22.5 million jobs—the most jobs ever produced under a single administration and more than were created in the previous twelve years combined. Of the total new jobs, 20.7 million, or 92 percent, were in the private sector.

All of these were worthy and significant achievements. But the Clinton administration failed at the one major progressive initiative that would have really moved the country forward: health-care reform. And having fallen short at that and then getting swamped in the 1994 elections, Clinton decided to play small ball the rest of his term. Thus, he had relatively little to show in terms of permanent progressive accomplishments.

Clinton's vice president, Al Gore, won the popular vote in 2000 and almost certainly would have won Florida had all the votes been counted in that state. But George W. Bush successfully stole the election, took office as president, and became arguably the most conservative and worst president in history.

The Economic Disaster of the George W. Bush Years

By the last year of his presidency, many historians were making the case that Bush beat out Harding, Coolidge, Hoover, Buchanan, and all the rest as the worst president in U.S. history—61 percent of historians in one survey thought Bush was the worst president of all time, and 98 percent rated his presidency a "failure." There are several reasons for that, including the disastrous consequences of the Iraq War, the erosion of civil liberties and the use of torture as a policy of the U.S. government, the lack of action on major urgent problems such as global warming, and the incredibly high levels of

corruption in this administration discussed in chapter 5. But one of
the biggest reasons has been Bush's economic policy. As Nobel
Prize–winning economist Joseph Stiglitz put it in December 2007:

> Up to now, the conventional wisdom has been that Herbert
> Hoover, whose policies aggravated the Great Depression, is
> the odds-on claimant for the mantle of "worst president"
> when it comes to stewardship of the American economy.
> Once Franklin Roosevelt assumed office and reversed
> Hoover's policies, the country began to recover. The eco-
> nomic effects of Bush's presidency are more insidious than
> those of Hoover's, harder to reverse, and likely to be long-
> lasting. There is no threat of America's being displaced from
> its position as the world's richest economy. But our grandchil-
> dren will still be living with, and struggling with, the economic
> consequences of Mr. Bush.

Here are some of the grim facts about Bush's economic record:

- The number of new jobs that need to be created every month
  in the American economy to keep pace with growth in the
  labor force is 122,000. During the Clinton era, that pace
  was easily exceeded, with an average of 237,000 new jobs
  per month. During the Bush era, we fell way short, averaging
  only 59,000 jobs per month as of July 2008.

- Bill Clinton inherited a massive annual federal deficit from
  the Reagan and Bush I presidencies and turned it around into
  a healthy and growing surplus. The projected surplus at the
  beginning of Bush II's presidency for the next decade (fiscal
  years 2002–2011) was projected to be $5.6 trillion. Bush's
  massive tax cut and other economic policies quickly wiped
  out that surplus, and we are instead on track to have a $2.4
  trillion deficit for this decade.

- Our foreign-held public debt ballooned from $1 trillion in
  2001 to $2.2 trillion in 2007.

- Our trade deficit set all-time record levels, ballooning to $850 billion over Bush's presidency as of July 2008.

- Oil prices have surged dramatically higher than they have ever been. When Bush came into office, oil went for $35 a barrel. By mid-2008, oil cost well over $100 a barrel and seemed likely to stay higher for the long term.

- The dollar is weak, having hit a record low of $1.60 against the euro in July 2008, the lowest it has been since the euro was introduced in 1999.

- The middle class got squeezed with declining incomes and rising inflation. According to Harvard professor Elizabeth Warren, the decline in median family income from 2001 to 2007 has been an average of $1,146. Meanwhile, the yearly increase in inflation-adjusted dollars during the same time period is an average of $200 more for food; $657 in child care; $1,150 for gasoline; $1,488 in mortgage payments; and $3,436 for yearly college tuition at a public university. Families were making less and having to pay far more in everyday expenses.

- Personal bankruptcy rates stayed high throughout Bush's term. Between March 2006 and March 2007, before the housing bubble burst and the recessionary waters began to deepen, personal bankruptcy rates went up more than 60 percent.

- The number of people without health insurance kept going up as well. When Bush took office, it was 41 million. By 2008, it was over 47 million.

- Bush vetoed (an action he has taken only four times in his presidency) a reauthorization of the State Children's Health Insurance Plan, which subsidizes health coverage for 6.6 million children from families that earn too much to qualify for Medicaid but not enough to afford their own private coverage.

- The housing sector was in freefall. During 2007, nearly 1.3 million U.S. housing properties were subject to foreclosure activity, up 79 percent from 2006. As of December 22,

2007, the *Economist* estimated that subprime defaults would reach a level of between $200 and $300 billion.

- The financial markets, mostly unregulated by the Bush administration, took their worst hit since the Great Depression, as one blue-chip financial company after another has been forced to write down tens of billions of dollars in debt.

- Bush's economic policies of tax cuts for the rich, little regulation of corporate fraud, and financial market shenanigans have left the country in its most precarious economic situation since Coolidge's and Hoover's policies created the Great Depression.

What is clear when you look at our country's economic history is that conservative policies have been at the heart of our worst economic times, and progressive policies have given us our best economic times. Lincoln's landmark economic policies gave us a prosperous economy for years afterward, but the Social Darwinist policies of the 1880s and 1890s created economic depression and havoc for farmers and workers. The Progressive Era policies produced a sound economy for the first generation after the turn of the century, but Coolidge and Hoover gave us the Great Depression. The New Deal helped us out of the Great Depression and kept us from having another depression ever since. The Democratic presidencies of the 1960s and 1990s made us prosperous, but the conservative policies of Nixon, Reagan, Bush I, and Bush II made us vulnerable to recession and long-term economic problems. When our country has chosen progressive policies, we've done well. When we haven't, we've paid the price—literally—for those mistakes.

7

The Dream and
the Backlash

T he general historical assumption is that the 1950s were a
time of calm, quiet conservatism in America, whereas the
1960s were the decade of massive change. In one way,
that's true. But the 1950s were also the beginning of the modern
progressive movement, which changed the country, and of the
right-wing backlash, which also became a movement and changed
things in its own way. The intense struggle between modern progressivism and modern conservatism that started in the 1950s and
raged openly—literally in the streets during the 1960s—has been
fundamentally shaping the country ever since. And it will come as
no surprise to you, if you've followed along with the theme of
the book, that both movements were deeply rooted in the past.

The "calm, quiet" 1950s actually started with an ugly jolt:
McCarthyism. As did conservative demagogues before and after
him, Joe McCarthy flourished on the back of that simple emotion:
fear. The Soviet Union had emerged after World War II as the
principal threat to American power. With Mao's Communist Revolution in China, the USSR's new ability to produce atomic bombs,
and the Korean War flaring up, Americans who were just recover-
ing from the trauma of World War II felt understandably on edge
because of the new perils. Just as Southern conservatives had used
threats to the "Southern way of life" to stoke the Civil War, and

George W. Bush would exploit fears of terrorism after 9/11, Joe McCarthy brilliantly capitalized on anxiety about communism to unleash a campaign against civil liberties and progressive ideas.

Any writer, artist, or political leader who had ever expressed sympathy for any "socialist" ideas (defined by McCarthy as pretty much anything to the left of Eisenhower) was subject to being called in front of congressional committees or being blacklisted. Any politician who objected to McCarthy's tactics was called a "red," and several fine political leaders, including the great Senator Claude Pepper, whom McCarthy mocked as "Red Pepper," went down to defeat. Despite, or perhaps because of, his tactics, McCarthy was lauded, honored, and assisted by conservatives all over the country. Phyllis Schlafly, who later led the opposition to the Equal Rights Amendment and started the far-right group Concerned Women for America, got her start as an aide to McCarthy. Barry Goldwater championed McCarthy to the bitter end and praised him for many years after he was discredited. Southern segregationist leaders such as Jesse Helms loved McCarthy and defended him against all attacks, again long after he fell into disrepute. And even to this day, despite all of the documentation of his lies and all of the lives he ruined, conservatives still align themselves with him: a new book by the longtime right-wing writer M. Stanton Evans, titled *Blacklisted by History*, gives a stalwart defense of McCarthy.

As we saw in chapter 2, the McCarthy era's antagonism toward anything defined as socialist had broad influence because even books by historical figures like Tom Paine were considered suspect. This was a period where fear was used to crush any kind of progressive ideas or initiatives.

Fortunately, courageous people such as Edward R. Murrow stood up to McCarthy, and his demagoguery was so over the top, and his lies so blatant, that once a few people confronted him and refused to back down, it broke the wave of hysteria that had gripped the country. McCarthy got the censure and humiliation he so richly deserved. The fear of communism would not go away until the end of the Cold War, but the panic around it subsided to some degree.

In the same year—1954—that McCarthy was finally being de-fanged as a major political force, the Warren Court came out with its historic *Brown v. Board of Education* decision. The civil rights movement had been quietly toiling away in all those years since African Americans were left to fend for themselves in the post-Reconstruction period. Now the movement got the heat on its burn-ers turned up a notch, and a new generation of leaders came to the fore. Rosa Parks was hardly the first person to protest segregation in the South, but the combination of her courage, the *Brown v. Board of Education* decision, and the leadership of a young man still in his first year as a minister at a modest-size church in Montgomery, Alabama, sparked a movement fire that burns yet today.

Martin Luther King Jr. and a Growing Progressive Movement

The success of the Montgomery bus boycott probably had at least as much to do with Rosa Parks's courage, and the grit of working-class African Americans walking miles to work instead of taking the bus, as it did with Martin Luther King Jr. But King's charisma, elo-quence, and strategic insights into how to build a movement cap-tured people's attention, and after the success in Montgomery, civil rights leaders throughout the South started to ask for his help to inspire people and develop organizing strategies. Not all of his organizing campaigns succeeded, but the wave of resistance to Jim Crow kept building, and new leaders stepped into the fray: the African American students who organized the sit-ins at lunch counters, the organizers of the Freedom Rides and of Mississippi Summer, and the African American students who applied to the white universities of the South.

The movement kept building, and Southern whites either gave way or looked awful when they refused. Southern segregation-ists continued to use every means at their disposal to fight back, in-cluding violence and terrorism. As a result, however, they became more politically isolated, and the civil rights movement made great progress.

But King was not only a civil rights leader. He was also part of a broader school of American progressive thought. He took his ideas on movement building and political philosophy from a wide variety of sources: from the Bible and from great modern theologians like Niebuhr and Tillich; from Mohandas Gandhi, Henry David Thoreau, and Saul Alinsky; from past civil rights leaders such as Frederick Douglass, W. E. B. DuBois, and A. Philip Randolph; from labor leaders like John L. Lewis and Walter Reuther; and from great men such as Paine, Jefferson, and Lincoln, who provided progressives with historic reference points.

The genius of King was that he reached back into history and connected it to the dreams and aspirations of African Americans who were then fighting Jim Crow. As a result, his movement resonated with and connected to the vast majority of Americans. King's "I Have a Dream" speech became the second-most important oration in American history, second only to the Gettysburg Address, because King succeeded so beautifully in building his vision on the structure of the past. Like Lincoln going back to Jefferson, King went back to Jefferson and Lincoln.

Standing in front of the Lincoln Memorial, King began his speech with language modeled on the Gettysburg Address: "Five score years ago, a great American, in whose symbolic shadow we stand today, signed the Emancipation Proclamation. This momentous decree came as a great beacon of hope in the flames of withering injustice. It came as a joyous daybreak to end the long night of their captivity. But one hundred years later, the Negro still is not free."

A paragraph later, King called upon the nation to redeem the promise of Jefferson's Declaration of Independence: "In a sense, we've come to our nation's capital to cash a check. When the architects of our republic wrote the magnificent words of the Constitution and the Declaration of Independence, they were signing a promissory note to which every American was to fall heir. This note was a promise that all men—yes, black men as well as white men—would be guaranteed the unalienable rights of life, liberty, and the pursuit of happiness."

Building his speech on those cornerstones of American progressive thought, King then spelled out his dream in words from scripture ("I have a dream that one day every valley shall be exalted, and every hill and mountain shall be made low, the rough places will be made plain, and the crooked places will be made straight and the glory of the Lord shall be revealed and all flesh shall see it together") and from beloved patriotic songs ("My country 'tis of thee, sweet land of liberty, of thee I sing. Land where my fathers died, land of the pilgrims' pride, from every mountainside, let freedom ring"), and from old African American church hymns ("Free at last, free at last, thank God Almighty, we are free at last").

Like the Declaration of Independence and the Gettysburg Address, King's "I Have a Dream" speech became American scripture. In a moment of great conflict and divisiveness, King forged a unified vision of what America should be: a nation built on the concepts of equal rights and opportunities, of political and personal freedom, and of fairness, justice, and dignity for all of its people. Like Lincoln, King answered the conservatives forcefully and directly and won the argument about how to interpret American history: "I have a dream that one day, down in Alabama, with its vicious racists, with its governor having his lips dripping with the words of interposition and nullification, one day, right there in Alabama, little black boys and black girls will be able to join hands with little white boys and white girls as sisters and brothers."

King's vision was too compelling to ignore. At the time, his speech was like a thunderclap. It has grown in power over the years and become part of America's deepest understanding of itself. Especially after King's death, the speech became so fundamental to our idea of America that conservatives tried to appropriate the words for their own causes, rather than argue directly against them. The words, like Jefferson's Declaration and Lincoln's Gettysburg Address, have become so iconic and familiar that it is too easy to forget their revolutionary nature. But like those other American scriptures, King's words have continued to inspire progressive leaders, thinkers, and activists to fight for progress at every level.

Inherent in King's legacy is that he was more than merely a civil rights leader or an African American leader: he was a leading light in America's broad progressive tradition. His "I Have a Dream" speech, like the Declaration of Independence and the Gettysburg Address, created an idea of an American identity built on progressive ideals. In his other discourses and books, he built on these broader ideals as well. In referencing his own "I Have a Dream" speech four years later, for example, King said, "I still have a dream that one day the idle industries of Appalachia will be revitalized, and the empty stomachs of Mississippi will be filled, and brotherhood will be more than a few words at the end of a prayer, but rather the first order of business on every legislative agenda."

King spoke repeatedly about economic justice issues linking with the issues of poverty and freedom. Only a few weeks before his death, he said, "And . . . there is no point in going around acting like we are free. We are still not free, we are still facing slavery. And you know why we aren't free? Because we are poor. We are poor."

King's last public action was to speak on behalf of striking workers in Memphis, Tennessee, on the night before he was shot. He also spoke frequently of the power and importance of community, of working together and looking out for one another, not only in terms of the movement or the African American community but in all of society. His speeches, including the "I Have a Dream" speech, are laced with images of people holding hands in fellowship and "sitting down at the table of brotherhood together." But even beyond that, he spoke more directly on the topic of community and interdependence. In a sermon called "Ingratitude," he spoke of ingratitude as being one of the worst sins because a person "fails to realize his dependence on others." He said that our fates are "inextricably linked in a garment of destiny."

King's broad progressivism wasn't merely theoretical, either. In addition to championing economic causes and union organizing, he came out, at great political risk to himself, against the Vietnam War. To LBJ and even certain other people in the civil rights community, this was wrong because they thought he should be focused only on civil rights. But King understood too well the connection between the various issues and the importance of being on the right side of all progressive debates. When he came out in opposition to the war, his remarkable speech had a depth of vision that was breathtaking. It clearly showed that King saw himself not only as a civil rights leader but also as a leader of the broader progressive cause:

> I come to this magnificent house of worship tonight because my conscience leaves me no other choice. . . . Many persons have questioned me about the wisdom of my path. At the heart of their concerns this query has often loomed large and loud: Why are you speaking about war, Dr. King? Why are you joining the voices of dissent? Peace and civil rights don't mix, they say. Aren't you hurting the cause of your people, they ask? And when I hear them, though I often understand the source of their concern, I am nevertheless greatly saddened, for such questions mean that the inquirers have not really known me, my commitment or my calling. . . . There is at the outset a very obvious and almost facile connection between the war in Vietnam and the struggle I, and others, have been waging in America. A few years ago there was a shining moment in that struggle. It seemed as if there was a real promise of hope for the poor—both black and white—through the poverty program. There were experiments, hopes, new beginnings. Then came the buildup in Vietnam and I watched the program broken and eviscerated as if it were some idle political plaything of a society gone mad on war, and I knew that America would never invest the necessary funds or energies in rehabilitation of its poor so long as adventures like Vietnam continued to draw men and skills and money like some demonic destructive suction tube. So I was increasingly compelled to see the war as an enemy of the poor and to attack it as such. . . .
>
> For those who ask the question, "Aren't you a civil rights leader?" and thereby mean to exclude me from the movement for peace, I have this further answer. In 1957 when a group of

us formed the Southern Christian Leadership Conference, we chose as our motto: "To save the soul of America." We were convinced that we could not limit our vision to certain rights for black people, but instead affirmed the conviction that America would never be free or saved from itself unless the descendants of its slaves were loosed completely from the shackles they still wear.

The vision that King laid out in that stunning speech, on the values that should underlie both domestic and foreign policy, is representative of the best of American progressivism.

The civil rights movement and the philosophy of Martin Luther King Jr. inspired a progressive resurgence in America. At that time, the complacency that resulted from the New Deal's great economic achievements and the establishment-oriented conservatism of the 1950s had sunk American politics into a sleepy inertia. America in the 1950s had a relatively moderate Republican president (Eisenhower) who was not interested in challenging the basic structure of the New Deal and a Congress that for most of the decade was narrowly divided between relatively moderate Democratic leadership and relatively moderate Republican leadership. This was arguably the most bipartisan decade in American history, but bipartisanship is not always a good thing. The sleepy status quo was about to break apart.

The civil rights movement inspired other progressives not only to help in the civil rights cause but also to come together around a range of other issues and constituencies. A renewed wave of feminism was sparked in great part by Betty Friedan's influential book *The Feminine Mystique*. The environmental movement gained broad public appeal when Rachel Carson's *Silent Spring* became a best seller. Students began to organize themselves. The Port Huron statement, written by Tom Hayden and others, prompted young people to get involved in politics through the student and antiwar movements. Students for a Democratic Society (SDS) was founded. Cesar Chavez used many of King's organizing tactics, as well as new ones of his own, to unionize farm workers in the agricultural fields of California. And as the 1960s wore on, progressives of all stripes looked with growing concern at the Vietnam War and began to protest in earnest against it.

What is truly astounding is how many of these movements were created in exactly the same window of time: the publication of *Silent Spring* and *The Feminine Mystique*, the Port Huron statement and the founding of SDS, and King's "I Have a Dream" speech all happened in a two-year period during 1962 and 1963. Chavez's organizing also began in the early 1960s. It was a flashpoint moment in American history, as movements and leaders inspired one another, and pent-up frustrations over injustice came spilling out. It was no accident that the Civil Rights Act, the Voting Rights Act, Medicare, Medicaid, the War on Poverty, the Fair Housing Act, the Clean Air Act and the Clean Water Act, Head Start, the creation of legal services for the poor, the establishment of the Occupational Safety and Health Administration and the Environmental Protection Agency, the *Roe v. Wade* decision, and the end of the Vietnam War all happened in the decade that followed.

This record of progressive achievements was competitive in scope and impact with those in the 1930s and 1860s. Lyndon Johnson, believing that "education was the only valid passport from poverty," pushed Congress to pass the Elementary and Secondary Education Act, which was the federal government's first and largest investment in elementary and secondary education. This act included the Title I program of federal aid to disadvantaged children, to address the problems of the poor in urban and rural areas. Johnson's War on Poverty and his Great Society programs— food stamps, Medicaid, Head Start, Job Corps, and community action programs—served as a catalyst to move people above the poverty line, as I discussed in chapter 6. Head Start, for example, in addition to helping thousands of children get medical attention, served as a job-creation program. Thirty thousand parents worked in the regular full-year program, while twelve thousand parents received college credit for their work in the program and a thousand parents were able to finish up their associate's or bachelor's degrees. The environment became dramatically cleaner. Landmark civil rights legislation, such as the Civil Rights Act of 1964 and the Voting Rights Act of 1965, ended Jim Crow for good. The lives of women changed fundamentally for the better, as did those of senior citizens. It was an amazing time.

The 1960s were an intense period, one of the most tumultuous in U.S. history. Many good things happened, but there was enormous pain as well. Nothing was more damaging to the country's psyche, and to the progressive cause, than the cutting down of three of our nation's most gifted and charismatic young progressive leaders—Martin Luther King Jr., John F. Kennedy, and Robert F. Kennedy. All of them were killed before they even made it to their late forties. All of them left painful questions of what might have been had they lived.

Whatever might-have-beens had King lived, the legacy he established in his thirty-nine short years was on a par with any other figure in history. JFK was still feeling his way as president and hadn't accomplished an enormous amount in terms of new legislation before he died, but his legacy in terms of saving the world from nuclear war is about as big as can be imagined, and his inspiring a generation of progressives to get involved in public service is an enormous monument to him.

The person who raises the most questions in terms of what might have been is Robert Kennedy. RFK probably had more raw potential to change American politics for the good than any politician in history. Although his earlier career had some blemishes, including his working with Joe McCarthy for a while, and he started out very cautious on civil rights as attorney general, by the end of his career, his heart and conscience had moved him dramatically to the left.

RFK's white-hot passion for justice and a better society gave him an intensity that bonded him to voters in a different way than his far cooler and more cerebral older brother. Robert Kennedy's ability to reach Catholics, working-class white voters, liberal professionals, and African American voters was a powerful electoral combination that would not only have likely won him the 1968 presidential race but also would have made him a formidable president, able to bring the country together in those years rather than tearing it apart as Nixon so successfully did.

RFK's philosophy by the end of his life had evolved into a powerfully progressive formulation of American community. Here he speaks on contrasting violence with the value of mutuality:

Victims of the violence are black and white, rich and poor, young and old, famous and unknown. They are most important of all, human beings whom other human beings loved and needed. What has violence ever accomplished, what has it ever created? Violence breeds violence, retaliation breeds retaliation, and only a cleansing of our whole society can remove this sickness from our souls. For when you teach a man to hate and to fear his brother, when you teach that he is a lesser man because of his color, or his beliefs or the policies that he pursues, when you teach that those who are different from you threaten your freedom or your job or your home or your family, then you also learn to confront others not as fellow citizens, but as enemies. Our lives on this planet are too short, the work to be done is too great. But we can perhaps remember, that those who live with us are our brothers, that they share with us the same short moment of life, that they seek as do we, nothing but the chance to live out their lives in purpose and in happiness, surely this bond of common fate, this bond of common roles can begin to teach us something, that we can begin to work a little harder, to become in our hearts brothers and countrymen once again.

In a speech at the University of Kansas shortly before his death, he contrasted the value of community with that of being focused in wealth:

Another great task is to confront the poverty of satisfaction—a lack of purpose and dignity—that afflicts us all. Too much and too long, we seem to have surrendered community excellence and community values in the mere accumulation of material things.

And in this great definition of what the modern Democratic Party was and should be, he makes clear his progressive philosophy:

> In this entire century the Democratic Party has never been invested with power on the basis of a program which promised to keep things as they were. We have won when we pledged to meet the new challenges of each succeeding year. We have triumphed not in spite of controversy, but because of it; not because we avoided problems, but because we faced them. We have won not because we bent and diluted our principles, but because we stood fast to the ideals which represent the most noble and generous portion of the American spirit.

RFK might have become the greatest political leader in U.S. history, greater than even FDR or Lincoln. But we shall never know, and that is one of history's great tragedies.

Kirk, Buckley, Goldwater, and Helms Create the Modern Conservative Movement

McCarthyism was hardly the last gasp of conservatism in the 1950s and 1960s. Commentators in the decades since have sometimes acted as if modern conservatism was simply a reaction to all the liberalism of the 1960s, but the seeds of the powerful modern conservative movement were planted in the 1950s. The primary founders of the modern conservative movement—Russell Kirk, William Buckley Jr., Barry Goldwater, and Jesse Helms—all rose to prominence in that decade. Together, they built the machine that would produce Reagan, Gingrich, DeLay, and the two Bush presidencies, along with the movement leaders, machinery, and echo chamber we see today.

Russell Kirk

Kirk was the intellectual cornerstone. His book *The Conservative Mind*, from which I have quoted a number of times, was published in 1953. It was a landmark for intellectual conservatives everywhere who were beleaguered by the longtime majority that FDR had built. The book starts rather defensively with this sentence: "The stupid party: this is John Stuart Mills's description of conservatives." Kirk was, of course, determined to prove Mills and all the liberals wrong, asserting that "the conservative principle has been defended, these past two centuries, by men of learning and genius," although he did note that his hero Edmund Burke "was not ashamed to acknowledge the allegiance of humble men whose sureties are prejudice and prescription." Indeed not, as Kirk and his followers were happy to be allied with segregationists and bigots throughout U.S. history.

Kirk decried "a world that damns tradition, exalts equality, and welcomes change." He described a conservative philosophy that "requires orders and classes, against the notion of a 'classless society.'" His conservatism argued that "freedom and property are closely linked," that "hasty innovation may be a devouring conflagration," and that tradition is of the highest priority.

Kirk's book became scripture for the generation of right-wing think tanks and neoconservatives that would follow. His formulation of what conservatism stood for and his admiring history of conservative thinkers and politicians of the past gave the growing conservative movement a confidence in itself. This certainty of its intellectual grounding would grow increasingly important as conservatism became more allied with the outright bigots of the South and distinctly unintellectual politicians such as Reagan and George W. Bush.

William F. Buckley Jr.

Buckley was literally a one-man media echo chamber. In addition to founding and running *National Review*, which has been and remains the most important magazine of the conservative movement, Buckley also did the following:

- Wrote fifty-six hundred columns syndicated in hundreds of newspapers across the country

- Created, produced, and hosted *Firing Line*, one of the longest-running talk shows on TV
- Authored more than fifty books
- Averaged more than seventy speeches a year
- Helped start Young Americans for Freedom, one of the most influential groups that organizes young conservatives
- Cofounded New York's Conservative Party, which helped his brother win a U.S. Senate seat in 1970

Buckley was a charming, sophisticated, and funny man, and reporters loved him. There probably was not a single newspaper obituary written after his death that did not include the word *erudite*. He took pride in being elitist and intellectual. But that sophisticated side did not keep him from being on the same team as some pretty nasty lowlifes.

As noted previously, he coauthored a book that passionately defended Joe McCarthy. He advocated forcing people with AIDS to be tattooed. He attacked John F. Kennedy for making peace with the Soviet Union during the Cuban missile crisis, rather than provoking nuclear war. He was openly in favor of denying the right to vote to the "uneducated." Perhaps most appallingly, he wrote a strong editorial in defense of Jim Crow, in which he said,

> The central question that emerges—and it is not a parliamentary question or a question that is answered by merely consulting a catalog of the rights of American citizens, born Equal—is whether the White community in the South is entitled to take such measures as are necessary to prevail, politically and culturally, in areas in which it does not predominate numerically? The sobering answer is Yes—the White community is so entitled because, for the time being, it is the advanced race. It is not easy, and it is unpleasant, to adduce statistics evidencing the median cultural superiority of White over Negro: but it is [a] fact that obtrudes, one that cannot be hidden by ever-so-busy egalitarians and anthropologists. The question, as far

as the White community is concerned, is whether the claims of civilization supersede those of universal suffrage. The British believe they do, and acted accordingly, in Kenya, where the choice was dramatically one between civilization and barbarism, and elsewhere; the South, where the conflict is by no means dramatic, as in Kenya, nevertheless perceives important qualitative differences between its culture and the Negroes', and intends to assert its own.

National Review believes that the South's premises are correct. If the majority wills what is socially atavistic, then to thwart the majority may be, though undemocratic, enlightened. It is more important for any community, anywhere in the world, to affirm and live by civilized standards, than to bow to the demands of the numerical majority. Sometimes it becomes impossible to assert the will of a minority, in which case it must give way, and the society will regress; sometimes the numerical minority cannot prevail except by violence: then it must determine whether the prevalence of its will is worth the terrible price of violence.

The axiom on which many of the arguments supporting the original version of the Civil Rights bill were based was Universal Suffrage. Everyone in America is entitled to the vote, period. No right is prior to that, no obligation subordinate to it; from this premise all else proceeds.

That, of course, is demagogy. Twenty-year-olds do not generally have the vote, and it is not seriously argued that the difference between 20 and 21-year-olds is the difference between slavery and freedom. The residents of the District of Columbia do not vote: and the population of D.C. increases by geometric proportion. Millions who have the vote do not care to exercise it; millions who have it do not know how to exercise it and do not care to learn. The great majority of the Negroes of the South who do not vote do not care to vote, and would not know for what to vote if they could. Overwhelming numbers of White people in the South do not vote. Universal suffrage is not the beginning of wisdom or the beginning of freedom. Reasonable limitations upon the vote are not exclusively the recommendations of tyrants or oligarchists (was Jefferson either?). The problem in the South is not how to get the vote for the Negro, but how to equip the Negro—and a great many Whites—to cast an enlightened and responsible vote.

Here you see not only open racism but also conservatism in all its glory: the preference for tradition over justice, the elitism that suggests that some people aren't ready for the vote, and the complete comfort with the idea that civilization requires some classes of people to be permanently in power over others.

This philosophy allowed people who prided themselves on sophistication and intellectualism to be perfectly comfortable hanging out with stone-cold racists such as Jesse Helms and George Wallace.

Barry Goldwater

Barry Goldwater was a successful and well-known businessman in Arizona who was elected to the Senate in 1952. He immediately started to build an impressive political machine, both in Arizona, which had been dominated by Democrats, and nationwide, through his role as head of the National Republican Senate Committee. Goldwater was strongly antiunion and made himself a hero to antilabor factory owners all over the country with his virulent and unrelenting attacks on the United Auto Workers' Walter Reuther. (It is worth noting, however, that Goldwater did nothing to oppose Jimmy Hoffa, who had ties to organized crime, and even made friends with the more conservative Hoffa because they both hated Reuther so much.)

Goldwater received substantial financial and political support from Robert Welch, the founder of the John Birch Society; from the far-right-wing Texas oilman H. L. Hunt; and from a highly influential radio talk show host and conservative movement organizer named Clarence Manion, who was a John Birch board member. These conservatives were excited about pushing Goldwater to run for president. They wanted to build a movement around him that was far more conservative than the more moderate Republican Party of that era.

It is worth stopping to note the reach and influence of the rather strange John Birch Society. The society was founded by Welch and a group of eleven wealthy businessmen in 1958. In addition to Manion, who was probably the single most important player in the Goldwater campaign for president in 1964, another of the cofounders was Harry Bradley, the CEO of a major electronics manufacturer in Milwaukee and the founder of the Bradley Foundation, which has been one of the biggest funders of right-wing think tanks and media projects in the country over the last fifty years.

One would be hard-pressed to describe the Birchers as anything other than the lunatic fringe. According to them, churches, schools, and the government had all been infiltrated by communists, and the civil rights movement was, lock, stock, and barrel a communist plot. Even Eisenhower, according to Welch, "has been sympathetic to ultimate Communist aims, realistically willing to use Communist means to help them achieve their goals, knowingly accepting and abiding by Communist orders, and consciously serving the Communist conspiracy for all his adult life." Welch demanded absolute loyalty from his members. He said that infighting would kill the effort and that the communists would not hesitate to demand such allegiance to achieve their goals.

The Birch approach was McCarthyism on steroids. But despite, or maybe because of, the craziness, the movement spread quickly and gained power. And some politicians began to align themselves with the Birchers, including Southern segregationists such as Senator James Hand of Mississippi, who praised the society as "patriotic." Goldwater was happy to endorse them, saying, "A lot of people in my hometown have been attracted to the Society, and I am impressed by the type of people in it. They are the kind we need in politics."

In addition to embracing the John Birch Society, Goldwater did one other thing that solidified his position as leader of the emerging conservative movement: he began to support the Southern segregationists. Although Goldwater had earlier in his career bragged about his lack of prejudice toward blacks and had voted in the 1950s for some mild civil rights bills, he gave a speech in South Carolina saying that *Brown v. Board of Education* should not be enforced by arms because it was "not based on law." He started to vote with Southern segregationists, including voting against the 1964 Civil Rights Act, saying that he based his opposition on the states' rights doctrine. He became enough of a hero in the South that the only states he won outside of his home state of Arizona in his 1964 landslide loss to LBJ were five Deep South states.

Goldwater's embrace of the movement that the Birchers were building and of the segregationists in the South allowed him to become a movement candidate for a unified conservatism. Although he was slaughtered by LBJ in 1964, in winning the nomination fight Goldwater fundamentally reshaped the Republican Party (much as William Jennings Bryan had realigned the Democratic Party in 1896, despite his loss to McKinley). And the movement that was forged around Goldwater's candidacy would keep building.

Rick Perlstein, in his superb 2001 book on the Goldwater campaign and the movement it launched, from whom I took much of the information in my previous section about Goldwater, summed it up this way:

> Scratch a conservative today—a think-tank bookworm at Washington's Heritage Foundation or Milwaukee's Bradley Foundation (the people whose studies and position papers blazed the trails for ending welfare as we know it, for the school voucher movement, for the discussion over privatizing Social Security); a door-knocking church lady pressing pamphlets into her neighbors' palms about partial-birth abortion; the owner of a small or large business sitting across the table from a lobbyist plotting strategy on how to decimate corporate tax rates; an organizer of a training center for aspiring conservative activists or journalists; Republican precinct workers, fund-raisers, county chairs, state chairs, presidential candidates, congressmen, senators, even a Supreme Court

justice—and the story comes out. How it all began for them: in the Goldwater campaign.

Jesse Helms

The final pillar of this new version of the conservative movement was carved by the Southern conservatives, those believers in John C. Calhoun's states' rights ideology, Jim Crow, and fundamentalist Christianity. Although there were many leaders of this movement—senators Thurmond and Eastland and Governor Wallace and all the rest of those names who will go down forever as being on the wrong side of history—no one became a bigger hero to their cause than Jesse Helms. Jesse Helms was a U.S. senator from 1973 to 2003, but before that, starting in the early 1950s, he was a radio and TV commentator, a lobbyist for the banking industry, and a race-baiting political operative who used dirty tactics to fight for the most hard-core segregationist politicians. Helms never backed off those beliefs or apologized for his opposition to civil rights and in the 1980s led the opposition to the Martin Luther King Jr. holiday, calling King a communist. He used racially charged ads and rhetoric in his campaigns up until the very end of his career.

Helms was important because he understood the importance of radio and TV in building the conservative media machine, and he was one of the earliest adherents of investing substantial amounts of money to build a big direct-mail list—his Congressional Club organization became one of the largest and most effective direct mail–based political operations on the right. He also helped make the critical link between the conservative movement and fundamentalist churches, something a civil libertarian like Goldwater, a sophisticated New Yorker like Buckley, or an intellectual like Kirk never could have or would have done. Helms was active early in the 1970s in reaching out to church-based conservatives and was instrumental in helping both Jerry Falwell's Moral Majority and Pat Robertson's Christian Coalition get off the ground and gain power.

As with the other three conservatives I have highlighted in this section, Helms had no problems with blatant extremism. He opposed gay rights and money for AIDS research, using the same nastiness with which he had opposed civil rights earlier in his career. He expressed irritation that gays referred to themselves as "normal." He opposed AIDS education, saying that AIDS was primarily a homosexual disease and that "sodomy, adultery and fornication are not now, nor have they ever been, safe." He vehemently opposed the Equal Rights Amendment and any other civil rights for women, including funds for victims of domestic abuse. He strongly supported right-wing dictators around the world, including Chile's Pinochet (whose torture and mass murder of his political opponents were well known from the 1970s on), and was an enthusiastic booster of the apartheid regime in South Africa. He opposed any government funding for the arts and dismissed scientific thought on issues ranging from evolution to tobacco causing cancer. There was virtually no right-wing cause that Helms did not champion. Helms's stridency, rather than turning people off, won him great love among conservatives, and he became their leading spokesman on Capitol Hill. Every time he gained headlines with his right-wing attacks on gays, artists, feminists, liberals, or the people he called communists, such as King and Nelson Mandela, he raised even more money from direct mail.

These four pillars of modern conservatism—the intellectual underpinning developed by Kirk; the media echo chamber created by Buckley; the small government, antiunion libertarianism of Goldwater; and the moralistic, racially tinged Southern conservatism represented by Helms—combined to create the powerful political moment we see today. These parts of the movement weren't always comfortable with one another—Buckley was libertarian enough to try marijuana and then brag about it, and he denounced the anti-Semitism of some of his right-wing friends; Goldwater got cranky with the Southern moralists at the end of his career—but they made common cause and almost always loyally supported one another, even when one branch or the other would go off the deep end on certain issues.

The pivotal political decision made by conservatives of all stripes in the 1950s and 1960s was to ally themselves with Southerners on

civil rights, using Calhoun's old states' rights strategy as the philosophical edifice that allowed them to pretend the issue was not
about race (just as conservative historians have pretended the
Civil War was not about slavery). Buckley and Goldwater probably weren't particularly comfortable embracing Jim Crow, but
they did because they could see that breaking the South, along
with working-class white ethnics in the North, apart from the New
Deal coalition of FDR was the linchpin of a strategy that would give
them political power. Goldwater, who had been a moderate on civil
rights, moved hard right on the issue, followed by Richard Nixon,
also formerly a moderate, with his famous Southern Strategy. Reagan
did so with his states' rights speech in Philadelphia, Mississippi,
about which I wrote in chapter 4. The old right-wing Democrats
such as Thurmond and Helms followed them into the Republican
Party, and, as we have seen in chapter 4, the South moved overnight from being a one-party Democratic stronghold to the most
Republican region in the country.

Along with their deal with the devil on race, the libertarian conservatives were willing to give in to the Christian conservatives on
social issues. As feminists, gay rights activists, poor people, and liberal students began to assert themselves in the 1960s, traditional
white working-class voters in all regions of the country grew more
uncomfortable, and the unified and newly energized conservative
movement was happy to exploit those fears. In 1972, George
McGovern was attacked by Republicans as being the candidate of
abortion, amnesty, and acid, and every candidate since has been
attacked as soft on crime, welfare, drugs, gays, illegal immigrants,
communists, and/or terrorists.

The Republican and right-wing rhetoric increasingly became
centered on the idea that Democrats and liberals, in the words of
former Speaker Newt Gingrich, had become "the enemy of normal
Americans." Republicans and conservatives (the two had become
increasingly the same thing, as moderate Republicans no longer
had a political base), they said, were for small government, low
taxes, strong defense, and traditional values, while Democrats
and liberals were for blacks, gays, immigrants, welfare queens,

letting criminals off easy, permissive sexuality, and abortion on demand.

Like conservatives throughout America's history, this new infra-structure of conservatism loved to mock and loved to invoke fear. To radio talk-show hosts like Limbaugh, feminists became "femina-zis," and African American politicians were ridiculed with songs like "Barack the Magic Negro." When communism faded as a threat and 9/11 made terrorism the new challenge, conservatives accused progressives of being terrorist dupes, just as the McCarthyites and the Birchers had accused them of being com-mies. After the 9/11 attacks, Karl Rove, the chief strategist for George W. Bush, said this about liberals' response to terrorism:

> Conservatives saw the savagery of 9/11 and the attacks and prepared for war; liberals saw the savagery of the 9/11 attacks and wanted to prepare indictments and offer therapy and understanding for our attackers. In the wake of 9/11, conserv-atives believed it was time to unleash the might and power of the United States military against the Taliban; in the wake of 9/11, liberals believed it was time to . . . submit a petition. I am not joking. Submitting a petition is precisely what MoveOn .org did. It was a petition imploring the powers that be to use moderation and restraint in responding to the terrorist attacks against the United States. . . . MoveOn.org, Michael Moore and Howard Dean may not have agreed with this, but the American people did. Conservatives saw what happened to us on 9/11 and said: We will defeat our enemies. Liberals saw what happened to us and said: We must understand our enemies.

A new generation of conservative political operatives, many of them raised in a South that was being forced out of its Jim Crow ways, came of age as part of this newly merged movement. Lee Atwater (South Carolina), Ralph Reed (Georgia), and Karl Rove (Texas), as well as aggrieved white suburbanites from the North such as Grover Norquist, all understood that the white working class, Northern and Southern, was the key to winning a conservative majority. Atwater frequently reminded his Republican colleagues, "The populist vote is always the swing vote."

Progressives Lose Their Way

In the forty years from 1933 to 1973, progressives had accomplished a truly remarkable set of achievements. They had saved the country from the economic panic and despair of the 1930s; passed banking regulations that protected consumers and stabilized the economy; enacted Social Security and Medicare for senior citizens; helped workers win their rights to unionize; mobilized the country to defeat the Nazis and Japan; passed the GI Bill, allowing most of a generation of Americans to go to college; passed the Marshall Plan, which saved the European economy after the war; jettisoned Jim Crow; ended a flawed war in Vietnam; dramatically cleaned up the air and the water from pollution; instituted new rights and expectations in terms of women's equality; and cut the poverty rate dramatically in this country. It was a stunning improvement in economic and civil rights, along with the quality of life, for all Americans.

But with conservatives newly energized and empowered, progressivism lost its way. In the early 1970s, when the right wing began in earnest to build its infrastructure, Democrats felt that they were the natural majority party, and progressives were accustomed to winning substantive policy victories as well. The party had held the White House for twenty-eight of the thirty-six years that began in 1932, when Franklin Roosevelt swept the Democrats into power, until Nixon took office by the slimmest of margins in 1968. Democrats had been in control of both houses of Congress during all but four years in that same period and were still on top, even with Nixon's landslide reelection victory in 1972. After the Watergate scandal, when Democrats swept the table in the 1974 congressional elections and then Jimmy Carter won back the presidency in 1976, things seemed to be returning to their natural order.

With the kind of forty-year track record of political and policy success I describe here, Democratic and progressive leaders of that era did not see the need for big new institution-building projects similar to the ones the right wingers were undertaking. Democrats made the assumption that they would always be a natural majority, and that assumption had some very unhealthy consequences for the progressive side, including:

- **Becoming defenders of the status quo.** When you have passed a lot of big initiatives and are running things, you start to think things are pretty okay in the world. The openness to new ideas by the powers that be in the Democratic Party faded, and the congressional leadership became very well entrenched. When Republican presidents started to get elected on a more regular basis, the natural reaction was to defend the programs of the past without coming up with new ones, which made our side sound increasingly defensive and whiny to the general public.

- **Promoting intellectual laziness.** Along with becoming defenders of the status quo came a certain intellectual laziness. Democrats felt that they had solved many of the problems of the world, and that voters would keep rewarding them for their historic accomplishments. They didn't see much need to rethink their overall ideology or assumptions about governing.

- **Protecting incumbents versus building the farm team or shaking things up.** When you assume that you are in a permanent-majority situation, it's natural to think first and foremost about protecting incumbents. This emphasis hurt us by lending an overall flabbiness to our message and in terms of recruiting, training, mentoring, and supporting promising young people who were coming up through the ranks. Entrenched incumbents never want to rock the boat too much by espousing a populist change message, either in general or on particular issues such as health care, and they just don't pay as much attention to the young turks on the way up.

- **Not building for the long term.** Conservatives felt perfectly comfortable digging in for the long haul on issues and messages because they felt that they had no choice. Progressives, not worried about having a long-term majority and believing any electoral setback to be a short-term aberration, tended to focus on whatever fight about a short-term issue that was at hand.

- **Expressing no ideological coherence or urgency about institution building.** This was the most important failing of all. Republicans and conservatives knew they had to build their case with the American public for a more conservative America, and they acted accordingly. They systematically built think tanks and advocated issues that had a coherent conservative message, ideology, and agenda at their heart. Progressives and Democrats assumed that the public was ultimately with them and tended to focus on specific policy areas to defend or do better on (the environment, choice, gun control, and so on) or on specific consistency groups to help (labor, blacks, women, Hispanics, gays/lesbians, the disabled, and so on). Progressives had a status quo mind-set, rather than being focused on building institutions or a broader message that could help win in the long term.

The end result of this fundamental difference in vantage points resulted in Republicans and conservatives building a movement and an infrastructure that held together both philosophically and in terms of political strategy. In the meantime, Democrats and progressives were more and more on the defensive and built issue-based or demographically based groups that had few common goals. The conservatives built themselves a movement; progressives built a series of narrowly defined interest groups.

The lack of movement-building took its toll. From 1968 until 2008, Democrats have controlled the presidency for only twelve years. And during those forty years, we have had only six years— Carter's four-year term and the first two years of Clinton's first term—where there was a Democratic president and a Democratic Congress. Even in those six years, progressives did not succeed in their efforts to get major legislation passed. Both Carter and Clinton fell short of getting labor law reform passed, and Clinton failed spectacularly at getting health-care reform through. The progressive movement was just not strong enough to get it done—I can attest to that personally because I was in the Clinton White House working on health care and other major issues of concern to progressives. The conservative movement dramatically out-organized, out-fought, out-lobbied, and outspent progressive efforts.

After the assassinations of King and John and Robert Kennedy, after all of the trauma and upheaval of those years, and after the many accomplishments of that era, progressivism allowed itself to forget the broader vision spelled out by King, proclaimed in the Port Huron statement, and embraced by others who had come earlier. The movement quite literally allowed itself to fall to pieces by focusing on identity politics and single-issue causes. No matter how important all of those individual things were, the broader reasons that have always called Americans to be progressive—economic and political equality, fairness, a government of the people—got lost. And conservatives stepped into the political vacuum that was created.

Fortunately, a democracy always affords its people new opportunities. And we are now at a point in our history that may allow us to build another wave of progressive change.

8

Hope, Fear, and the Culture of Caution

W hen Barack Obama based much of his 2008 presidential campaign on the theme of hope, he certainly wasn't
the first candidate to make that pitch. And when John
McCain, George W. Bush, and Dick Cheney, during the years since
9/11, preached fear and more fear and nothing but fear, they
weren't the first to do that, either. The entire history of American
political debate can, in some sense, be described as the argument
between the hope of progressives for a better future vs. the fear of
conservatives who want to protect the way things are now.

In recent decades, neither party has been able to get a toehold as
an enduring political majority. The Republicans' problem has been
that they aggressively overreach, and then their rather extreme policy prescriptions just don't work. We get wars with no exit plans,
market-based solutions that don't actually solve anything, supply-
side tax cuts that result in gigantic deficits, and voluntary goals for
industry that never result in anything tangible happening.

For Democrats, the problem has been the opposite. They have
been so beaten down by the conservative attack machine that they
have allowed themselves to get into the habit of being cautious.
When in power, they have had decent policy ideas that have produced pretty good results, but the results aren't substantial enough
to make permanent changes or get voters excited about what

Democrats are trying to accomplish. Since the tumultuous change decade of the 1960s and the ugly backlash that followed it, Democrats have often been too scared to think big about progressive change, and it has hurt them.

Hope, Fear, and Tom Paine

My main focus in this chapter is on the modern debate between hope and fear, but, as in the rest of this book, I want to take some time to ground this discussion with a few thoughts on the way things have played out historically.

The American Revolution was all about the hope vs. fear debate. As we saw in chapter 2, the pro-British Tories did everything they could to beat back the revolutionary impulse by preaching fear: fear that the rebels would be crushed and fear of what might actually happen if the democratic mob were to govern in America. All of the Tories' debating points were dominated by the fear motif. It was our old friend Tom Paine who answered them most convincingly, at one of the worst moments of the war while this country was heading into the winter of Valley Forge. Paine began his remarkable reverie to hope, *The American Crisis*, with these immortal words:

> These are the times that try men's souls. The summer soldier and the sunshine patriot will, in this crisis, shrink from the service of their country; but he that stands it now, deserves the love and thanks of men and women. Tyranny, like hell, is not easily conquered; yet we have this consolation with us, that the harder the conflict the more glorious the triumph.

From this stirring beginning, Paine laid out why there were no grounds for panic or despair. In fact, he bluntly said, "'Tis surprising to see how rapidly a panic will sometimes run through a country. All nations and ages have been subject to them." He went on to calmly describe why the Americans would prevail if only they didn't give in to their fears. He himself, he said, saw "no real case for fear. I know our situation well, and can see our way out of it."

Paine called for a unity of patriots, a sense of true American community. "I call not upon a few, but upon all: not on this state or that state, but on every state: up and help us. . . . Let it be told to the future world, that in the depth of winter, when nothing but hope and virtue could survive, that the city and the country, alarmed at one common danger, came forth to meet and repulse it."

Like *Common Sense* before it, Paine's words in *The American Crisis* came at the most critical time and inspired the revolutionaries who were at their most desperate and fearful. But beyond its immediate significance in keeping the revolutionary fires burning, it is a remarkable testimony to the idea of hope over fear.

Fear and Conservatism

Fear has been the staple of every generation of conservatives, and in this book we have seen many examples of what they have said through the years. Fear of the democratic mob. Fear of the freed slave. Fear of a liberated woman destroying the traditional family. Fear of freethinkers destroying traditional religion. Fear of communism. Fear of gays and lesbians. Fear of hippies, "free love," and the drug culture. Fear of the immigrant. In a bizarre twist, Social Darwinism gave us fear of the weak, and in the modern version of Social Darwinism, Reagan gave us fear of the poor on welfare. Post-9/11, you can now add in the ever-potent fear of terrorism.

Sadly, while some of those fears have faded with the passage of history, many remain with us, still powerful.

Many conservatives still fear feminism, sometimes to a hilarious degree. Here is one of my all-time favorite quotes, from the inimitable Pat Robertson: "[Feminism] is about a socialist, anti-family political movement that encourages women to leave their husbands, kill their children, practice witchcraft, destroy capitalism and become lesbians."

I had no idea feminism was so comprehensive, but there you have it. Of course, many men who are threatened by strong women aren't quite so hysterical, but like threatened people everywhere, they love to mock. Rush Limbaugh, who coined the term *feminazi*, has this definition of feminism: "Feminism was established so as to allow unattractive women easier access to the mainstream of society."

The prospect of empowered women isn't the only fear that conservatives have carried throughout the years of our nation's existence. They have always feared freethinking, which opens the door to a range of ideas and beliefs. The notion that their children might be exposed to any ideas or scientific theories that are different from what is being taught at home, as exemplified by the battles that are fought daily about public education, still scares conservatives a great deal. Read articles from any local newspaper about the nature of their resistance—to the teaching of evolution, the discussion of global warming, the assignment of certain books by English teachers, and so on—and you will see parents who are terrified that their children might learn a way of thinking contrary to their own.

Fears of communism and welfare have faded somewhat in the last twenty years because of the fall of the Soviet Union and the passage of welfare reform, but they have been quickly replaced by conservatives' finding new things to scare voters with. Terrorism and immigrants have become the new hot-button excuses for pushing the political fear button. Or maybe I should amend that: terrorism, at least, is relatively new as a major fear for voters because until 9/11, people knew it could be a problem but didn't worry about it much. After 9/11, it became the biggest thing Americans were scared of. Immigration, on the other hand, is a very old fear that conservatives have been exploiting with renewed vigor in recent years.

In the early days of the United States, immigrants were generally quite welcome because the country had an ever-expanding need for new workers, farmers, and pioneers to go out West. But by the 1850s, as more poor and working-class Irish journeyed across the Atlantic to settle here, the combination of antipoor and anti-Catholic bigotry stirred up the vicious anti-immigrant movement called, appropriately enough, the Know-Nothings (the name came from the fact that their leaders swore an oath of secrecy about being involved in the movement, so that if asked about it, they said they knew nothing).

To join the organization of the original Know-Nothing movement, the Order of the Star-Spangled Banner, you had to be white and male, be born in the United States, and not only be Protestant but have no family connection whatsoever to Catholicism. The Know-Nothing political party, called the American Party, won nine gubernatorial seats and controlled at least one branch of the legislature in six states during the mid-1850s. It ran former president Millard Fillmore as its presidential candidate in the 1856 election, and he received about a quarter of the votes. But the movement quickly faded because the slavery issue soon overwhelmed everything else.

Throughout the late 1800s, another conservative period in U.S. history, immigration was regularly featured in the American political debate. Concerns about Chinese immigrants in California and Irish immigrants in the East were a constant refrain in the arguments against voting rights and civil rights. Sadly, even the populist movement was tainted by anti-immigrant rhetoric, as well as by its alliance with Southern segregationists.

The Chinese Exclusion Act was the first major restriction on immigration. Passed in 1882, it prohibited most immigration from Asia and took away the right of Chinese immigrants to become citizens. However, it was after World War I that anti-immigrant zeal truly reached its peak. Fearing a wave of postwar refugees and gripped by the conservative frenzy of the times, Congress passed legislation, in 1921 and 1924, that restricted immigration. The Emergency Quota Act of 1921 limited European immigration to 3 percent of the total population of each European nationality living in the United States as of 1910. The Immigration Act of 1924 went much further, limiting European immigration to 2 percent of each nationality living in the United States as of 1890.

Just as conservatives do today, back then they also used people's fear of immigrants to attack other progressive ideas and legislation. Congressional opponents of the 14th and 15th amendments, for example, worried that immigrants would take advantage of these new voting rights. In the 1920s and earlier, immigrant bashers were anxious about what kinds of communists, socialists, and anarchists might be coming over to contaminate our population.

For example, a San Francisco newspaper, the *Daily American*, printed the following editorial in April 1881:

> Steamships are vomiting forth rotten cargoes of a thousand Chinese fortnightly, smitten and cursed with the plague of small-pox, and with other and deadly plagues. The one-hundred thousand Chinese on this coast today, without family ties, with no elements of a prosperous immigration, the bronze locusts from Asia, plague-bearing[,] are eating out the substance which rightly belongs to the patrimony of the people. . . . The single Chinese immigrant does, in this sense, usurp the place of a family. Trades and industries languish. . . . The evils of Chinese immigration are upon us full force, aggravated by obstructions which originated with politicians who care more for some petty interest of party (the democratic party) than for the great and vital interests of the country.

If you think that was then and that things have progressed, here are a couple of quotes from the current leadership of the anti-immigration movement. The first comes from Congressman Virgil Goode of Virginia, who gained notoriety when he criticized Keith Ellison's choice to be sworn in using a copy of the Koran, rather than the Bible. Goode warned his constituents, "If American citizens don't wake up and adopt the Virgil Goode position on immigration, there will likely be many more Muslims elected to office." He also had this to say about Hispanic immigration: "My message to them is, not in two weeks, not in two months, not in two years, never! We must be clear that we will not surrender America and we will not turn the United States over to the invaders from south of the border."

Another anti-immigration leader, Joseph Turner—a staff member of the most powerful anti-immigration lobbying group, Federation for American Immigration Reform (FAIR)—recently said this in a letter to anti-immigration contributors: "Our enemies are blood-ied and beaten. We cannot relent. Our boot is on their throat and we must have the willingness to crush their 'throat' so that we can put our enemy down for good. The sovereignty of our nation and the future of our culture and civilization are at stake. The United States is a beacon of salvation unto the rest of the world. Our freedoms, our culture is man's salvation. If we perish, man perishes."

These statements were made in 2006 and 2007, not in some long-ago debate when social conventions and attitudes were differ-ent. And they were not the ravings of marginal crazies or rabid talk-show hosts; they were made by a senior member of the Re-publican caucus in Congress and by a leader of one of the biggest organizations working on the anti-immigration side of the aisle.

There are legitimate issues to debate in terms of immigration policy. Having better border security is a good thing, and we should be worried about corporations that try to exploit immigrant labor. But we can work those issues through and create a legitimate path to citizenship for immigrants without resorting to the fearmonger-ing of the right wing.

Just as stopping the spread of totalitarian communism and keep-ing us safe from Soviet aggression during the Cold War were important objectives, today we need to deal with the real threat of terrorism. Many thoughtful suggestions, such as those generated by the Hart-Rudman Commission and the 9/11 Commission, have been put forward. Important issues like securing the uranium from old Soviet weapons sites and keeping it away from the hands of ter-rorists, as well as safeguarding our own country's nuclear and chemical facilities to a greater degree, ought to be priorities for the U.S. government. What is fundamentally wrong, though, is turning the fear of terrorism into a political football, as Bush, Cheney, and other right-wingers have done.

Here's George W. Bush in 2004: "The Democrat approach in Iraq comes down to this: The terrorists win and America loses. That's what's at stake in this election."

And Dick Cheney: "If we make the wrong choice, then the danger is that we'll get hit again—that we'll be hit in a way that will be devastating from the standpoint of the United States."

Comparing a politician to Joe McCarthy is pretty strong stuff, but I find it hard to avoid the comparison when we live in a time when government officials spout the rhetoric I've just quoted. Using fear to justify virtually everything you want to do—from torture to absurd levels of government secrecy, to a war with no exit plan, to no-bid contracts for your biggest contributors, to violating the law and the Constitution with warrantless wiretapping—is fundamentally wrong. Just as John Dean said that the Bush administration scandals have been worse than Watergate, I'd be inclined to argue that Bush's and the Republicans' fearmongering over terrorism has been worse than McCarthy's fearmongering over Communism.

The Right-Wing Echo Chamber and the Democratic Response

Besides the fact that communism and terrorism have been genuinely scary, the right-wing movement in this country has, during the last forty years, built a truly powerful echo chamber that has allowed it to maximize and heighten the fear factor. This echo chamber consists of a wide array of mutually reinforcing institutions that repeat the same messages, themes, and issue frames over and over, to a point where more mainstream media outlets, and all too often even Democratic political leaders, pick up the right-wing language and begin to use it themselves.

The conservative movement's media machine has received plenty of commentary elsewhere, so I won't go into details here, but it's worth providing a quick outline of how it works. This echo chamber consists of the following elements:

- Big, extremely well-funded think tanks whose communications and media-training budgets are often larger than their research budgets.

- An extensive network of radio and TV talk-show hosts, led by well-known national figures such as Rush Limbaugh, Bill O'Reilly, Sean Hannity, and convicted felons G. Gordon Liddy and Oliver North. The group also includes hundreds of local and regional talk-show hosts with their own homegrown followings. According to a joint report by two groups, the Center for American Progress and the Free Press, the hours of conservative talk that are broadcast on the 257 news-talk stations owned by the top five commercial station owners outnumber the hours of progressive talk 10 to 1.

- A large and well-funded training arm led by an organization called the Leadership Institute.

- An aggressive media-monitoring function spearheaded by the Media Research Center that constantly attacks the traditional media for supposed "liberal bias."

- An array of media companies, including Fox News, Sinclair Broadcasting, and Salem Communications (conservative Christian radio and the Internet), that have a strong conservative bias in their news and commentary.

- TV and radio televangelists such as Pat Robertson and James Dobson, as well as many other regional and local conservative Christians with their own shows, who talk as much about politics as they do about religion.

- A swarm of pundits, columnists, authors, and all-around conservative gadflies such as Ann Coulter, Tucker Carlson, and Robert Novak, who write and pontificate with a hard-line conservative message.

- Conservative magazines such as the *American Spectator, National Review*, and the *Weekly Standard*, which push out conservative commentary and analysis on a weekly or monthly basis.

- Grassroots organizations of all shapes and sizes, some single-issue and some multi-issue, ranging from the huge National Rifle Association to small but very effective local chapters of right-to-life groups or gun clubs.

- A group of important movement strategists led by Grover Norquist that coordinates tactics and makes sure movement people are working together.

This infrastructure has largely sprung up since the 1960s and has become extraordinarily well funded and remarkably well coordinated. This disciplined right-wing echo chamber has been extremely effective in jumping on any mistakes or openings that Democrats give it, in manipulating events that happen in the news, and in penalizing any conservatives who cause trouble for the movement by going off the party line. Whether it is Republican politicians voting the wrong way or conservative commentators going off-message, the right-wing infrastructure has been very aggressive about getting its own people back in line, often using its financial connections as a tool to enforce obedience.

Because the modern progressive movement, as described in chapter 6, has been so fragmented and single-issue siloed, the conservative movement has been able to shape and dominate much of our political debate. Along with having a greater ability to stay on message, this hyper-aggressive and well-coordinated communications infrastructure has produced one other crucial development: because Democrats have been attacked with such viciousness and discipline, and defended so weakly by our side, they have become far too cautious and halting in their politics.

You can see this in big ways and small. When Rush Limbaugh, Pat Robertson, or the leader of FAIR says something outrageous, offensive, or even truly racist, Republican elected officials tend to gloss over it, laugh it off, and sometimes even defend it. But when John Kerry did a bad job of telling a joke in 2007, other Democrats rushed to distance themselves from him. And when MoveOn.org ran a controversial ad raising legitimate questions about whether a general in Iraq was becoming an inappropriately political cheerleader for Bush's Iraq policies, more than half of the Democrats in Congress joined a Republican vote to censure the ad.

Many times, even when Democrats raise completely legitimate points in public debates, the right-wing attack machine does such a good job of twisting their words and Democrats are so cautious about defending one another that the Democrat in question is forced to back down. A recent example is Senator Dick Durbin of Illinois, who read from an FBI report about prisoners at Guantánamo being tortured and then noted, "If I read this to you and did not tell you it was an FBI agent describing what Americans had done to prisoners in their control, you would most certainly believe this must have been done by Nazis, Soviets in their gulags or some mad regime—Pol Pot or others—that had no concern for human beings." It was a legitimate point in an important debate, but the right-wing media machine and the Republicans attacked Durbin immediately, aggressively, and repeatedly, saying that Durbin was comparing American soldiers to Nazis. Durbin, who was left virtually undefended except by the progressive blogosphere, quickly apologized on the Senate floor.

My point here is not to get into an argument over whether Kerry's joke was well told, whether Durbin might have overstated his case, or whether MoveOn.org's ad was politically effective. You wouldn't get much of a fight from me over that. But the difference between the Democrats and the Republicans is striking: Republicans do not condemn their members of Congress or their right-wing groups or their right-wing talk-show hosts for saying all kinds of wildly outrageous things, whereas Democrats have become so scared by the conservative echo chamber that they throw their allies under the bus the first time that controversy raises its head.

On my blog, OpenLeft.com, I have written about the timidity of Democrats in terms of both policy and politics. I call it the "culture of caution," a name I thought of in 2005 when my Democratic friends on Capitol Hill began to talk about the Republicans' culture of corruption. I liked that phrase and used it a lot myself in attacking the Republicans in 2005 and 2006, but I also thought, well, that is their problem, while ours is a culture of caution.

The culture of caution feeds on all of the political problems I describe herein, but, more fundamental and more important, it has created caution on the policy side. For the most part, since their extraordinary policy achievements of the 1960s and early 1970s, Democrats have been hesitant to push big new ideas.

It's not that Democrats and progressives have accomplished nothing since the 1970s. They have championed a series of solid and well-earned achievements during the last thirty years, usually in the face of fierce opposition from Republicans and conservatives (who have mostly become one and the same since the "Rockefeller Republican" moderates were almost entirely driven out of the party). Democratic policy successes in these last three decades included the following:

- A Superfund, paid for by polluters, to clean up some of the worst toxic dumpsites in the country (which the Republicans let expire in 2004).

- The Martin Luther King Jr. holiday (which was passed over Reagan's veto).

- The Family and Medical Leave Act (unlike in most industrialized countries, it is unpaid, and it exempted many small businesses, but it was still a very good first step).

- The Motor Voter law, making it easier for citizens to register to vote.

- The National Service Initiative, which allowed thousands of young people to volunteer for social service and environmental programs in exchange for a small stipend and help with college tuition.

- The Reinventing Government Initiative (many readers may not think of this as progressive, but I would argue that it was actually an important progressive accomplishment. We made government less bureaucratic, cut paperwork dramatically, and made it easier for people to get services delivered to them effectively. Any time you can improve the actual workings of government and make people feel better about what it is delivering, that is a progressive achievement).

- Cutting crime dramatically in the 1990s by putting more cops on the streets, adding to crime-prevention programs, and using the Brady Bill and the ban on assault rifles to keep more guns out of the hands of criminals.

- The S-CHIP program, which expanded health-care coverage to millions of children.
- Increases in the minimum wage in 1996 and 2007.
- New congressional ethics legislation that was passed in 2007 and 2008 to clean up the stench left behind by the scandals of the previous few years.
- The Sarbanes-Oxley Bill, which created modest regulatory oversight of corporate finances in the wake of the Enron, WorldCom, and other accounting scandals. .

In addition, Democrats and progressives fought off some of the worst conservative ideas, even when Democrats were in the minority in Congress. Social Security has not been privatized, abortion is still legal, the National Endowment for the Arts and the Department of Education still exist, the school lunch program is still in place—all of these faced fierce attacks by conservatives during the last twenty years, and progressives deserve credit for saving them. None of these accomplishments, whether positive or defensive, should be minimized. But it is also undeniable that the scale and scope of Democratic initiatives have been modest in comparison to the great achievements of progressivism in the 1860s, 1900s–1910s, 1930s, and 1960s through the early 1970s.

Democrats have made only two serious attempts since the 1960s to pass legislation that would have fundamentally changed the country in the way that it was transformed during those earlier eras, and both attempts failed. The first was in 1978, when Jimmy Carter was president and Democrats controlled both houses of Congress by wide margins. The labor movement came within one vote of passing a comprehensive labor law reform bill. This bill would have considerably strengthened labor's hand in organizing unions and made labor stronger during the assault on it by Reagan and the two Bushes. The bill didn't pass because Dale Bumpers from Arkansas, who is normally a fairly progressive senator, didn't want to irritate all of the antilabor businesses back home, such as Wal-Mart, and because Carter didn't care enough to really push

Bumpers to vote for it. Given labor's central importance to the health of the Democratic Party, the party has paid bitterly for that failure ever since. And given the stagnation and stress the middle class has dealt with in this country since 1978, the weakened power of labor—which is the greatest champion for the economic health of the middle class—has been a devastating blow.

Health-Care Reform

The second time that Democrats tried and failed to do something really big was on health care in 1993–1994. I was a part of that bitter fight, serving in the White House war room on the issue. Given the issue's centrality to everything that has happened since, it is worth taking a moment to discuss it.

Trying to comprehensively reform the U.S. health-care system, which comprises one-seventh of the U.S. economy and is intensely important to Americans' quality of life, is a gargantuan undertaking. Democrats were up against the odds under any set of circumstances. We made our share of tactical mistakes along the way. But the irony of the health-care battle is that although our policy ambitions were big, we ultimately failed because of our political caution and our opposition's political aggression.

Some moderate Republicans such as John Chafee wanted to work with us on the legislation, but conservative leaders understood from the beginning that if Democrats succeeded in giving Americans comprehensive, lower-cost health-care security, it would be as devastating to Republicans politically over the long run as FDR's creation of Social Security was in 1935. Leading conservative strategist Bill Kristol wrote a famous memo that made this argument. In it, he said, "Passage of the Clinton health care plan in any form [underlined in the original] would be disastrous. . . . Its success would signal the rebirth of centralized welfare-state policy at the very moment that such policy is being perceived as a failure in other areas." Kristol, Newt Gingrich, and other conservative leaders vowed an all-out war against passing anything related to health-care reform. They knew that Democratic success on this central issue would be both a long-term political disaster for them and a setback in their drive to win a majority of seats in Congress in 1994.

Although some Democrats grasped that reality as well (I remember Hillary Clinton and Dick Gephardt making those arguments in closed-door meetings with Democratic members of Congress), all too many didn't see that fundamental dynamic, and they diddled around and put roadblocks in our way. Senators such as Pat Moynihan, Bill Bradley, Joe Lieberman, and Bob Kerrey and House members like Jim Cooper could have been major players in helping us get something done, but they either opposed us outright or moved slowly and lethargically on the issue.

The central problem, though, was our message, and this was where caution really destroyed us. On a complicated issue like health care, so many voters felt nervous about messing with what they were used to. Only a strong, compelling message would succeed at selling the plan in the face of the hundreds of millions of dollars being spent by the insurance and pharmaceutical industries. In our public opinion research, we had discovered two such powerful messages.

One was a straightforward assault on the very industries that were spending so much money to oppose our plan. We could attack them as the culprits and get the public to understand that our plan would help protect people against the power of those corporations. I wrote such a speech for Hillary Clinton to give to a convention of union activists from the Service Employees International Union, and she gave it with gusto. It got big headlines in the media and an incredible response from activists, but the more cautious staffers in the White House were worried that we were being too tough and going too far, and they convinced the first lady and the president not to be so bold.

The other approach was to say that all Americans ought to have the same right to health coverage that their members of Congress had. Again, it was a simple, compelling way of describing our fundamental idea, and it played very well. But this time, Democratic members of Congress got nervous; they worried that it might feed on the already building anti-incumbent sentiment of 1994. So we didn't use this message either, not until close to the end, when a few members of the pro-reform coalition began use it in earnest in spite of congressional Democrats' objections. But by that time, it was too late. The plan was already dead.

Caution not only permeated our message but was also inherent in other parts of the Democrats' strategy for health-care reform. President Clinton decided to put NAFTA before health care, which badly divided the progressive coalition. A hundred delays slowed our introduction of the plan. The progressive movement was generally too fragmented and obsessed with its particular health care–related issue to be of much help with the entire package. Congressional leaders who didn't want to irritate entrenched committee chairs didn't push as hard as was warranted to get the bill moving.

When we lost the health-care fight, voters who were already irritated at Democrats for not delivering more of what we had promised turned on us with a vengeance. The 1994 blowout, when we lost fifty-two House seats and eight Senate seats, was the biggest congressional landslide since 1964. We lost control of both houses of Congress, including the House of Representatives, for the first time in forty years and didn't win back control of Congress until 2006. It was the most sweeping defeat of either party in an off-year election in modern American history.

The Culture of Caution

In the culture of caution that dominates Democratic politics in the modern era, when you try something big and fail, even if the failure is due in great part to your own timidity, you only become more cautious. The failure of health-care reform made President Clinton more cautious, and he started playing small ball. President Clinton famously advocated for things like school uniforms and agreed to support bad Republican bills on welfare reform and telecommunications reform. Clinton deserves credit for standing up to Republicans in the 1995 budget showdown, a decision that was the most important factor in his winning reelection, and for the other achievements I mentioned previously. For the most part, however, his last six years in office were a time of very modest policy ideas.

The culture of caution hurt the Democrats' political strategy as well. When the Lewinsky scandal and the impeachment fight with the Republicans reared their ugly heads in 1998, I was working for the progressive group People for the American Way. We got heavily involved in opposing impeachment and worked alongside the activists who eventually started MoveOn.org. We ran ads saying that it was time for the country to stop worrying about a sex scandal and "move on." Many Democratic politicians were horrified at those ads, convinced that by mentioning the issue we would just remind voters of what they didn't like about Clinton. We were asked by the party committees and the top members of Congress to pull them, but our focus groups had convinced us that we were right and should stand our ground. The message worked so well that candidates running in competitive races started to use the message in the ads, and, eventually, even the party committees did as well. Democrats picked up five seats in the 1998 elections and thereby stunned the pundits of conventional wisdom, who had widely predicted Democratic losses of thirty seats or more in Congress. It was the best showing for the party of a president in his sixth year in office in history since 1822, when James Monroe essentially had no opposition party. But Democrats would likely have won control of Congress if the Democratic establishment had not been so cautious for so long about facing the impeachment issue.

When Bush took over and exhibited an aggressive form of ideological partisanship never before seen in modern history, Democrats sometimes stood up to him, but all too frequently, they rolled over. This was especially true on national security and civil liberties issues after 9/11.

In 2002, when the authorization vote on the Iraq War came up, I was told in great confidence by a top aide to Dick Gephardt that if Democrats would cut a deal with Bush on the war, the issue would go away and Democrats would win the 2002 election on domestic issues. That same cycle, I was told by a top pollster for the party committees that Democrats should just avoid talking about national security altogether because it wasn't our strongest issue.

Of course, this strategy didn't work out so well, as Democrats went down to an ugly defeat in the 2002 election, where security issues dominated. In fact, Gephardt's strategy of cutting a deal with Bush was a political disaster. Progressive antiwar Democrats were divided and discouraged, and the Republicans attacked the Democrats just as hard as they would have otherwise on national security. The deal also played out poorly in the 2004 elections because John Kerry could never quite explain why he had voted for the war, even though he later said that he opposed it.

The most aggravating thing about the Democratic culture of caution is how strong it is, even when more aggressive approaches are working. Too many Democrats remained cautious despite their win in 2006 using heavily populist and antiwar campaigns, and even when Bush's approval ratings and credibility had gone down the tubes. In 2007 and 2008, Democrats caved multiple times on war-related votes and on civil liberties; they lived in fear that a president with a 30 percent approval rating would call them soft on terrorism.

Although I regret that the Democrats haven't stood up to Bush more on security and civil liberties issues, and I think they could have easily survived politically if they had, there is at least a stronger argument for being politically careful on those issues—voters are really scared of terrorism, and the message for Democrats on security issues is complicated. On domestic policy, though, Democrats have also failed to be strong advocates of dramatic new initiatives. The minimum wage and ethics initiatives they passed were solid achievements; forcing Bush to veto S-CHIP has been a worthy political fight to engage in, as was compelling him to veto legislation to withdraw troops from Iraq. The compromise energy bill that the Democrats passed and got Bush to sign had some respectable policy initiatives in it although it also had some poor ideas. But Democrats have failed to provoke major battles with Bush and the Republicans to illustrate how important their policy differences are.

Money, Conventional Wisdom, and Caution

Caution is not the only reason for the Democrats' lack of boldness. The power of money and inside-the-Beltway conventional
wisdom have made it harder to get Democratic votes for big ideas.

Since the 1970s, the cost of campaigns has skyrocketed. When I
started to work in politics in the early 1980s, you could run a
respectable race for Congress in a competitive district at a cost of
$150,000. Now, competitive congressional campaigns average much
more than $1 million, and party committees frequently spend an
additional $1.5 to $3 million per race on top of those expenditures.
When you need to raise that kind of money, standing up to wealthy
corporate interests becomes a lot tougher.

Another thing that has skyrocketed is big-business spending
on lobbying. The number of registered lobbyists in D.C.—more
than 34,750 in 2005—was double the number that existed in 2000.
The vast majority of those new lobbyists are on the corporate and
business trade association side. These corporate interests tend to
have both Democratic and Republican congressional staffers so
that they will have plenty of access to both parties, and when the
Democrats took back Congress in 2006, the corporate interests
dramatically beefed up their hiring of Democrats, along with
their contributions to top Democratic leaders. Corporate lobbyists get very big paychecks or retainers for their work, so a
Capitol Hill staffer who is used to making $80,000 or $100,000 a
year can quickly jump to making $250,000, $300,000, or even
$500,000, and sometimes more, if he or she crosses over to the
lobbying side.

These businesses pay not only for lobbyists but for much more.
They spend tens of millions of dollars each year for public relations
consultants, public opinion research, and sophisticated advertising.
They also pour their money into what's called "Astroturf" lobbying—paying veterans of political campaigns to go into key districts and do field organizing, or funding phone banks to call
constituents of targeted members of Congress to get them worked
up over an issue.

Another way that big businesses spend money is in contributions to organizations. Conservative think tanks are delighted to have corporate contributions to pay for research and reports that, shockingly, back up the agendas of those corporations. Conservatives set up phony grassroots groups with corporate money, such as the senior citizen's organization United Seniors, which takes in millions of dollars in drug-company money every election cycle to run advertisements that praise members of Congress for voting with the drug companies. Yet not only conservative organizations take corporate money and tend to argue for more corporate-friendly policies. The Democratic Leadership Council (DLC), which was started in the 1980s to support centrist Democratic ideas, gets most of its funding from corporate contributors and argues strongly against Democrats using rhetoric that is too populist or pushing policies that are too progressive. The DLC has had some good ideas in its day—Clinton's National Service Initiative, the Reinventing Government Initiative, community policing, and a hundred thousand cops on the streets were all ideas that the DLC pushed strongly—but because so much of its money comes from big business, it has consistently been a strong pro–big business voice in the party.

Besides the corporate money, one other major factor has pushed Democrats to the small-idea mushy middle, and that is the powerful pull of conventional wisdom. There are two aspects of this conventional wisdom: the first is the acceptance of conservative frames around issues and politics, and the second is the belief inside the Beltway that bipartisan compromise is almost always a good thing, no matter what the nature of the deal is.

One area where the right-wing media have been very successful is in getting the rest of the media, and even many Democrats, to adopt its framing language on issues. The right-wing media have been consistently effective at inducing reporters to substitute phrases like *pro-life* for *anti-abortion*, *death tax* for *estate tax*, and *supporting the troops* for *funding the war*. Fox News, Limbaugh, and all the rest have influenced more traditional media sources to be obsessed with Clinton scandals that weren't scandals, such as when the Clintons lost money on a fourteen-year-old

Whitewater land deal. The right-wing media have convinced reporters that Gore said he had invented the Internet when he never actually said this; they successfully pushed the ridiculous idea that Osama bin Laden wanted the Democrats to win (when even CIA intelligence has suggested that bin Laden is perfectly happy with Bush, who inadvertently aids him in recruiting so many new terrorists).

Of course, part of the traditional media's acceptance of conservative frames is that traditional media have begun to look more and more like other big-business conglomerates. With media consolidation and media companies being brought up by defense contractors such as General Electric, traditional media's interests have been lining up more frequently with conservative politics. Although there are still plenty of liberal reporters, the people who make decisions about what to cover and how to cover it are becoming more conservative all the time.

The other way that conventional wisdom in D.C. works is that the golden ideal for so many media people and D.C. movers and shakers is bipartisan compromise. It's a tendency some of my friends in the blogosphere call "High Broderism," in honor of the *Washington Post* columnist David Broder, who loves to write about the benefits of bipartisanship. There are many politicians in D.C. to whom the art of the deal is far more important than whether the deal is actually any good.

To me, the quintessential art-of-the-deal politician during my time in D.C. has been retired Louisiana senator John Breaux. Breaux was a classic back-slapping politician, a highly social guy who always seemed to be enjoying himself. And, boy, did he love to be in the middle of a deal. One friend of mine, a strong environmental activist, met Breaux at a party early in Breaux's career. Breaux struck up an animated conversation and asked my friend what issues he was most interested in. When my friend said, "The environment," Breaux looked disappointed. "Well, I'm not much of an environmentalist," Breaux said, "but I can do business with anybody—I'm always up for trying to make a deal." And he was. Breaux is now making big money as a corporate lobbyist.

Don't get me wrong. I know politics is the art of the possible, and I can accept half a loaf if I can't get the full one. Deal making and bipartisan compromise are not bad things if they actually move the ball down the field. But there is such a mania right now for bipartisan deal-making above all else, including good policy, that the conventional wisdom of bipartisanship has become a roadblock to actually making real progress on anything important.

The fervor over bipartisanship also ignores the state of our politics at this moment of history. Republicans have become an overwhelmingly hard-right conservative party, with only a very small group of GOP moderates left in Congress. And those moderates always have to be wary of primary challenges from the right.

Finally, the love of bipartisanship ignores much of history. There have been only two times in American history where progressive change has happened in any kind of bipartisan way: in the Progressive Era of the early 1900s, when a strong-willed Republican president, Teddy Roosevelt, made an alliance with populists and progressives in the Democratic Party to push through a series of progressive reforms over the opposition of most of his party; and in the 1960s, when a few liberal Republicans, mostly from the Northeast, helped Northern Democrats overcome opposition from Southern Democratic conservatives and most of the Republican Party to win civil rights and environmental reforms (although those same moderate Republicans were generally far less helpful on economic issues than on civil rights or the environment).

In the early 1800s, in contrast, Jefferson ran the government with virtually no help from the Federalists. Andrew Jackson opposed big-money interests and brought the working class into power with almost no support from the upper-class Whig Party. Lincoln and the Radical Republicans pushed through major changes in policy with no help from the opposition party. And FDR passed bills on Social Security, labor law, and the rest of the New Deal with little or no Republican backing.

If Democrats have good margins of support in the House and the Senate and a Democratic president in 2009, they should look for bipartisan deals wherever they can get them. They should always be civil to Republicans and reach out genuinely to their opponents wherever they can. But they need to be prepared to use presidential executive orders, the budget process, conference committees, and hardball politics if they are to deliver the vital changes this country needs.

Obama's Message of Hope and Change

Because I'm writing these words without knowing the outcome of the 2008 election, and you are reading this with the knowledge of how it came out, I won't comment much about the 2008 race, except to say how striking and overt Obama's theme of hope versus fear has been. I think the greatest mistake Clinton made in the primary was to suggest the dangers of "promoting false hope." It was an odd attack for a candidate whose husband had run sixteen years earlier as "the man from Hope," even more so because she was running as a candidate from a party and a movement that had been arguing for hope and change for more than a century.

Obama has, more than any other candidate in my lifetime, built his candidacy on the legacy of progressive hope and change. He has used Cesar Chavez's organizing cry from the 1960s, "Sí se puede/ Yes, we can"; repeatedly invoked the Declaration of Independence; announced his presidential run at Lincoln's home in Springfield, Illinois; and recalled the hope of progressive pioneers of our country's history to create a campaign dominated by the imagery of past progressive victories. It is fitting that I close my chapter on hope and fear with a quote from his speech that responds to Clinton's line about promising false hope:

> We have been told we cannot do this by a chorus of cynics. And they will only grow louder and more dissonant in the weeks and months to come.
>
> We've been asked to pause for a reality check. We've been warned against offering the people of this nation false hope. But in the unlikely story that is America, there has never been anything false about hope.

For when we have faced down impossible odds, when we've been told we're not ready or that we shouldn't try or that we can't, generations of Americans have responded with a simple creed that sums up the spirit of a people: Yes, we can. Yes, we can. Yes, we can.

It was a creed written into the founding documents that declared the destiny of a nation: Yes, we can.

It was whispered by slaves and abolitionists as they blazed a trail towards freedom through the darkest of nights: Yes, we can.

It was sung by immigrants as they struck out from distant shores and pioneers who pushed westward against an unforgiving wilderness: Yes, we can.

It was the call of workers who organized, women who reached for the ballot, a president who chose the moon as our new frontier, and a king who took us to the mountaintop and pointed the way to the promised land: Yes, we can, to justice and equality.

Yes, we can, to opportunity and prosperity. Yes, we can heal this nation. Yes, we can repair this world. Yes, we can.

And so, tomorrow, as we take the campaign south and west, as we learn that the struggles of the textile workers in Spartanburg are not so different than the plight of the dishwasher in Las Vegas, that the hopes of the little girl who goes to the crumbling school in Dillon are the same as the dreams of the boy who learns on the streets of L.A., we will remember that there is something happening in America, that we are not as divided as our politics suggest, that we are one people, we are one nation.

And, together, we will begin the next great chapter in the American story, with three words that will ring from coast to coast, from sea to shining sea: Yes, we can.

For an author who is making the case that we ought to connect modern progressivism to our historical roots, that is a speech to love.

9

The Next Big Change
Moment

I n Arthur Schlesinger Jr.'s classic book *The Cycles of American History*, written in the mid-1980s, he talked about "public opinion" and "private purpose" consolidation cycles in history. He suggested that in the twentieth century, history had run in thirty-year cycles: a decade when change exploded into the political environment (1900s, 1930s, and 1960s), followed by a decade when momentum from the earlier decade kept going but gradually slowed (1910s, 1940s, and 1970s). This was followed by a politically conservative decade when people were exhausted from public change and turned to private interests and pursuits (1920s, 1950s, and 1980s). Based on this pattern, he was expecting another big decade of progressive change in the 1990s. It seemed that his prediction would be fulfilled when Clinton was elected with big Democratic margins in both the Senate and the House in 1992.

But it was not to be. As we have seen, when we Clintonistas failed to deliver on health-care reform in 1993–1994, disappointed Democratic voters stayed home, and the Republicans took control of Congress. And when Clinton turned to a triangulation strategy instead of a stronger progressive strategy in 1996 to win reelection, Republicans kept control of Congress. Even when Republicans overreached, on the budget fight of 1995 and an impeachment attempt in 1998, Democrats were too timid to take advantage of the opportunity and drive them out of power. Gore's cautious 2000 campaign and his tentative response to Republican vote stealing in Florida ended a stalemated decade and brought a new period of conservative ascendance.

History has big patterns and trends, but very little is inevitable. The decisions, courage, and failures of individual leaders and mass movements of people determine its course.

If Paine had not written *Common Sense* in the closing months of 1775 and *The American Crisis* in the year that Washington's troops experienced such a difficult winter at Valley Forge, there probably would not have been a successful revolution. If Jefferson had not opened an otherwise fairly pedestrian list of grievances against the British with his soaring egalitarian vision, the nature of American political debate would have been forever lessened. If conservatives had not dominated the Constitutional Convention in 1787, maybe Jefferson's ideas about phasing out slavery would have been adopted, rather than delegates giving in to the demands of the hard-line slave owners; instead of seventy years of the horrors of slavery and the Civil War, slavery might have faded away. If abolitionists in the mid-1800s had not stirred the pot, the reign of slavery would have been far longer. If a weak, ineffectual president, like the previous several ones, had been in office rather than Lincoln, the South's secession would have been a success. If the generation of Republicans who followed the radicals of the 1860s hadn't been more interested in taking bribes from the robber barons than in defending the hard-won rights of African Americans, the almost century-long tragedy of Jim Crow would not have happened. If women activists had not hung in there against great derision and battled with great courage year after year for almost a century, it is not at all clear when women might have finally acquired the right to vote. If FDR had decided to listen to conservative Democrats rather than to people such as John L. Lewis and Walter Reuther, Social Security and the rest of the New Deal would not have happened. If Rosa Parks, Martin Luther King Jr., Rachel Carson, Cesar Chavez, and Betty Friedan had not inspired one another, the progressive changes of the 1960s would have been diminished.

Progressives had a chance to make the 1990s a big change moment in American history, but we failed. We have now had the longest period in our history without an era of far-reaching progressive change. Previously, the most protracted period of conservative dominance was from the early 1870s until 1901, after the trauma of the Civil War years. Following the early 1970s, we have had more than thirty-five years since the last time things moved dramatically in the right direction. I believe the time is now ripe for another of those big change moments, but making this moment happen will demand courage and boldness from our progressive movement and from our political leaders.

I say this for a number of reasons. The first is that after years of ignoring our enormous problems or making them worse, they have become too complex to manage without substantial changes. Look at the issues staring us in the face: an extreme climate-change crisis, an economy mired in debt and in serious long-term trouble; an intractable and fruitless war in Iraq; relations with our allies in disarray; a completely dysfunctional health-care system; an immigration policy that is also utterly dysfunctional; an education system with deep flaws; a media world dominated by a small number of conglomerates; a crumbling infrastructure of roads, bridges, schools, and electric grids that affects the public every day; and the list goes on.

These are major problems that will require boldness, courage, and ingenuity to solve. The longer we go without dealing with them, the worse off we are. Laissez-faire won't get it done, and neither will the cautious baby steps that were the hallmark of the Clinton years.

Second, when I look at public opinion polling over the last couple of decades, I am struck by how different people's attitudes are right now in comparison to the recent past.

In 2004, while agreeing with Democrats on some topics, Republicans fought us to a draw on enough issues that the fear message Bush was pushing successfully overcame voters' reluctance. But by 2006, Democrats had a significant edge on most issues—on health care and the war in Iraq, a very strong edge—and were behind

Bush only on certain security issues, depending on how you phrased the questions, and on equal rights for same-sex marriages. In addition, conservatism itself as a philosophy had become more negative in the minds of voters:

- The word *conservative* itself went from 18 points positive in 1994 to 3 points negative in 2006.
- The phrase "Bottom line, America's security depends on its own military strength" went from even in the polls in 2002 to a 24-point deficit after the most recent election, as compared with the phrase "America's security depends on building strong ties with other nations."
- Each year finds more public tolerance for gays, lesbians, bisexuals, and transgender individuals and for their rights in general, as well as for same-sex marriage (although it is still opposed by a majority of the population).
- By consistently big numbers (usually around 58–36 percent over the last few years), voters say they agree with the statement "Government regulation of businesses and corporations is necessary to protect the public," rather than with "Government regulation of businesses and corporations frequently does more harm than good." In the Reagan era and the 1990s, those numbers were much worse in terms of attitudes toward regulation.
- By a 53–41 percent margin in 2006, voters said that "Government should play a vital role in ensuring all individuals have the same opportunity to succeed," as opposed to "The government should stop providing social services and give people the tools to make their own choices on important issues."

On perhaps the most fundamental question of all, community versus individualism, voters choose community. In that same late-2006 poll I have been quoting, voters chose "America should promote the principle of strong community and taking responsibility, because we are all in this together" by 10 points, over "America should encourage individualism, personal responsibility and self-reliance." It's hard to get much more of a succinct summary of the progressive philosophy versus the conservative one.

These changes do not merely reflect weariness with Bush, although I believe that is part of it. There was a clear moment in 2005 when several events combined to show the American people how bankrupt conservatism had become: the Social Security privatization campaign that Bush launched, the Terri Schiavo overreach, weariness with the war in Iraq, and the Katrina disaster, which laid bare the conservatives' lack of concern for the problems of America's poor. That was when Bush's numbers went permanently into the lower 30s, when the numbers supporting the Democrats in Congress shot up, and when margins on key issues began to move dramatically in a progressive direction. It was the polling equivalent of a tectonic plate shift. When the economic repercussions of Bush's no-oversight regulatory state started to hit home with a vengeance in early 2008, the number of voters who understood the serious defects of conservatism increased.

Third, the progressive movement is finally beginning to emerge from its period of relative slumber. New organizations have sprung forth that are multi-issue, rather than single-issue, and that have a broader, more comprehensive view of progressivism than the narrow interest-group politics of the past. Progressive donors and foundations are beginning to think long-term and strategically, rather than being focused only on short-term tactics. The labor movement is showing some spunk and energy in organizing that I haven't seen in my lifetime, even though the actors in it spend too much time fighting one another. Young people are becoming engaged again in the political fray, voting and volunteering at levels one could only dream of just a few years ago—a trend that was helped, though not started, by Barack Obama's campaign.

Perhaps most important of all, the changes in media and technology have allowed a new kind of activist to get involved in an easy, efficient, relatively low-cost, and powerful way. For millions who were never previously active in politics, MoveOn.org, blogs, and other Internet-based structures have created tools that let people volunteer, give money, meet their neighbors at house parties, and contact their elected officials. Progressive bloggers have created a democratic, interactive medium where anyone with a computer can take part. An organization called ActBlue developed political fund-raising tools that, as of late April 2008, have enabled 368,763 people to donate nearly $44 million to candidates. This grassroots spigot of small-dollar contributions (the median contribution to ActBlue, as of April 2008, is $50) has given progressive candidates a way to compete with corporate fund-raising.

When you look back at American history, only the combination of strong progressive citizens' movements and progressive leaders in government have made big changes happen: Lincoln and the abolitionists; Teddy Roosevelt, Woodrow Wilson, and the populist and progressive movements; FDR and the labor movement; and JFK, LBJ, and the civil rights movement. With the newly revitalized progressive movement of today, if good people get elected, we will have that combination in place again.

The fourth reason I think the stage is set for a big change moment is the power of new media itself to intrinsically transform the political system. This capability goes far beyond the tools for activists I mentioned previously. Smart ideas can go viral at almost no cost, any individual can write his or her own blog post or be a video producer, and a young activist with a cheap camera can show up at a campaign event and make an impact (for example, the famous Macaca incident that tripped up Senator George Allen in 2006). All of this radically changes the nature of modern politics.

The top-down nature of television had a pacifying effect on politics and civic engagement in general. As I wrote on my blog, OpenLeft.com:

Those of us who do politics for a living are at a moment in history that feels similar to what political operatives must have felt like back in the late 1950s. The medium of television that had emerged a few years before was transforming the way politics was done. However, no one could imagine just how much it was going to revolutionize political campaigns, political organizing, and the political dialogue across the United States. In the 1950s, it was television. Today, it's the rapidly evolving world of new media. . . .

In the 1950s, the advent of the television era, Americans had greater faith [in] and a more direct connection to their government. At that time, they were more likely to be actively engaged in PTAs, labor unions, and local civic organizations. These groups were more likely to be involved in a substantive dialogue with politicians and political parties. Americans were much more likely to be active precinct captains or volunteers in their local political party organizations and were much more likely to read daily newspapers and weekly magazines that had in-depth articles covering local and national politics. I agree with Robert Putnam's compelling case in *Bowling Alone* that television played a dramatic role in the decline in civic participation, and I think that idea carries over even more into our political life.

Television played a major role in changing all that, making people more passive recipients of political information, and making 30-second ads the dominant way information was disseminated. Because politics shifted toward television advertising and away from grassroots organizing and direct voter contact, and because the expense of television advertising kept rising, campaigns became more and more dependent on big business and wealthy special interest donors. This added further distance between politicians and regular voters and it cheapened the political experience. Finally, as television became more corporatized (with the networks being bought up by corporate conglomerates), the quality, quantity and fairness of TV news coverage about politics, both national and local, slipped dramatically.

Organizing and communicating through the Internet—and now increasingly through mobile media—have begun to be an antidote to this poison. Between MoveOn.org, the blogosphere, and other Internet organizing structures, the progressive movement is revitalizing and transforming the Democratic

Party and the country. Now, as new technology and new media continue to open doors for organizing, we just have to keep building on what we've already started.

The final factor that bodes well for a new progressive change moment is the utter intellectual and political bankruptcy of modern American conservatism. Conservatives have built a great political machine and invested an extraordinary amount of money in their policy infrastructure, but for all their thunder and pomposity, they don't have a lot to show for their efforts. The Bush administration was a disaster, leaving an economy in shambles, a quagmire in Iraq, and foreign policy in crisis. The old Reaganite political coalition of Christian conservatives, economic conservatives, and foreign policy neoconservatives came apart at the seams in a dispirited 2008 primary that ended up with a Republican general election candidate whom nobody in the conservative coalition really liked very well. The Bush thematic agenda of the "ownership society" disappeared from Republican rhetoric years ago. The centerpiece policy proposal of Bush's second term, Social Security privatization, went down in flames long before the Republicans lost control of Congress.

The only big arguments remaining for conservatives are their old standbys, fear and the contention that government doesn't work, for which, ironically, their own failures provide the most powerful evidence. In fact, ever since the Katrina disaster, conservatives have said that what Katrina proves is that government is incompetent. They cynically use their own ineptitude to argue their philosophical point. When your most powerful argument is your own incompetence, you don't have a very strong hand.

If another of history's big progress moments is coming over the next decade, how can Democrats lead us toward that opportunity? Democrats need to reorient themselves to do two fundamental things, which are closely related to each other. One is to think big and bold, rather than small and cautious. The other is to be clear about running ideologically, as strong progressives, rather than as careful, defensive-sounding centrists. The American public wants change, big change, and Democrats should not be shy about offering it to them.

These thoughts will be counterintuitive to Democrats of my generation and the one just before it. Democrats who came of political age in the post-1960s, during the Nixon and Reagan years, are used to being on the defensive. Although the public has been with us on some issues (the environment, the minimum wage, spending on many domestic programs), we typically think in terms of how we can inoculate ourselves against conservative attacks and how we can seem like centrists, rather than liberals.

While we will always need to frame issues in a way that appeals to populist swing voters who are skeptical of government (certainly, the Republicans have proved that government is capable of great corruption and incompetence), I believe that the public is ready for a strong, confident progressive message. In addition to the polling I cited earlier, let me give a couple more examples from public opinion research projects I have been directly involved in.

The first is a project of the nationwide citizens' group USAction (a long-time client of mine), an agenda it calls "Invest in America's Future." This agenda was described as follows in a poll of swing voters done in February 2008:

> The Invest in America's Future plan represents a fundamental change in this government's priorities. Rather than spending billions on a war overseas or on tax cuts for millionaires and big corporations, this plan invests in our own people and in our own children.
>
> The Invest in America's Future plan will make government more accountable by reducing the influence of special interests through campaign finance laws, eliminating special loopholes for corporations and auditing federal departments to reduce waste.
>
> The Invest in America's Future Agenda is deficit neutral because it roots out waste, eliminates tax cuts on millionaires, closes corporate tax loopholes and would save billions of dollars by ending the war in Iraq.

The Invest in America's Future plan focuses on issues that affect every American family: guaranteeing high quality affordable health care, developing clean energy and achieving independence from oil, and investing to give our children an excellent education from pre-K through college.

This plan is supported by an overwhelming margin of 69 percent of swing voters in the survey (with 25 percent opposed), and 58 percent said they would be more likely to support a candidate for president and Congress if that person favored such an agenda. Although these swing voters are skeptical of government in general and are nervous about tax increases, the plan withstood conservative attacks and still came out of the survey with big support.

To give another example of how progressive language is working: an organization I founded and run, American Family Voices, sponsored a collaboration research project between Greenberg Quinlan Rosner Research and Emory University professor Drew Westen, the author of an insightful book (*The Political Brain*) on how people's brains react when they are thinking about politics. We tested message paragraphs coming from both a conservative and a progressive perspective on the most controversial issues around, including lesbian, gay, bisexual, and transgender rights, immigration, guns, civil liberties, national security, taxes, and the role of government.

To our delight (and sometimes surprise), we discovered that a well-crafted progressive message beats the strong conservative message on every issue we tested, generally by a more than 10-point margin.

Now, I will admit that these messages were carefully crafted and tested and retested to discover what kind of language worked, so I'm not suggesting that liberal Democrats will automatically start sweeping every election in every region of the country. There are too many years of stereotypes, emotional button-pushing, and ingrained voting habits to move voters in the habit of voting Republican that fast. What I am convinced of by these results, though, is that the American people, including more conservative voters, are open to a broadly progressive message that goes beyond the careful, cautious mushiness of the Democratic message in recent years. What this research conclusively shows is that the American public, by big majorities, is ready for a strong progressive change agenda.

What are the bold policies we should be pushing? I want to stay away from the long laundry list of programs and bills that so many Democrats have made a habit of running on. I will focus here on the main problems that really need to be solved to change the country. No doubt, I will leave things out that will irritate or offend some people because I'm not trying to cover every single item on the agenda. But the worst problems we have in this country have been ignored or exacerbated by eight years of Bush's rule and forty years of mostly conservative dominance. Addressing these failings will require a real sense of focus. The challenges we face are too crucial and fundamental not to be dealt with head on, with big, sweeping solutions. Here's what we have to work to repair in the next few years:

- **Climate change.** If you believe Al Gore and 95-plus percent of the scientists who have studied this issue, as I do, we desperately need to retool our economy in a fundamental way, moving it from running on a carbon-based energy system to clean and renewable sources of energy. This will require allotting substantial federal investments toward energy conservation, technology research, and the retooling of manufacturing and energy production; legislating serious and strict caps on carbon emissions; and making it a top priority to deal with climate change in terms of trade policy and diplomacy with other governments, especially China and India. We must immediately act to mitigate this crisis so that we can avoid dire problems in the future.

- **Health care.** We need a health-care system that covers all Americans; puts serious cost controls in place so that insurance companies and drug companies don't make such obscene profits; embraces a standard for health benefits that includes prevention but also fully treats people when they are ill; and stops insurance companies from gaming the system by cherry-picking the healthiest and screening out the old and the sick.

- **Immigration reform.** Yes, America's border security should be tightened. But undocumented people deserve a fair path to citizenship that is reasonably fast and efficient, and we need a policy designed so that people who want to immigrate to this country have a legitimate way to do so. At the same time, labor laws must be strictly enforced and strengthened so that corporations can't continue to exploit the cheap labor of illegal aliens, to the detriment of both immigrants and American workers.

- **Workers' rights.** We haven't changed labor law in a way that helps unions organize freely since the 1930s, and much of the legislation passed since then has reversed the labor movement's earlier progress. It should be easier to join a union, the minimum wage should be raised and adjusted to inflation, and laws regarding working conditions and worker safety should be strengthened.

- **Public financing of campaigns.** Candidates and elected officials should not have to continually raise money from wealthy people and corporations to be able to win elections. Creating a public system to finance congressional campaigns would lessen the power of big-money interests and would free candidates and lawmakers to actually talk to regular voters and work on legislation that might help their constituents. Making this reform would not end the role of money in politics, by any means, but it would be a significant improvement in our system.

- **Internet neutrality, universal broadband, and the break-up of media conglomerates.** There is nothing more important to our democracy, and few things more essential to our long-term economic health, than a progressive telecommunications policy that preserves the even playing field for content that we have on the Internet; assures that all of our citizens, regardless of income or geography, have fast and easy online access; and breaks up the current frightening levels of media consolidation.

In addition to these urgently important policy reforms, the two most immediate issues for our next president and Congress will be dealing with the mess that Bush has left us: the chaos in Iraq and the faltering U.S. economy. Resolving both problems will require broad, fearless measures.

In terms of ending the war, a number of plans have been put forward to do this, and many of them have merit. My own personal favorite, and the one I have been promoting in my work, is called the "Responsible Plan to End the War." It was written by Darcy Burner, a remarkable young congressional candidate from Washington State (and hopefully, by the time you are reading this, a member of Congress), with help from Major General Paul Eaton, who served in Iraq before retiring. You can find it on the following Web site: www.responsibleplan.com/plan. It gets us out of Iraq and also deals with the refugee problem and the political repercussions in Iraq and the Middle East. It even includes long-term solutions that will help us avoid getting mired in a war like this ever again.

On the economy, Bush's policies have put us in a world of hurt, worse than at any time since the Great Depression. If we increase wages, reform health care, create the green jobs and the new technology that climate change requires, and bring immigrants out of the shadow economy, as discussed earlier, all of that will provide a significant boost to the U.S. economy. We also desperately need to re-regulate our financial markets and enforce more accountability for CEOs and corporate accounting. And we must provide real relief to the middle class and poorer people who were caught up in predatory lending practices.

What we should be looking to do, in the phrase of columnist Harold Meyerson, is create "a new New Deal." Our economy has floated along on debt—government, trade, and personal—and bubbles in technology, housing, and stock prices, rather than on policies and practices that create a longer-lasting, more stable, broad-based prosperity for the middle class. As Meyerson wrote in March 2008:

> The key lesson Americans need to learn from today's troubles is how to distinguish faux prosperity from the genuine article. Over the past hundred years, we've experienced both. In the three decades after World War II we had the real thing. Led by our manufacturing sector, productivity increased at a rapid clip and median family incomes rose at a virtually identical rate. The value of the American work product grew significantly and that value was shared with American workers.
>
> But we've had other periods of apparent prosperity that were based not on broad increases in personal income but on the inflation of assets. So it was with stocks in the late 1920s, a time when most Americans lacked substantial purchasing power. So it was with the dot-com bubble of the late '90s. And so it was with the rising value of American homes in recent years.
>
> Our goal should be to re-orient our economy away from the highly individualistic, winner-take-all, free-market worshipping economic philosophy that has underlied the conservatism of the last four decades, and toward a philosophy that once again invests in regular people, lifts wages, and has as its primary goal an expanding and economically secure middle class. If we can leave caution and conservatism long enough to do that, and to achieve these major accomplishments, our country will once again deal with the challenges facing it, and we will move toward the future with confidence.

What many political observers, including too many Democrats looking for an excuse to be cautious and pundits caught up in the mania for bipartisan compromise, will argue is that even if we have Democratic majorities in both houses of Congress and a

Democratic president, a filibuster in the Senate will always stop us from doing big things (because it requires sixty votes rather than merely a fifty-one-vote majority). But that's not true, and here are the reasons:

- A great deal can be done through the budget process, which requires only fifty-one votes in the Senate. Instituting progressive tax increases on millionaires, discontinuing the hundreds of billions of dollars in corporate tax loopholes, abolishing tax subsidies for large agribusinesses and other industries that get tax help, ending the war in Iraq and other types of wasteful military spending—all of these things will free up funds to spend on health care, subsidies for green jobs to transform the economy's dependence on fossil fuels, and a variety of other domestic programs.

- We can add a lot of important progressive measures into popular bills' conference committee reports, making them part of a package that is much harder for Republicans to filibuster. This, by the way, was a tactic Republicans were happy to use when Democrats were in the minority.

- If we do a good job of framing the issues, win strong support from the American public, and partner with progressive movement activists who are fired up to put heat on their senators, filibusters become much harder to sustain. Republican senators will find it very difficult to say no to an aggressive president who is backed by public opinion and a vibrant core of millions of activists. This is especially true if Democrats force Republicans to expose their opposition by actually filibustering over a matter of weeks, rather than pulling bills on the threat of a filibuster or going along as Democrats have done with the faux filibusters of recent times, when we gave up after a very brief debate.

- Just as Democrats compromised on a range of issues in the face of Republican hardball when Republicans controlled every branch of government from 2003 to 2006, the fact that Republicans and corporate lobbyists know that we will employ these tough tactics will make them willing to come to us with compromises that are more on our terms, compared to the cave-in compromises we would have had to give them otherwise.

To Democrats who are accustomed to the tenor of business as usual in recent times, this kind of scenario may seem too hopeful. But when the public is behind you and an activist movement is mobilized, business as usual can change dramatically. And as Barack Obama puts it, "In America, hope has never been false."

Moving the Country Forward

Democracy gains strength from at least two competitive political traditions: one that agitates for change, and one that reveres tradition and warns against changing too fast. If either of them becomes dominant for too long, the system bogs down. The crustiness and lack of ambition I saw in our "change party" (Democrats) when I came to D.C. in the early 1990s, after forty years of rule in the U.S. House of Representatives, illustrates the value of political competitiveness. Schlesinger's point in *The Cycles of American History* is an important one as well: that democracies after a period of major change have an almost organic need for consolidation and rest as a society, that substantive change at this level wearies the body politic.

The competing tension between conservative and progressive philosophies has played out during our entire history as a nation. Paine's *Common Sense* and *The American Crisis* and Jefferson's opening paragraph of the Declaration of Independence were central in shaping Americans' understanding of their new nation. The one-third of colonists who sided with the British against the Revolution were quintessential conservatives, who opposed democracy, change, equal rights, and new ideas. Some conservative thinkers joined the Revolution and deservedly became highly revered Founding Fathers—George Washington and John Adams at the top of that list. In the early days of the nation, from the Revolutionary War through the framing of the Constitution and the first years of the Washington administration, as well as at other periods in U.S. history, our country has been shaped by a mix of conservative and progressive heroes and conservative and progressive ideas.

But having said all that, I also strongly believe that when you look back at American history and see the consequences we have reaped in picking conservatism over progressivism, it is clear which path is better for our country. When progressivism has been ascendant and progressive leaders have had the courage and support to fight for and win big changes, we have moved forward and become a better society. When conservatism has ruled politically, we have not only failed to make progress but have frequently gone backward or made big mistakes that cost the country dearly. From the earliest times until today, despite the contributions of conservative thinkers and leaders, the history revealed in this book supports this argument. Look at how that history has flowed.

We have seen that when conservatives prevailed on the issue of slavery—with Southern hard-liners demanding major concessions and Northern conservatives going along for the sake of a deal—it gave us seventy years of pure misery for millions of slaves, economic stagnation and political repression in the South, and a horrible civil war that almost destroyed the country.

The Electoral College was another mistake supported by conservatives, who feared electing a president by popular vote. The result has been a series of crises in our political system that has undermined Americans' faith in our democracy—the first one in 1800 also almost destroyed the country in its fragile early days.

Yet another harmful conservative error, not delineating a Bill of Rights, almost cost the framers the ratification of the Constitution itself. When grassroots progressives demanded that a Bill of Rights be added to the Constitution, the country was set on the path of having the freedoms we cherish today.

Conservatives forced through the Alien and Sedition Acts just a decade later during John Adams's term in 1798, and those freedoms were put to the test. The unity of the nation was again at risk.

Fortunately, Jefferson won the next election, and the instability of those first few rough years finally began to ease.

In 1824, we had another major crisis caused by the conservative invention of the Electoral College and by a deal between three conservative politicians: John Quincy Adams, John Calhoun, and Henry Clay. Following four unhappy and ineffective years of Adams's presidency, Andrew Jackson swept into power and pushed for policies that expanded democracy and opposed economic elitism. After that, the country had a twenty-four-year run of presidents who served one term or less (two presidents in that period died in office). Most of them were ineffectual and conservative, and none of them responded with any kind of courage or foresight to the rapidly developing conflict that would become the Civil War.

In the 1800s version of the 1960s, Lincoln and the Radical Republicans set the country on a profoundly different path. They won the Civil War, freed the slaves, established new rights for voting and citizenship, turned Calhoun's states' rights doctrine on its head, gave millions of pioneers free land, and afforded tens of millions of young people the chance to get a relatively inexpensive college education. Unfortunately, after that incredible wave of progress, a new generation of particularly nasty conservatives came into power for the rest of the century. They were fueled by robber baron money and a new Social Darwinist philosophy that justified stealing from the poor and giving to the rich. Their legacy was open corruption, child labor, big-city slums, millions of farmers losing their land, millions of workers being exploited, and terrible destruction of the country's environment.

We turned to the path of progress again in the early 1900s, as many of the reforms advocated by the populist and progressive movements became law. At least some of our country's natural beauty was preserved, food became safer to eat, the robber barons finally had a check on their power, and women won the right to vote. The country moved forward again.

When we turned back to conservatism in the 1920s, we got another massive wave of corruption and an economic depression so profound that it almost destroyed our country. Fortunately, America then elected progressive leadership. FDR, in alliance with the labor movement and other progressives, got the nation back on its feet. Banks and corporate finances were regulated, and people regained confidence in them. The jobless went back to work. Farmers were able to stay on their land. Senior citizens no longer lived in abject poverty. Wages and family incomes began a relatively steady forty-year rise. And the wrenching depressions of the past became milder economic downturns.

The 1960s gave us another period of progress. Life improved for African Americans, Hispanics, and women. Senior citizens and the poor got health care. The environment started to get cleaned up. A war we never should have been in finally ended. But, shaken by all the dramatic change and manipulated by a newly resurgent conservative movement, Americans again turned toward more conservative leaders.

Since the 1970s, we've had stagnant wages for the vast majority of American workers. We've made no progress on solving our addiction to foreign oil. The rich have gotten stupendously richer, while the middle class and the poor have been squeezed. We've entered another long, ugly war we shouldn't be in. Millions still have no health insurance, and health-care costs for those who do have it are soaring. We've done nothing despite twenty years of warnings about the terrible consequences of climate change, and scientists are now certain that we are in serious trouble. And we've had three conservative presidents—Nixon, Reagan, and the second Bush—who were seemingly in competition with one another to have headed the most corrupt administration in history.

The time has come again to choose a progressive path, to reject caution and embrace our history, and to rise to the example of progressive leaders of the past. Paine and Jefferson, Frederick Douglass and William Lloyd Garrison, Abraham Lincoln and the Radical Republicans, Elizabeth Cady Stanton and Susan B. Anthony, Teddy Roosevelt and Woodrow Wilson, FDR and John L. Lewis, JFK and RFK, Martin Luther King Jr. and Cesar Chavez, and Betty Friedan and Rachel Carson: their legacy calls us. We need to rise to the challenge and make the coming years a time to remember and record in our history, a period of transforming change that will lift up our nation and inspire future generations.

We can solve the immense problems of our time if we understand our history, throw fear and caution aside, and then choose the path that goes forward.

NOTES

1. The Big Change Moments

The Limbaugh quotes come from Rush Limbaugh's book *The Way Things Ought to Be* (New York: Pocket Books, 1992) and from an episode of *The Rush Limbaugh Show* that aired on March 19, 2007. The Emerson quote is taken from a lecture he gave in December 1841, titled "The Conservative."

2. A Progressive Revolution: How Tom Paine and Thomas Jefferson Literally Invented the Idea of America

For this chapter, my reference on Paine's writings was Phillip Sheldon Foner's *The Life and Major Writings of Thomas Paine: Includes Common Sense, the American Crisis, Rights of Man, the Age of Reason, and Agrarian Justice* (Chicago: Replica, 2000). My main reference on Paine's life and the reactions to him throughout history was Harvey J. Kaye's *Thomas Paine and the Promise of America* (New York: Hill and Wang, 2005).

Other sources include Albert Maltz's film *The House I Live In*; John Grafton's *Declaration of Independence and Other Great Documents of American History, 1775–1865* (New York: Dover, 2000); Arthur Schlesinger's *The Cycles of American History* (New York: Houghton Mifflin, 1999); *The Federalist Papers,* edited by Garry Wills (New York: Bantam, 1982); Saul Padover's *Jefferson: A Great American's Life and Ideas* (New York: Harcourt Brace Jovanovich, 1992); Russell Kirk's *The Conservative Mind: From Burke to Eliot* (Chicago: Regnery, 1986); Daniel Boorstin's *The Genius of American Politics* (Chicago: University of Chicago Press, 1953); Samuel Huntington's *The Clash of Civilizations? The Debate* (New

York: Simon & Schuster, 1996) and *The Remaking of the World Order* (New York: New York University Press, 1975); and Joseph Ellis's *American Creation: Triumphs and Tragedies at the Founding of the American Republic* (New York: Knopf, 2007).

Quotes from Reverend William Linn come from *Serious Considerations on the Election of a President Addressed to the Citizens of the United States* (New York: J. Furman, 1800).

3. The Constitution, the Bill of Rights, and the Right to Think and Speak Freely

The chief executive debates are discussed in Carol Berkin's *A Brilliant Solution: Inventing the American Constitution* (New York: Harcourt, 2002). Information for the section on the Devil's Bargain comes from both Berkin's book and Garrett Epps's *Democracy Reborn: The Fourteenth Amendment and the Fight for Equal Rights in Post–Civil War America* (Henry Holt, 2006). The section on the debate over the Bill of Rights relies on the Berkin book and on *Origins of the Bill of Rights* (New Haven, CT: Yale University Press, 1999) by Leonard Leavey. Salient facts in the passages about the freethinkers are taken from *Freethinkers: A History of American Secularism* (New York: Metropolitan Books, 2004) by Susan Jacoby.

4. Civil Rights, States' Rights, and the Re-Creation of the American Idea

My primary sources in this chapter are Garry Wills's *Lincoln at Gettysburg: The Words That Remade America* (New York: Simon & Schuster, 2006); James M. McPherson's *Battle Cry of Freedom: The Civil War Era* (New York: Ballantine, 1988); Garrett Epps's *Democracy Reborn: The Fourteenth Amendment and the Fight for Equal Rights in Post–Civil War America* (Henry Holt, 2006); and Doris Kearns Goodwin's *Team of Rivals: The Political Genius of Abraham Lincoln* (New York: Simon & Schuster, 2005).

Quotes attributed to John Calhoun come from Margaret L. Coit's *John C. Calhoun* (Englewood Cliffs, NJ: Prentice Hall, 1970); Russell Kirk's *The Conservative Mind: From Burke to Eliot* (Chicago: Regnery, 1986); and Kenneth Leish's *The American Heritage Pictorial History of the Presidents of the United States* (New York: American Heritage, 1968). The quote attributed to Bull Connor is from William A. Nunnelly's *Bull Connor* (Tuscaloosa: University of Alabama Press, 1991). The quote attributed to Tom Tancredo is taken from one of his presidential campaign ads, "Consequences," www.youtube.com/watch?v=wv4bYWBTgdw, accessed May 1, 2008. The Jesse Helms quotes are from UNC Television, "Jesse Helms: Senator No," www.unctv.org/senatorno/timeline/1960.html, accessed April 30, 2008. The quote attributed to Frederick Douglass comes from Lerone Bennett's *Before the Mayflower: A History of Black America* (New York: Penguin, 1993). Alexander Stephens's quote can be found in Henry Cleveland's *Alexander H. Stephens, in Public and Private: With Letters and Speeches, before, during, and since the War* (Philadelphia: National Publishing Company, 1866). Stokely Carmichael's quote can be located in Jo Freeman's *The Politics of Women's Liberation: A Case Study of an Emerging Social Movement and Its Relation to the Policy Process* (New York: McKay, 1975). The quote from Jackson to Calhoun also comes from Kenneth Leish's *The American Heritage Pictorial History of the Presidents of the United States.*

For information on *Brown v. Board of Education,* I used Robert Mann's *The Walls of Jericho: Lyndon Johnson, Hubert Humphrey, Richard Russell, and the Struggle for Civil Rights* (New York: Harcourt Brace, 1996).

For statistics on the Homestead Act, I referred to Martin K. Beutler and Matthew A. Diersen's "Pasture and Grazing Land Price Information," http://agbiopubs.sdstate.edu/articles/ExEx5048.pdf), accessed July 24, 2008.

5. The Battle over Democracy

Two primary sources for this chapter were Russell Kirk's *The Conservative Mind: From Burke to Eliot* (Chicago: Regnery, 1986) and *A Testament of Hope: The Essential Writings and Speeches of Martin Luther King, Jr.*, edited by James Washington (New York: HarperCollins, 1991).

My information about the Birchers and Barry Goldwater's biography comes from Rick Perlstein's *Before the Storm: Barry Goldwater and the Unmaking of the American Consensus* (New York: Hill and Wang, 2001). For the details about Jesse Helms, I referred to William Link's *Righteous Warrior: Jesse Helms and the Rise of Modern Conservatism* (New York: St. Martin's Press, 2008).

The statistics mentioned in my discussion of Johnson's Great Society programs came from Frank Stricker's *Why America Lost the War on Poverty, and How We Can Win It* (Chapel Hill: University of North Carolina Press, 2007).

The statistics about poverty rates can be found at the U.S. Census Bureau's online poverty resources at http://www.census.gov/hhes/www/poverty/histpov/hstpov3.html (for age-specific information on children and the elderly) and http://www.census.gov/hhes/www/poverty/histpov/hstpov2.html (for statistics on the poverty rate among the general population), both accessed April 28, 2008.

The rather uncouth quote from Richard Daley was one I found in Todd Gitlin's *The Sixties: Years of Hope, Days of Rage*, revised trade edition (New York: Bantam, 1993).

The quote from Newt Gingrich is taken from Charles Babcock and Ann Devroy's *Washington Post* article "Gingrich Speech Gives Lobbyists a Strategy for Midterm Elections," October 14, 1994. Quotes from Rush Limbaugh are from his book *The Way Things Ought to Be* (New York: Pocket, 1992) and his radio show, *The Rush Limbaugh Show*, March 19, 2007. Karl Rove's remarks were made on June 26, 2006, at the annual New York Conservative Party Dinner. The quote attributed to Lee Atwater can be found in William Greider's *Who Will Tell the People? The Betrayal of American Democracy* (New York: Simon & Schuster, 1992).

6. Trickle-Down vs. Bottom-Up

The two quotes from Schlesinger are in the text of his *Cycles of American History*, pp. 229 and 232, respectively. The wage slavery quote is from *The Story of American Freedom*. The quotes attributed to Truman were found in Jonathan Alter's *The Defining Moment: FDR's One Hundred Days and the Triumph of Hope* (New York: Simon & Schuster, 2006). I relied generally on David McCullough's *Truman* (New York: Touchstone/Simon & Schuster, 1992) in my passages about Truman throughout the book.

My information about populists came from Michael Kazin's *A Godly Hero: The Life of William Jennings Bryan* (New York: Knopf, 2006).

For my discussion of FDR and the agricultural economy, I relied on D. C. Brown's *Electricity for Rural America: The Fight for the REA (Contributions in Economics and Economic History)* (Westport, CT: Greenwood, 1980) and Laurence Malone's article "Rural Electrification Administration," *EH.Net Encyclopedia*, edited by Robert Whaples, March 16, 2008. The statistics on the New Deal and the elderly are reported in Roger Biles's *A New Deal for the American People* (DeKalb: Northern Illinois University Press, 1991). The details about the New Deal's Works Project

Administration came from Robert Leighninger's book *Long-Range Public Investment: The Forgotten Legacy of the New Deal* (Columbia: University of South Carolina Press, 2007).

The statistics on the GI Bill were taken from the *Congressional Research Report*'s "Montgomery GI Bill: Analysis of College Prices and Federal Student Aid under the Higher Education Act," January 25, 2008.

My description of Calvin Coolidge and his economic policy relies in part on David Greenberg's *Calvin Coolidge* (New York: Henry Holt, 2006).

The statistics I used in the sections on Lyndon Johnson and the creation of Medicare came from Patricia P. Martin's article "Social Security: A Program and Policy History," in the 2005 *Social Security Bulletin* 66, no. 1. Other LBJ-Great Society statistics were found in Frank Stricker's *Why America Lost the War on Poverty and How to Win It Back* (Chapel Hill: University of North Carolina Press, 2007).

The quotations from Republicans on the House Ways and Means Committee and generally from Republicans regarding Social Security were taken from Nancy Altman's *The Battle of Social Security: From FDR's Vision to Bush's Gamble* (Hoboken, NJ: John Wiley & Sons, 2005).

The discussion and statistics I used regarding Ronald Reagan's presidency can be found in Kevin Phillips's *The Politics of Rich and Poor: Wealth and the American Electorate in the Reagan Aftermath* (New York: Random House, 1990). For statistics on the Clinton administration's successes and difficulties, I consulted Nigel Hamilton's *Bill Clinton: Mastering the Presidency* (New York: Public Affairs, 2007).

For data on America's current state of affairs, including the rising cost of oil, health care, groceries, education, and tuition, I referred to a variety of sources, such as Edmund Andrews's article "Employment Falls for the Second Month," *New York Times*, March 7, 2008; "Short-Term Energy Outlook: Motor Gasoline Consumption 2008: A Historical Perspective and Long-Term Projections," *Energy Information Administration*, released April 2008, www .eia.doe.gov, accessed April 30, 2008; "Lara Moscrip's article "Dollar Hits New Low versus Euro," http://money.cnn.com/2008/07/15/markets/dollar/index.htm?postversion=2008071508, accessed September 8, 2008; Robert Gavin's article "Surging Costs of Groceries Hit Home," *Boston Globe*, www .boston.com/business/personalfinance/articles/2008/03/09/, accessed April 28, 2008; *Trends in Student Aid*, the College Board, 2006; *Calculations by the Project on Student Debt* from the National Center on Educational Statistics, National Post-Secondary Student Aid Study (NPSAS), 1993 and 2004 undergraduates, Data Analysis System; and Michael Fletcher's "Rising Health Care Costs Cut into Wages," *Washington Post*, March 24, 2008.

7. The Dream and the Backlash

I relied heavily on Alexander Keyssar's *The Right to Vote: The Contested History of Democracy in the United States* (New York: Basic Books, 2000) for much of the section on voting rights, including the quotes from John Adams, the Knights of Labor, and the delegate to the California Constitutional Convention. To a great extent, I also made use of my own experiences in politics for the last thirty years, particularly in the areas of voter registration, get-out-the-vote drives, and so forth, in writing about modern efforts to suppress voting.

In my discussion of Martin Luther King Jr., I took excerpts of his speeches from a wonderful compilation, *A Testament of Hope: The Essential Writings and Speeches of Martin Luther King, Jr.*, edited by James Melvin Washington (New York: HarperCollins, 1986). I also used Drew D. Hansen's *The Dream: Martin Luther King, Jr., and the Speech That Inspired a Nation* (New York: HarperCollins, 2003).

For the section on McCarthyism, I availed myself of M. Stanton Evans's book *Blacklisted by History: The Untold Story of Senator Joe McCarthy and His Fight against American Enemies* (New York: Crown Forum, 2007). I also relied on Rick Perlstein's *Before the Storm* (New York: Hill and Wang, 2001) and David Halberstam's *The Fifties* (New York: Fawcett Columbine, 1994).

For the section on corruption, I relied to some extent on Jack Beatty's *Age of Betrayal: The Triumph of Money in America, 1865–1900* (New York: Knopf, 2007).

For the section on Jesse Helms, I used William A. Link's excellent work *Righteous Warrior: Jesse Helms and the Rise of Modern Conservatism* (New York: St. Martin's Press, 2008).

The Schlesinger biography of Robert Kennedy that is referenced in this chapter is *Robert Kennedy and His Times* (New York: Ballantine, 1978).

8. Hope, Fear, and the Culture of Caution

I drew on my own experience working in the White House from 1993 to 1996 in many parts of this chapter, particularly on health-care reform.

Pat Robertson's quote on feminism can be found in a fund-raising letter published in the *New York Times* on August 26, 1992; that from

Rush Limbaugh was made on *The Rush Limbaugh Show*, broadcast on Premiere Radio Networks on August 12, 2005. The editorial that appeared in the *Daily American*, a newspaper printed in San Francisco, was published on April 18, 1881, issue 7, p. 2, col. A. The Virgil Goode quotes, respectively, were taken from a column by Michael D. Shear and Tim Craig, titled "Goode Has Often Inspired Political Ire," in the *Washington Post*, December 23, 2006; and in a column by Jim Malone, titled "Small Groups Dominate US Immigration Debate," in the *Voice of America*, June 18, 2007. The quote from Joseph Turner was in an e-mail to supporters of "Save Our State," an anti-immigrant group in California, on October 7, 2006. The quote from Rudy Giuliani appeared in an article by Roger Simon, titled "Giuliani Warns of New 9/11 If Dems Win," in *The Politico* on April 24, 2007. George W. Bush's quote about Democrats and terrorism can be found in an article by Michael Abramowitz, titled "Bush Says 'America Loses' under Democrats," in the *Washington Post*, October 31, 2006. The quote from Dick Cheney was in an article by Spencer S. Hsu and Dana Milbank, titled "Cheney: Kerry Victory Is Risky," in the *Washington Post*, September 8, 2004.

I discuss the phrase "culture of caution" and its underpinnings in some depth at the *Huffington Post* blog, in a post titled "D.C. Conventional Wisdom: Caution Equals Brilliance," which can be found at the link www.huffingtonpost.com/mike-lux/dc-conventional-wisdom_b_51881.html and which was written on June 13, 2007; and at OpenLeft.com, in a post titled "The Birth of a Movement," which is available at www.open left.com/showDiary.do?diaryId=18 and which was written on July 8, 2007.

Regarding John Dean's statement that George W. Bush's actions have been "worse than Watergate," Dean wrote a book titled *Worse Than Watergate: The Secret Presidency of George W. Bush* (New York: Little, Brown, 2004) and has since made corroborating comments in the press.

The research regarding the dominance of conservative talk radio comes from a report jointly released by the Center for American Progress and Free Press, titled *The Structural Imbalance of Political Talk Radio*, published on June 21, 2007, and updated on June 22, 2007.

Dick Durbin made his speech on the Senate floor. The full speech can be found in the *Congressional Record*, S6594, June 14, 2005.

The quote from Bill Kristol comes from his op-ed piece in the *Wall Street Journal*, titled "On Principle," January 11, 1994.

The excerpt by Barack Obama was from a speech he made in Nashua, New Hampshire, on January 8, 2008. The full text can be found at http://my.barackobama.com/page/community/post_group/ObamaHQ/CGTN, accessed April 15, 2008.

9. The Next Big Change Moment

I drew to some extent on Arthur M. Schlesinger Jr.'s *The Cycles of American History* (New York: Mariner, 1999) in my thinking for much of this chapter.

The polling data I cite come from a post-2006 election report released on November 8, 2006, by the Campaign for America's Future in conjunction with Greenberg Quinlan Rosner Research. Full polling data and analysis can be found at www.ourfuture.org/report/2006-post-election-poll-results-americans-issue-populist-anti-war-mandate, accessed April 25, 2008.

The data concerning the number of ActBlue donors and the size of donations were obtained through an interview with representatives of ActBlue via e-mail over a period from April 25 to 28, 2008.

The excerpt from my blog is from a post I wrote, titled "The Role of Television in Dumbing Down of American Politics," on my blog Open Left.com, on July 20, 2007.

The Harold Meyerson excerpt comes from a column he wrote, titled "A New New Deal," in the *Washington Post*, March 20, 2008.

INDEX